STEAMLUST

STEAMLUST

STEAMPUNK EROTIC ROMANCE

Edited by
Kristina Wright

Foreword by
Meljean Brook

CLEIS
PRESS

Published in the United States by Cleis Press, Inc., 2246 Sixth Street, Berkeley, California 94710.

Printed in the United States.
Cover design: Scott Idleman/Blink
Cover photograph: Axel Lauerer/Getty Images & Ole Graf/Corbis
Text design: Frank Wiedemann

First Edition.
10 9 8 7 6 5 4 3 2 1

Trade paper ISBN: 978-1-57344-721-8
E-book ISBN: 978-1-57344-741-6

Contents

FOREWORD

Meljean Brook

E ven if you haven't encountered the term *steampunk* before
picking up this anthology, you've probably read or seen
something that fits the genre: an episode of "Wild Wild West,"
perhaps, or a story in which a time-traveling hero uses his knowledge of future technologies to create a weapon to save the day,
or a novel by one of the two forefathers of modern steampunk,
Jules Verne and H. G. Wells. Typically set during the Victorian
era and featuring advanced steam engine or clockwork technology, steampunk is historical fiction with a speculative twist;
it's silk and steel, corsets and gears, parasols and airships. Tales
of alternate histories, extraordinary inventions and their fascinating creators abound in steampunk, all driven by a hands-
on, do-it-yourself attitude that is beautifully represented in this
collection of erotic steampunk romances.

Do it yourself. In an erotic anthology, such a phrase might
signal a writer gearing up for a pun, but that hands-on approach
has been a lynchpin at the heart of steampunk's rising popu-

larity. The aesthetic provides enormous appeal—who can resist the amenable collision of industrial grit and the elegance and refinement of upper-crust Victoriana?—but one glance online or at a steampunk convention reveals that this is a genre and subculture powered by do-it-yourselfers: those who have fitted brass and gears to their slick computer cases and music players, clothiers and jewelry designers who craft one-of-a-kind items for sale, and those industrious individuals who build their own steam-powered machines from the ground up.

In the literary field, authors have taken that attitude and built a steam-powered rocket with it. The very act of writing is, of course, hands-on creation, but steampunk takes it a step farther and throws in a little (or a lot of) do-it-yourself history...and erotic romance gives that history a focus.

Unlike science fiction writers who speculate on the future, steampunk authors have the unique perspective of being able to view the historical period they are writing in—and they are looking at it through twenty-first-century goggles. As beautiful as the dresses are, as civil as the manners were, steampunk writers can't ignore the constrictions of corsets and gender roles, the effects of imperialism and colonization, the barbaric labor practices and the rigidity of the class system. That do-it-yourself history often becomes a revisionist history that either alters the boundaries of societal structures or keeps those boundaries and includes more voices. In this collection, we see that revisionist history in many forms, but one recurring theme is the liberation of women, the rejection of a defined role and a celebration of their sexuality. These heroines might be wearing beautiful clothes, but the women inside those dresses are much more fascinating.

In "Sparks," Anna Meadows's heroine opens her tale with, "I would have been the first to concede how much better things were for me back when I behaved myself." The same could be said for most of the women in these stories: life would be easier if they didn't step outside society's proscribed boundaries. Life would be easier, safer—but constrained, and steampunk heroines aren't the type to remain still when told to. They seek their freedom and independence, and although that freedom exacts a price from them, it's one they are willing to pay...particularly when the rewards are so pleasurable. In Elizabeth Coldwell's "A Demonstration of Affection," a young woman apprentice knows that her choice to pursue her education voids any chance of a proper marriage, but who needs a proper marriage when one can have the professor? In Christine d'Abo's poignant "The Undeciphered Heart," the melding of invention and body means being cast completely from society and life, but also heralds the reunion of lovers parted by war.

In these erotic tales, release becomes more than just a physical event. It propels characters beyond the constraints of social class and gender. As the stories open, some of the heroines have already found that release and broken free of their bonds, as did the fascinating Maddy from Sacchi Green's "Fog, Flight and Moonlight," whose sexual history would have a proper miss reaching for her smelling salts, but a steampunk heroine takes in stride.

Nothing is handed to these steampunk heroines; they, too, must do it themselves. Most of the women utilize their hands or intellect, and the celebration of steampunk's do-it-yourself spirit lies within the stories, as well. These women aren't afraid to get their fingernails dirty, though their work leads to rather unusual occupations, such as in Andrea Dale's "Lost Souls," where a heroine invents devices that serve as otherworldy distractions in a greater game, or the time-traveling thieves in Vida Bailey's "Undergrounded." They don't have to work alone, however; the partnerships in these stories are critical to success, and allow them to find ecstasy—both physical and intellectual—along the way.

Steampunk allows for a revised and reimagined history, but not everything from the eighteenth and nineteenth centuries is tossed away. It was an era of exploration and conflict, and that spirit lives on in steampunk, even when it leads our heroines into dangerous and unexpected territories, as when Lisabet Sarai's Caroline Fortescue-Smythe seeks to persuade a young Siamese man to her side of a raging war in her unique way in "Green Cheese." It was also an age of invention and discovery, and the celebration of ingenuity. That is aptly demonstrated in Sylvia Day's "Iron Hard," in which the finely wrought craftsmanship of a man's prosthetic arm arouses the heroine's intellect before a touch from that mechanized hand does the same to her flesh.

Gadgets and inventions often play a large role in steampunk tales, providing conflict with or a reflection of the society— providing freedom or oppression, depending upon who uses them—but they cannot fulfill every need. In a subtle turn on Victorian doctors and their treatment of women's hysteria, the heroine of Nikki Magennis's "Make Your Own Miracles," orders a machine to be built that will ease the need within her, but finds that a connection with a living being, albeit partly clockwork, was all that she required.

In other tales, it is through a machine that the connection is made. Saskia Walker's clever inventor and formidable engineer come together inside "The Heart of the Daedalus," and in Lynn Townsend's "Golden Moment," an invention which measures the auspiciousness of a particular moment leads the heroine to the right lover at exactly the right time. In the grips of "Mr. Hartley's Infernal Device," Charlotte Stein's wonderful heroine's eyes are opened to beauty and wonder, and the revelation that "I have real freedom here, for the first time in my life..." That is a sentiment that might also be echoed by the automaton heroine in Mary Borsellino's beautifully written "Liberated," who works to fix a broken world and seeks connection and life in the arms of a lover.

Turn the page with me, and step into the new worlds these authors have built—worlds where airships rule the skies, where romance and intellect are valued over money and social status, where lovers boldly discover each other's bodies, minds, and hearts.

This is steampunk...written extra hot, for double the steam.

INTRODUCTION: A PASSION FOR STEAMPUNK

The term *steampunk* first came on my radar several years ago when I was hunting around on Etsy.com for a necklace as a gift for a friend. I kept running into the word in relation to these beautifully unique pieces of wearable art that combined copper, brass, glass, tiny cogs and other delights. I wasn't sure what *steampunk* was, but I knew I at least liked how it translated into jewelry. Soon, I was seeing references to steampunk fiction and I was intrigued. What was this new genre all about? Who was writing it?

Turns out, steampunk is a relatively new word for a rather old genre. If you've read Jules Verne or H. G. Wells, you already know what steampunk is. While the term came onto the literary scene a couple of decades or so ago (depending on your source), referring primarily to a niche of science fiction, the idea of making steampunk *steamy* is a very new idea. It makes sense, though. What is sexier than combining history and fantasy with exciting voyages and exploration? Victorian costumes and futuristic gadgets, airships and automatons—steampunk is a genre that was meant to be romanticized and eroticized. And so, with *Steamlust: Steampunk Erotic Romance*, that's just what we have done!

The stories in *Steamlust* are about characters willing to take tremendous risks or make great sacrifices in the name of freedom, invention and love, but steampunk is also about rebellion—and this collection offers up some of the best bad boys (and girls) to be found. Between these covers you will find stories of high adventure and dangerous intrigue, not to mention imaginative gadgets and clever automatons. But at the heart of every story is the immeasurable passion of the free-spirited rebels and dreamers steampunk is known for, passion that transcends all boundaries and limitations because there is no greater motivator of the human spirit than erotic love. As Sylvia Day's dashing hero in "Iron Hard" says, "Once we find the other half of ourselves, we are never again whole without them."

Steamlust: Steampunk Erotic Romance is an amalgam of authorial inspiration resulting in a collection of stories that blend the historical, the scientific, the fantastical, the romantic and the erotic. These tantalizing crystalline and clockwork visions capture a time and place that never existed except in the authors' imaginations. And—now—*your* imagination. This is steampunk that goes beyond the magic and science of Verne and Wells and explores the hearts and desires of the intrepid characters behind the machines—and leaves the bedroom door open for your voyeuristic pleasure.

To further spur your steampunk imaginings, I invite you to visit *steam * lust * animation* (steamlustanimation.blogspot. com). This lovely blog is an Internet version of a leather-bound journal—chockfull of clever creations and a dash of enchantment. It is the brainchild of talented artist and writer Nikki

Magennis and offers an account of her adventures in creating an animated book trailer for this anthology (extra special thanks and a bouquet of crystalline roses to Nikki for her creative genius) as well as providing a comprehensive compendium of all things steampunk. Nikki's film is a spectacular visual rendering of the book you hold in your hands and her account of the process is as entertaining and amusing as it is educational. The steampunk band Escape the Clouds deserves grateful acknowledgment, as well, for giving us permission to use their song "Marrakesh" as the soundtrack for the book trailer. I listened to their music as I compiled the final version of the book and I think their sound embodies the adventure, romance and passion I was looking for in this collection.

I would like to offer a very hearty thank-you to my fabulous team at Cleis Press for believing in my steampunk dreams and to Scott Idleman of Blink for proving that you can, in fact, judge a book by its gorgeous cover.

I hope you enjoy *Steamlust: Steampunk Erotic Romance*, dear reader. May these stories inspire your clockwork dreams and fuel your steamy fantasies!

Kristina Wright
Chesapeake, Virginia

IRON HARD

Sylvia Day

London, 1820

Y ou are attached to them."

Annabelle Waters took one last, lingering look at the mechanized lovebirds in their velvet-lined delivery box, then closed the lid. "I'm attached to all my creations."

"Let me rephrase," her brother said. "You are *especially* attached to these."

She met her twin's blue-eyed stare. "Have you any notion of how difficult it was to calibrate the resonance frequencies so that if one should fail the other will also?"

"They are your best work yet," Thomas agreed. "But that isn't why you favor them so, and we both know it."

Annie looked at the empty birdcage in the corner of her workroom, then shifted her attention to the clock on the mantle. With a sigh, she pulled the safety goggles off the top of her head and ruffled her short cap of dark curls. "I have to make myself presentable."

"Allow me to deliver this one."

"The baron asked that I personally demonstrate how they work. Considering the obscene sum we charged him, it is the least I can do."

"Annie—"

"I promise to speak of you," she rushed on, knowing what he desired, "if the opportunity presents itself. But the subject must be delicately approached. His lordship's future patronage and endorsement could change our fortunes in profound ways."

"I know. But you've no notion of what it is like at his shipyard," he complained. "I have waited in that line for nearly a year and am no closer to gaining employment than I was when I began. Every man in England wishes to apprentice under his banner."

She knew that; it was impossible not to know. Baron de la Warren had returned from the war a hero, a sky captain lauded for his brilliant strategies and swashbuckling boldness. He was credited with the destruction of Boney's dirigible fleet and romanticized for his patched eye, which gave him the appearance of a pirate. Peacetime had done nothing to lessen his appeal. He was, in fact, more popular now. His import empire offered well-paying work and apprenticeship to many destitute yet able-bodied young men, like her brother. Annie had been startled when his lordship had commissioned the lovebirds, wondering at the private man who lived beneath the public personage. What manner of warrior thought of such a lover's gift? She was more than a little eager to see for herself.

The long case clock in the hall began to chime with the hour. Annie proceeded with her egress. "I will find an excuse to mention you. Perhaps I can convince his lordship to visit under the guise of viewing some of my other creations. He could find nothing untoward about meeting you here, and once he does, he'll certainly engage you. How could he not? You're just the sort of intelligent, ambitious young fellow he cultivates in his employ."

"It's not working," he grumbled after her. "Your flattery."

"Yes, it is." She slowed at the sound of creaking floorboards and heavy footsteps.

The soothing whirring of gears preceded the appearance of their butler as he rounded the balustrade in the visitors' foyer. He slowed his steady forward momentum when he saw her, his striated glass lenses turning to adjust his polarized vision.

"Please have the coach brought around, Alfred."

He acknowledged her request with an eminently regal dip of his head.

"Thank you," she said, unable to refrain from smiling.

The servant was one of her most prized creations, albeit one lacking the painful sentimentality of the lovebirds. As much as she longed to keep them, she also could not wait to be parted from them. They awakened memories she'd learned to suppress through an intense focus on her work.

It had been five years since Waterloo. *Five years.*

He wasn't coming back.

Annie secured her hat to her head with an ivory pin and collected the boxed birds with gloved hands. Alfred pulled the front door open, allowing the low-lying fog to roll in over the cracked marble floors with the sinuousness of a lover. She left the house, skipping over the shattered second step to reach the street, which was deserted aside from her steam coach.

What had once been a fashionable neighborhood for the wealthy was now home to a pile of rubble. When Prinny had urged the willing and able to stake claims on salvageable abandoned properties, she and Thomas had chosen a row house that stood as a lone sentinel on a ravaged street. It was quiet here. She was spared the distraction of belching delivery wagons and the repetitious *tick tick tick* of insectile vendor cart legs picking their way over pockmarked cobblestones.

Lifting her skirts, Annie climbed onto the box seat and settled herself. She pulled her driving goggles over her eyes, then gripped the wheel as she let the break, holding on tightly as the coach lurched forward.

In short order, she left the city behind. Baron de la Warren lived on the outskirts, away from the smoke and fog that shrouded London. When she arrived at the massive iron gates that kept the fawning world at bay, she rang the bell. The locking mechanism had been built as a work of art, with copper meshing gears and tin ornamentation. She watched admiringly as the chains slid smoothly over well-oiled sprockets, causing the gates to swing inward and grant her entrance.

Within the high brick perimeter walls, the baron's property was massive. A dirigible landing pad was situated on the left side of the brick manse and a large carriage house was visible in the distance on the right. Sleek hounds followed her progress up the lane, their iron plates flexing with the ease of snakeskin.

Once she reached the circular front drive, Annie reined in her delight and focused on the meeting ahead. Clearly his lordship held an appreciation for mechanization and she had no qualms in saying that she was the best engineer in London.

Squaring her shoulders, Annie caught the brass ring held in the jaws of a massive lion's head doorknocker and rapped it sharply. She was initially surprised when a human butler opened the door, but that passed swiftly. The baron could afford the luxury of live servants and their wages. She, on the other hand, had created Alfred from scrap parts.

The butler took her hat, gloves and pelisse before showing her into a shadowed study.

As he bowed and moved to turn away, she said, "I will require more light, please."

The striking of a match preceded the flaring of illumination from one of the room's corners. Her head turned swiftly, her breath catching as a man stepped forward. She scarcely paid any mind to the door clicking shut behind the retreating servant.

"Will this do?" he asked in a low, rumbling voice. He turned up the flame in the gas lamp he carried and joined her at the desk where she'd deposited the birds.

She stared, riveted by the savage beauty of his face and the intensity with which he regarded her. His dark hair was long, hanging to his shoulders in a thick, glossy mane. A wide band of pure white strands embellished his left temple, framing a silver eye. Even as she watched, the metallic iris turned, the lens adjusting to accommodate the brighter light. A scar ran diagonally from his temple, across the eyelid and over his upper lip, explaining how he'd lost the eye he had been born with. The blemish did nothing to mitigate his comeliness. While it altered her perception of the symmetry of his features, it was in a manner she found highly appealing, as she did the air of danger surrounding him.

The provocation she felt was far from fear.

Breathing shallowly, her gaze raked over his face, admiring his dark winged brows, brilliant green iris and the impossibly sensual shape of his mouth. His jaw was square and bold, his cheekbones high and expertly sculpted. He was far too masculine to be pretty, but he was certainly magnificent, and younger than the strip of white hair and his world-weary gaze would suggest. The drawings of him in the gazettes had never done him justice.

"Miss Waters," he greeted her, extending his gloved hand. "I cannot tell you what a pleasure it is to receive you."

"My Lord. The pleasure is mine." She curtsied and placed her fingers within his palm, shivering as he clasped her. There was a sincerity in his commonplace greeting that startled her. Then something else unexpected—the unforgiving strength of metal curling around her fingers—stole her attention. "Your hand...?"

"My arm," he corrected.

An entire arm. Mechanized. Excitement coursed through her.

He watched her with searing intensity. "Would you like to see it?"

"Yes. Please."

Releasing her, he stepped back and shrugged out of his beautifully tailored velvet jacket. He tugged off his gloves; first the one on his mechanical hand, then its mate covering his physical one. She was amazed by the dexterity of his copper fingers as he freed the button at his cuff and rolled his sleeve up.

Her lungs seized at the wondrous sight. She took a step forward without her volition, her gaze riveted to the softly whirring copper and steel gears. They had been fashioned into the shape of an arm and so precisely meshed that she doubted even air could slip between the cogs. Encased in what appeared to be thin glass, it was worthy of museum exhibition.

"How extensive is the replacement?" she asked, fighting the urge to run her hands over it.

"To the shoulder."

Her tongue darted out to lick suddenly dry lips.

His green eye flashed with heat and his mouth—that wicked, wonderful mouth—curved in a rakish smile. "I would gladly show you the whole, but I'd have to undress further. Do you object?"

"No." She quivered with anticipation. "Please."

The baron loosened his cravat. She was so mesmerized by the expert craftsmanship of his artificial appendage, she scarcely registered that he was disrobing. Until the tight lacing of his abdomen was bared. Followed by the rippling expanse of his powerful chest.

"Oh, my…" Her arousal spiked. Her blood was hot for him, her body softening to accommodate the hardness of his. Unseemly thoughts filled her mind. Naughty thoughts. Highly sexual.

He was scarred on his chest as well. As with his face, the puckered bullet hole and multiple knife slashes only made him more delicious. Annie's lips parted on lightly panting breaths, her breasts swelling within her bodice.

She flushed and tore her gaze away from the seductive expanse of flame-lit muscle and golden skin. It shocked her to realize how much effort was required to focus on his finely wrought arm instead. In truth, it had been far too long since flesh and blood had held more appeal than steel and grease. She found herself at a loss over which arm was more skillfully cast—the one afforded him by the grace of God or the one crafted by an earthly engineer.

"Exquisite." Annie referred to the entirety of him, not merely the manmade pieces.

Judging by his sudden low growl, the baron knew it.

Sharp tension spiked between them, a heightened awareness that swept across her skin in a prickling wave. An aching need built between her legs, a reminder that she had suppressed her desires for years. Or, more accurately, it had been that length of time since a man had proven capable of rousing them. After the loss of Gaspard, she'd wondered if grief had made her immune to masculine charms. But the baron was proving her wrong.

Her gratitude for that was as potent as her attraction.

Turning away abruptly, she faced the desk and lifted the lid on the delivery box with unsteady hands. The lovebirds glimmered in the firelight, their tin feathers flexing as they moved closer to each other. "I hope these are satisfactory, my Lord."

He came up behind her, his greater height enabling him to look over her shoulder. He stood so close she could smell him: warm, virile male with the faintest touch of clove and bergamot.

"My god," he said gruffly, reaching around her to slide his hand beneath a bird and lift it out. "I have never seen the like."

Annie's stomach quivered with delight at his praise. The way the baron hefted the small creature—curling his palm around it and testing its weight—incited scorching thoughts of his hand on her breasts, cupping them from his position behind her, admiring her form with equal warmth.

"Do not remove them too far from one another," she warned. Her voice softened with the memory of another pair of birds, a gift from a man she'd once thought to spend her life with. "They cannot be parted, if you don't wish them broken."

"Broken." His warm breath blew across the shell of her ear. "Is that not true of us all? Once we find the other half of ourselves, we are never again whole without them."

"Yes." Her gaze remained riveted on his hand, the warm live flesh carefully holding her delicate creation. "Will they be a gift? For your other half, perhaps?"

"They are for you, Annabelle," he said softly. "To replace the ones you lost."

"My lord?" Her chest lifted and fell in an elevated rhythm. She wondered if he knew how the soft hum of his turning gears affected her. The low sound coursed over her senses in a constant tingling stream.

"Gaspard Vangess served under me. He spoke of you. As

beautifully as you create things with your hands, he created you in words." There was the veriest hint of his lips against her ear. "Before I saw you in truth, I dreamed of you. Wanted you."

With shaking hands, she took the bird from him and set it carefully back in the box. Its partner cooed and shifted closer.

"Have I frightened you?" he asked hoarsely. "I meant to woo you carefully. That remains my intent. I apologize that I wasn't prepared for your effect on me. The moment you entered the room, I was ensnared. But I won't press you beyond your allowance."

"I'm not frightened." She exhaled in a rush. "He is gone, then?"

"Yes."

"I knew it. Felt it." But she also felt a quiet, painful relief to know her first love's fate for a certainty. Not knowing had become the most painful aspect of all.

"His last words were of you. He secured my promise to replace the birds he'd once given you, the ones you lost during the London invasion. He went to war to make the world a safe place for you to have precious and fragile things, and he wanted to see that goal met and come full circle. I chose to present you with a gift that won't die. I cannot replace Vangess, but I can give you something of him that will never leave you."

A tear slipped free, along with an aching weight she hadn't realized she was carrying. "My poor, sweet Gaspard."

The baron stood at military rest behind her, a stoic yet soothing presence. "My heart aches for your loss."

"Thank you." Annie watched the small parrots nuzzle against each other. She was powerfully aware of her desire to do the same with the man behind her. A man with whom she felt an undeniable affinity and appreciation. "I am no longer the girl he told you about."

"No. That girl was his. Annie, he called you. But I think Bella better suits the lush and courageous woman you've become."

And the woman she'd become was suddenly unencumbered. And so very lonely. She watched the lovebirds and envied their bond. "For a time, I was broken."

He touched the top button of her jacket where it lay against her nape. "And now?"

"Now...I am whole but empty." And mantled by a man who stirred her blood while desiring her in return. An unexpected yet welcome miracle.

"What you would have of me? You have only to ask."

Her head fell forward, her eyes drifting closed. "I want you to touch me, my Lord. I want to be the Bella you see when you look at me. I want to be filled again."

He nuzzled against her upswept hair. The first of her coat's buttons was urged free of its hole. The rest swiftly followed, coaxed into surrender—as she was herself—by the baron's agile and dexterous mechanical hand. When he pushed the garment forward, over her shoulders and down her arms, she reveled in the rush of air that cooled her fevered skin.

"I must tell you," she whispered. "My brother, Thomas, aspires to work for you."

"I will train him myself."

The largesse of his quick offer and the joy it would bring to Thomas softened her heart. "That isn't why I want you."

"I wouldn't care if it was."

Annie glanced over her shoulder, her heartbeat faltering at his beauty. "Why not?"

He brushed the backs of his fingers across her cheek. "Clearly a man with my embellishments would benefit considerably by an association with an engineer of your skill, but that does not mitigate the fact that it's the living parts of me that need you most. Requiring each other for more than sex is a blessing, Bella, not a curse."

She lifted her arms over her head, wrapping them around his neck and pulling his mouth down to hers. His kiss curled her toes. Lush and deep, he took her mouth with a fierce possessiveness. He ate at her, licking and suckling in a manner that had her writhing against him, seeking the kind of closeness that required bared skin.

The remainder of her clothes were swiftly shed—her shirt and skirt, pantalettes and stockings. When he freed the stays of her corset with a hiss of compressed air, she sighed along with the sound, her inhibitions stripped away with her attire. Not that she'd had all that many by the time he touched her. The baron had been seducing her from the moment he commissioned the lovebirds. The journey to this point, both mental and actual, had only lured her deeper under his spell.

"Annabelle." He cupped her breasts through her chemise, lifting their moderate weight and kneading gently, just as she'd imagined mere moments before. He rolled her nipples between thumb and forefinger, and her head fell back against his shoulder, her lips parting on rapid breaths. Both of his hands were warm, his touch both reverent and rapacious. Her nerve endings woke from their extended dormancy, prickling with near-painful intensity. She grew slick and hot between her legs, her sex throbbing with greedy hunger.

Her fingers slid through the long, thick strands of his hair to reach his nape. She stroked him there, shivering when he groaned. Her hips began to rock in small circles, deliberately massaging his cock with her derriere. "My Lord..."

The baron nipped her ear with his teeth and clutched her possessively between her thighs. "Raphael," he corrected. "I want to hear you say it."

His lips moved across her nape, caressing, goading without words. Her heartbeat stuttered.

"*Raphael.*" Clutching fistfuls of courage along with her chemise, Annie pulled the garment's hem to her waist, the material sliding between his gentle grip and her tender flesh.

He parted the lips of her sex with scissoring fingers. "I'm going to put my mouth here and lick you. Make you come."

Annie sagged against him, slicking his artificial hand with the liquid proof of her desire.

The use of that hand told her that he knew her. Understood her. There were few who collected her appreciation for mechanization. Even Thomas wondered at her fascination with well-oiled and effortlessly moving parts. He didn't comprehend the thrill she felt, the rush of excitement and pleasure. She wasn't certain she understood it, but there was no denying her attraction to the baron. All of him. The parts pulsing and breathing with life, and the metallic ones having those very effects on her.

"I want my mouth on you, too," she confessed. She would start at his lips and work her way down his arm, sucking each copper finger before performing the same service to his cock.

"It will be." Raphael caught her by the waist and lifted her, eliciting a soft cry of surprise. He carried her to the damask-covered settee and arranged her on her back, sinking to his knees on the floor beside her. Gooseflesh raced across her skin. One of her legs was lifted and draped over his muscular shoulder, then his head lowered to the glistening flesh between her thighs.

The first teasing lick made her arch upward with heated lust. Sweat misted skin that felt too tight and hot. "I am too fast with you," she gasped.

"Am I not equally so with you?"

"You are a man."

"I promise to make you happy about that."

Annie laughed, then caught her breath, her stomach concaving as he covered her with his mouth. *"Yes."*

Her moan echoed through the cavernous room, her fingers pushing into the silky curtain of his hair. He tongued her gently, the pointed tip stroking feather light over her distended clitoris. Pleasure coiled like a compressed spring. Too swiftly. "Raphael. Please."

"Not yet." Lips curving against her, he angled his head and speared his tongue into her quivering sex.

Beyond shyness or shame, she tightened her leg over his shoulder, tugging him closer. Raphael obliged with a growl, fucking her aching flesh with quick fierce stabs. She rocked into his working mouth, circling her hips without thought or reason. Effortlessly, he lifted her, balancing her with one hand as he pushed two unyielding copper fingers inside her.

Fingers that *vibrated*.

Annie jerked in startled delight. The slightly ribbed texture of the flexing joint meshing sent tremors through her limbs. She sobbed as the vibration increased, beading her nipples into painfully hard points. He began to thrust, his fingers pumping through her spasming tissues with tender purpose. Determined. Expert. Knowing just the spot to rub with those wickedly pulsating fingertips. All the while he sucked her clitoris, tugging and worrying the sensitive point with frenzied flicks of his tongue.

She gasped his name as she shuddered into an orgasm so powerful it blackened her vision. Violent trembling racked her body and she clung to the edge of the settee, seeking an anchor as reality fell away.

The baron lowered her gently to the cushion, his wet mouth nuzzling against her inner thigh before he withdrew from her and pushed to his feet with powerful grace. He undressed swiftly and unabashedly, his abdomen lacing tightly as he dispensed with his boots, a task impossible for most men without the aid of a valet. Flushed with lust, lips wet and swollen from the attention he'd paid to her, the baron's gaze slid over her like a tangible caress: soft, yet resolute; his mind clearly occupied with all the ways he wanted her and how he would have her.

It was a novel and highly exciting perusal for her. Gaspard had been nearly as untried as she had been, their love having grown from adolescence. Raphael was mature and delectably well practiced.

He set one knee on the cushion between her sprawled legs and stabilized himself with one hand around the wooden lip of the seatback. "What are you thinking?"

She realized then how exposed she was, how immodest and unguarded. "What have you done to me?"

He cupped her cheek with his free hand. "No more than you have done to me. This arm you admire is not the one given to me on the battlefield. Such craftsmanship could not be found in that hell. The grafting of the first, crude replacement was excruciating. Death would have been a kindness and there were days when I prayed for it. Gaspard Vangess—awash in needless guilt that I had shielded him from the blast that took my arm—would sit with me and distract me with tales of you. He regaled me with stories of a rambunctious girl with freckles on her nose and mischief in her blue eyes. Mindless with agony and laudanum, my mind took possession of the memories he shared. For a time in my delirium, you were mine and I loved you beyond all reason. It was for you that I recovered, only to realize you were a dream that belonged to another man, a promising airman who was killed a fortnight before I returned to the fleet."

"Raphael—" She cupped his hip in her palm.

His breath hissed out. He mounted her, his patience seemingly at an end. The thick head of his cock tucked into the slick and swollen entrance to her body. She held her breath, waiting.

"Please," she whispered. At his first slow push, her head fell back.

"Christ." His luxurious hair brushed her cheek. "Your cunt is tight and hot. So wet. Perfect."

Catching her leg behind the knee, he anchored it on his hip, opening her wider. He withdrew slightly, then returned in a practiced roll of his hips.

Her nails dug into his clenching buttocks. "Faster," she urged in a voice so hoarse she scarcely knew it.

He laughed, and the arrogant maleness inherent in the sound spurred her further. She threw her hips upward, taking more of him.

"Vixen." Raphael kissed her even as he pinned her to the settee with a firm but gentle grip on her hip. "I won't allow you to rush me."

Her fingers kneaded restlessly into the hard muscles of his back. "You cannot command me as you would your crew."

"No?"

"You said you would fill me, not tease me to madness!"

All levity fled his breathtakingly handsome features. He pulled back, then pushed deeper, exhaling in a rush when she tightened greedily around him. He was hot to the touch, his skin slick with sweat, his muscles rigid. But he would not be spurred into rutting atop her as she wished. "I want something from you in return, Bella."

Wrapping both legs around him, she tried to draw him closer. "What more can I give you?"

"This," he purred, working his thick cock inexorably deeper. "Your passion, your need. I want to be the one you hunger for, the one who shares your bed. The only one, from this day 'til my last."

Even in the extremity of her lust, her mind raced with the impossibility of their mutual infatuation. And yet...something more profound was between them as well.

"You know," he went on, altering the angle of her hips to slide farther into her, "as I have known, that we are what the other needs or you would not be arching beneath me now."

Dear god, she wanted the baron with a primitive hunger. She wanted him as she knew him to be: Bold. Dauntless. A force of tremendous will. What an adventure it would be to become the mistress of such a man... "Yes, I know."

He stilled, staring down at her with those gloriously dissimilar eyes; one as brilliant as an emerald, the other like polished silver. "But I cannot be a kept man."

She blinked up at him. "Beg your pardon?"

His mouth curved with wicked amusement. "Young men emulate me. I have a reputation to uphold. You must make an honest man of me."

"Raphael." Her chest tightened painfully. With hope. With fear. With lingering grief. "I—"

With an exaggerated sigh, he straightened his arms and began to withdraw. When she realized he intended to cease their bedsport completely, she narrowed her gaze. Two could play.

Tightening her legs around him, she caught his shoulders and wrenched to the side, rolling them both to the floor.

The drop was short, mere inches. He landed on his back. *Laughing.* Jaw set with determination, she reached between them to position the cock that was as impressive as the man himself, then sheathed him in her body with a swift plunge of her hips.

A soft cry escaped her. His mirth fled with a serrated groan.

She set her hands palms down on his chest and gave a tentative swivel of her hips, easing the pressing fullness of his deep penetration.

"I'm conquered," he said hoarsely. "My surrender is unconditional and absolute."

"But I've yet to state my terms."

"I concede to them all."

Her brow arched even as she rose up on her knees, stroking her eager sex with the length of his throbbing erection. The sensation was exquisite, as was he, this legendary man who awakened a stirring emotion she'd thought forever lost to her. "Where is the strategy in that, Captain?"

Raphael caught her hips and surged upward, filling her. "One must lay claim to a territory before one can cultivate it."

Clutching his wrists for balance, Annie began to move in earnest. Her spine arched with heated pleasure as he worked with her, lifting his lean hips to meet her downward drives. Beneath the onslaught of sensation, her body moved as a thing separate from her mind, the need to ride his pumping cock too potent for moderation. An approaching orgasm drummed through her blood, coaxing wrenching cries from her with every desperate thrust.

He pushed the low table aside with a powerful sweep of his arm, then rolled her beneath him. Fisting the thick Aubusson rug in his mechanical hand, he anchored her by the shoulder and pounded his lust into her with heavy, rhythmic lunges. Her legs fell open, inviting him deeper, her neck arching with the brutal rush of desire.

"Bella," he growled, an instant before he jerked inside her. The first hard pulse of semen made her gasp, spurring the climax that joined with his. She tightened around his spending cock, milking his seed with rippling spasms. He groaned with every clinging grasp, circling his hips to hit the end of her.

Her arms encircled him as he lowered his chest to hers, his back slick with sweat and his muscles quivering like a stallion run hard and long. Her eyes closed on a shuddering sigh. She contemplated possessing such a lavishly splendid creature as the baron and being possessed by him in return. The endeavor, when committed to so early in their association, was not without tremendous risk. But the rewards... Already she felt like a butterfly newly emerged from its cocoon.

He pulled her tighter against him and breathed her name. Turning her head, Annabelle claimed him with a kiss.

HEART OF THE DAEDALUS

Saskia Walker

Moonlight carved an eerie path through the low-lying landscape of the Romney Marshes, solidifying the patches of mist that gathered over the sodden ground. The area was riddled with inlets of water and bog, making a treacherous journey for anyone who dared go there. Nina Ashford scanned the ground ahead and soothed her mount, encouraging the horse along the narrow path. It was a familiar track to Nina for she had grown up in a nearby village, but it was dangerous nonetheless. Her mount huffed on the cold night air, picking its way carefully.

The clear sky was in her favor, which was some mercy, but her attire was not. She'd come straight from a formal supper and hadn't had time to change out of her best gown. Word had reached her of the whereabouts of the Daedalus and she'd grasped the opportunity to view it in secret. Fetching her cloak, she'd paused only to strap her pistol to her ankle boot and her sword to her flank—wary of brigands and smugglers on the marshes—then raced out into the night lest the Daedalus be moved elsewhere. The man who had so callously stolen her designs for the machine had enormous wealth at his disposal. He could easily toy with it, then cast it aside. The knot in her chest tightened as she thought on it, but this only served to strengthen her resolve. She had to see her beloved creation, now. Pursing her lips, she pressed on determinedly.

Up ahead she spied her quarry, a smuggler's den—a long and low shelter in a dugout pit, built from old planks covered over with slabs of peat and tufts of grass to conceal the moorings and storage space within. It was here that she'd been told the prototype had been hidden. The machine had been engineered and built elsewhere, so why was it here? The question went unanswered as the lure of the Daedalus drew her on. A steady plume of smoke rose from the rear of the shelter, making her wary. Her informant, an old friend, had told her no guards had been employed. Apparently it had been deemed unnecessary in this lonely, barren place. However she approached with caution. Dismounting, she secured her horse beneath a cluster of trees and edged closer to the ramshackle building by foot.

At the entrance she peered inside the gloomy interior. Somewhere a light shone. As she became accustomed to the limited light she realized it was coming from inside the huge metal construction. Her breath caught as her chin lifted to take in the outline of the immense machine. *Mine.* Her pride swelled. How she had pored over drawings of this creation, this beautiful machine. Inspired by her research on insects, she had imagined a machine that would emulate their ability to react, to leap, to track and to hunt. And here it was—part spider, part praying mantis, engineered in metal and powered by combustion engine.

The pod-like body was designed to rise from the ground on eight legs, strong but spindly, each leg made invincible by internal springs that provided enormous flexibility. She wrapped her hand around one of the legs, her emotions running high. It had been a fanciful artistic creation, but seeing it constructed in solid metal took her breath away. Awestruck, she made her way around the machine. At the side she heard the low throb of the combustion engine. She ran her hand along the underbelly and felt its heat. Smiling fondly, she felt as if she had been reunited with long-lost kin. She'd come there angry, possessive and thwarted, and yet seeing her design realized as a complete construction made her hands tremble with excitement.

At the rear she found a metal ladder that dropped from the vessel to the ground. She hitched her skirts and clambered up. Cautiously, she opened the hatch. Inside it was gloomy but toward the front of the pod an oil lamp stood on a brass surface, giving out a warm, inviting light. She paused, still wary, but heard no sound other than the low rumble of the combustion engine in dormant mode. Unable to resist, she climbed inside.

Nothing could have prepared her for the beauty of the interior. Where solid sheets of sturdy welded metal characterized the exterior, inside it was all gleaming brass dials and copper pipes. The construction was immaculate and finished to a high standard. She stepped over to the control panel and ran her fingers along the casement. She was so fascinated that she did not sense the human presence behind her until it was too late. When she did she tensed and turned on her heel.

The man rose from a seat in the darkness beyond the hatch.

Her hand went to the pommel of her sword.

"What have we here," the man drawled, "a thief in the night who dares to touch my precious creation?"

The statement was meant to provoke, she knew that. Nevertheless her anger flared. "I am no thief." She drew her sword, pointing it around the gleaming interior of the Daedalus. "What is this, if not theft of my design?"

He laughed softly.

She assumed an *en garde* position, challenging him.

He stepped into the fall of light. Built tall and large, he towered over her. She cast an eye over his greatcoat and polished knee-length boots, taking in the fitted breeches and open necked shirt beneath. His dark hair fell loosely to his shoulders and his eyes were shadowed under drawn-down brows. Stubble marked his jaw. The rugged build of his features looked starker still in the half-light. The sight of him made her will strong and her legs weak.

"Thief!" she declared.

He moved swiftly, his sword out and clashing against hers. "And you?" he responded, with amusement. "Lurking on the marshes in the midnight hours, like a common smuggler." With consummate skill he traded thrusts and parries with her, his blade ringing against hers.

Her heart raced wildly, but gritty determination to equal him drove her on.

He nodded approvingly at her maneuvers. "I have to admit your fencing has improved somewhat since our last meeting, my dear."

Nina smiled. She had been taking lessons. However his compliment distracted her and before she could draw breath he knocked the sword from her hand. Cursing, she glared at him. His blade flashed again, slicing the fabric of her bodice between her breasts.

Furious, she backed away and clutched her hands to the polished brass panel behind her. "Dishonorable as ever, I see, Dominic Bartleby."

"Particularly where you are concerned, my beauty." He ran the tip of his finely crafted blade into the torn fabric at her cleavage, as if daring her to move.

In an attempt to stifle the rise and fall of her chest, she bit into her lower lip. When the blade skimmed over the surface of her corset, a quiet moan escaped her.

Dominic raised an eyebrow, his mouth lifting in a faint smile.

"You never did play fair," she stated. Smarting, she pushed his blade aside and covered her torn gown with her cloak. "The least you can do is allow me to experience the Daedalus now that it has been built."

He stepped back and bowed, but his pleasured smile didn't escape her notice. He wanted this—he wanted her to be needy and grateful for the chance to see it and touch her own creation. How infuriating it was to have been caught here. Even so, her body responded as it always did to his proximity and attitude, as if his very presence infected her blood with a fever of longing that she could neither deny nor ignore. *Damn him.* Bracing herself for his mockery and cheek, she took another look at the control area of the vessel, studiously avoiding the place where he stood. "Why did you do it? Why did you build it?"

He took an age before he responded. "Because it was a superlative design."

She shot him a glance. He'd teased her about her designs, calling them impossible frippery. She'd always known that his engineering skills could make them solid and true, but he'd not taken her seriously when they'd been together. "The real reason."

He nodded, deferring to her skepticism. "Your design was outrageous...wild, and seemingly unattainable." His gaze roved over her. "It was perfect in every other way."

He met her stare. She scowled at him.

"The Crimean War raised many issues," he continued in a more serious tone. "The world is changing. Britain may be an empire and an island but our coastline is still vulnerable. I presented your design to Parliament and offered to build a prototype from my own funds. I suggested it could be used to guard shallow waters and low-lying areas such as the Romney Marshes, places that would be our frontline if invasion should threaten." He gave a sardonic grin. "Given the problem we already have with smugglers here on the marshes, Parliament practically snatched the contract from my fingertips."

Nina's fury built. The way he so blatantly told her what he'd done with *her* design was utterly galling.

"Now that the minister of defense has seen it," Dominic continued, "he wants more of your beautiful machines." He paused, observing her reaction. "Imagine it, Nina, a frontline of Daedalus spiders, cunning workers observing our coastline, able to march through any terrain and confront the enemy."

Her emotions twisted and turned. Pride flared in her chest, but at the very same moment the sense of injustice she felt bit deep into her. If she had taken the project to Parliament she would have been cast out as a foolish woman. "I suppose you expect me to be grateful that you took charge of it?"

"Of course not. You are far too contrary and stubborn to be grateful for anything."

The tone of his comment irked her even more.

Then he licked his lips as if he was relishing his power over her. "I've engineered your design successfully, improved on it, made it solid and real and useful, but all you can do is glare at me." He shrugged one shoulder. "I'm disappointed. Frankly, my dear, I expected more fire." His handsome mouth lifted at one corner, as if he was daring her to lash out at him. He knew her rebellious spirit far too well.

"I always knew it could be done," she retorted. "What annoys me is that you stole my designs and you ruined my reputation, and now you expect me to be pleased because you've sold it to Parliament, the very establishment I detest?"

"What better way to mutiny Parliament than from within?" He was quite serious, and she loved that. The suggestion was there in his eyes: bright, devilish and promising her many an adventure. Her body responded, aching for him. "Besides," he continued, "as I recall you were quite willing to have your reputation ruined, eager in fact." He looked her over with undisguised appraisal, as if recalling their more intimate encounters.

Nina bristled. "Heat of the moment, nothing more."

"Is that so? And there was me thinking it was so much more than that."

He was right of course. Studying together meant that their mutual attraction had built steadily, until it could not be denied. And how well matched they had turned out to be in matters of sexual congress. Her body throbbed with arousal as treasured memories flitted through her mind. But that was behind them now, and that's where it had to stay.

Dominic strolled closer. He parted her cloak and gazed at her chest, then trailed the back of his knuckles along her jaw, his touch inflaming her. "In fact, being a vicar's daughter only seemed to make you more rebellious in matters of morals."

Fury bit into her. She slapped him.

With lightning reactions he gripped her around the upper arms and kissed her, his mouth hungry and possessive on hers.

Stunned, she froze, then melted. Her lips parted under his, her fisted hands pressed to his chest. His wicked charms always had made her weak.

"I want you," he demanded as he drew back, "right here and now, at the heart of the Daedalus." Bending her back over the area for map reading that was stationed next to the controls, he pinned her down to the flat surface with his hands on her shoulders.

"No!" Nina gasped, torn between fighting him and submitting. She hated the way he affected her so, but heat gathered between her thighs with startling speed. "Not until we discuss my rights."

Dominic's eyes glinted, as if that was the very thing he wanted her to say. He undid her cloak where it was latched at her collarbone then his hands moved to her skirt. He moved it in his hands, pausing to speak. "You have no rights whatsoever, but that is not because I took them from you."

Oh, how she reviled that fact, and he knew it. She'd ranted about it often enough, much to his amusement. It felt far too much as if he was making her face the paltry existence her sex was fated to, something she balked against as a woman who could outthink most men.

"The patent in your name," he offered, "in exchange for something I want."

Her lips parted, objection hovering there, but need put its own spin on her reaction, making her moan with longing instead. Without further ado he tugged her skirts and petticoats up, handling them roughly, until the material was bunched at her waist.

Desire tugged at her will, unraveling it. "You cannot put the patent in my name," she blurted, attempting to cling to reason. "As a woman I do not have the status to carry it." Heated emotions flared in her. Having a female monarch made not one jot of difference. "A scholarship to Cambridge for a woman of humble background does not change the fact she is a worthless woman."

He stroked her woolen stockings over her knees and his eyes flickered, dark and possessive, his mouth pursed as he observed her. "Don't be bitter, Nina. It doesn't suit you. Besides, you were more intelligent than most of the men at Cambridge."

More intelligent than most of them, except him. If she was, she wouldn't have been captured here and at his will, all for the sight and touch of a machine that she could never own. Her thoughts were in chaos, because the position he had put her in splayed her intimate parts against his hard erection. Fighting to stifle her response, she pressed her lips together and turned her face away, when what she really wanted to do was rub against the hard bulk of his erection. He bent to kiss her in the dip of her cleavage.

"And more desirable than all of the women I have ever known," he added. "Why else do you think I arranged this?"

She stared down at him, her eyes widening. This was an elaborate trap? He'd used the Daedalus to bait her, knowing that she would have to see her dream made real? All the evidence suggested it was so, but she could not believe it. Dominic had the world at his feet. He did not need to toy with her, a vicar's daughter who had ideas and intelligence above her station—a burden if ever there was one.

"Ah, you see it now. Yes, that is how much I want you. I knew that you could not resist seeing it so I secreted it in the place that the local vicar's daughter knows so well." He ran his fingers down her cheek, and there was longing in his eyes. "If only I could lure you as easily as this machine has."

"You can lure me all too well," she shot back at him, "that is why I stayed away."

"Why did you run from me?"

His question disarmed her. Months had gone by. She didn't even think he cared, and had for a long time assumed he'd moved on to his future bride. "I left you a note," she muttered.

"All it told me was that our relationship was over. Why?"

His fingers stroked up and down the soft skin of her inner thighs, maddening her. The way he touched her while he quizzed her made her vulnerable, her desire undermining her will to defy him.

"I heard of your impending engagement to Lady Lucy Etherington." The old familiar pain uncoiled in her gut. She lashed out. "I have too much wit and will to be designated the role of secret mistress until you cast me aside!" Her body rose against his, attempting to buck him off.

He pinned her down with his hands on her hips. "And you also have too much pride to ask me if the rumors were true." He quirked an eyebrow to emphasize his point. "The match was discussed, but it was not for me. My father has been set straight on that matter." He shrugged off his greatcoat, casting it aside. "There's only one woman I want in my bed."

The fine lawn of his shirt clung to the heat of his body, drawing her attention, making her want him even more. Ducking his head, he breathed along the skin of her cleavage. His mouth on her breast stole her breath away. Meanwhile, he pushed her farther up the flat surface, so that her bottom rested on it and her legs dangled, then his fingers breached her drawers, finding their way into the gap there. He stroked her puss. "I want you, Nina Ashford."

His demanding approach made her pulse race. The damp heat between her thighs was impossible to ignore. She felt exposed, emotionally and physically stripped to the core, her will and being made freely available to him because she craved him so. Dominic did this to her as only he could. Moaning aloud, her head rolled.

He ran his fingers into the slit in her drawers, then stroked them up and down her damp folds. "Ah, yes, but you're lush and ready for this."

His voice was hoarse. She cried out, because the tantalizing touch made her want to rub against him. She hated him for disarming her so thoroughly and turned her face away.

"Your absence in my bed has driven me close to madness." He held her jaw in one hand, forcing her to meet his gaze. "I must be inside you or I will not be held accountable for what occurs."

The provocative statement left her speechless, but he moved his hand, rolling his thumb back and forth over her seat of pleasure. The relief she felt was immense. Then he shifted and ducked. His mouth engulfed her swollen nub. He grazed her tender flesh with his teeth and release barreled through her. He pushed his tongue inside her, collecting her copious juices. She was still gasping for breath when he rose up and tugged at her bodice, making her breasts rise from the tight fabric. Nina was so shocked by his actions that she stared up at him, then his hands moved and he arranged her legs around his hips.

As he did so he looked at the pistol strapped to her ankle boot with both admiration and amusement. Again his fingers roved over her puss. "Are you ready for me?"

She turned her face away. Ready? Her body clamored for him, her center alight with expectation, her core slick with her juices. "Make haste," she blurted, "before I change my mind."

Dominic gave a wry laugh and then unbuttoned his breeches. When she felt the blunt head of his cock pushing at her slippery opening, she clutched at his shirt. Then he reached past her and pushed a lever. The Daedalus roared into action, the engines huffing and whirring, the pipes that ran around the pod vibrating. One of the dials to the side of her head pinged loudly, startling her. Then the entire machine jolted, lifting up onto its legs—first at the front, then at the rear where she had climbed up the ladder.

Staggered by the sense of power and the sudden movement, she tugged on his shirt. "Dominic!"

The shunt and jolt of the machine as it rose up only seemed to assist his approach, angling her body to him. His cock thrust deep into her, stretching her open and filling her. She cried out, intense sensation rolling through her when he touched her center.

The machine swayed as it leveled, making her head spin.

"Oh, dear lord, how it rolls!" Delighted laughter escaped her.

"I took the liberty of lengthening its rise." As he spoke humor flitted through his eyes and he put his hands beneath her bottom, lifting her in order to probe her deeper. Her corset seemed tighter still, pressing down against her womb where heat built and swelled. Meanwhile the Daedalus remained poised and pumping, as if waiting instruction.

The feeling of being filled by him was too good. Her thighs locked around his waist, her body arching up to meet his. The pressure of his rod at her center sent a wild flare through her entire body, a fiery reaction akin to that of the combustion engine that stoked the Daedalus. She was back at the precipice in moments, her groin alive with sensation.

He worked his length in and out of her sensitized puss, his hands locked around her bottom while he drove himself into her, relentlessly. "There is a way," he stated, between thrusts. "Marry me, Nina. Take my name and it will be on the patent. The Daedalus is ours and there will be many more inventions with you as designer and me as engineer...it's not the same without you."

Her breath caught.

"Answer me!"

Defiance still underpinned her will. "You indicated the patent was for this favor."

He shook his head, and his expression was thoroughly wicked as he clarified his meaning. He drove his slick cock in and out of her in measured strides, working her closer to spilling while holding his own release in abeyance. "You're here. I'm claiming my reward. I want the rest...your name on the patent."

She could see it was taking intense concentration for him to work her while he spoke, but he did so. "Marry me, Nina, make it so." His fingers trailed along her throat, his expression growing serious. "Please, I need you."

She loved him so much that his plea broke her apart inside. Never before had he shown her that need, that affection. Her fingers dug deep into his powerful shoulders and her core clenched at his rod. He groaned and leaned closer still, bending her legs under him, his weight against her tender folds. Again she flooded. The release was so great that she felt dizzy even though she was flat on her back, but the hard rod of his cock inside and the pressure of his body against her sensitive, intimate parts kept her there.

The muscles in his shoulders and neck stood out, his eyes closing. His cock stiffened, stilled and jerked repeatedly. Another wave hit, her thighs shuddering as her entire body burned with the raw pleasure he'd brought about.

When he withdrew he rained kisses on her face, throat and chest, then reached out and pushed another lever. "Hold on tight," he murmured.

Taking her hands in his, he guided them to a metal strut above her head then he rested over her. He held her steady while the engines roared and the Daedalus rose to its full height, bursting through the ramshackle covering above them.

Only then did she realize that Dominic had incorporated a glass panel above their heads, and she was bathed in moonlight. In the gloom of the old moorings, the panels were not visible.

Now they were. She was in ecstasy. With her eyelids lowered she felt every swift movement the machine made, how it emulated the leap and stride of the insects that had inspired it, as it made its way across the marshland. It rose and fell as it gained the measure of the uneven landscape beneath it, the pod acting like a massive spirit level just as she had dreamed. All the while Dominic held her tightly, staring down at her face as she took in the intensity of what they were sharing and what had passed between them. Pleasure spiraled through her. From her core, where she still throbbed in the aftermath of her release, it radiated through every part of her.

She stared up into his eyes, adoring him for his brazen cheek. "I can scarcely believe this," she whispered.

"It is magnificent. Your talent for design is like a beacon showing the way to the future."

It wasn't what she meant, but she went with his flow. "You made it happen."

He raised his eyebrows. "I get to share a little of the credit?"

Humility was not something she was used to him showing, and it made her heart swell. "A little. Come now, Dominic, it's yours as much as it is mine."

He fixed her in a glance. "And you? Say you will be mine."

"Perhaps." Nina smiled and rolled her hips against his, delighted when she felt him harden again.

"Nina Ashford, you will be mine," he stated gruffly.

He claimed her mouth, not waiting for her to reply, but Nina didn't care, because this time she didn't want to disagree with Dominic Bartleby. He'd built her machine to win her back, but her heart was already his.

FOG,
FLIGHT AND
MOONLIGHT

Sacchi Green

Fog lay heavy on the city, muffling sound, blurring those few gaslights still lit, slowing life like a pocket watch in need of winding. To tell the truth, though, San Francisco even in winter is generally lively enough to make up for some dreary days, and this one had a hint of spring to it. In the past two years I'd learned to read the weather patterns of San Francisco Bay as well as ever I'd known those of Wyoming; this was a low fog that would burn off within the hour.

A hundred feet up I saw I'd been right. Above that dense, narrow layer, a nimbus of thinning mist glowed pale gold, and by two hundred feet it gave way to sunlight bright enough in the east to make me yank tinted goggles down across my eyes. Rising through dimness into light, from earthbound cloud into limitless freedom, always gave me a thrill keener than any other—except sex, and even then such peak encounters had been few. The only time I would have gladly traded for had been the day back in Wyoming when Miss Lily had first shown me the delights two women could draw from each other's bodies.

That had been in this very wicker gondola beneath this same hot air balloon, patched with fancy silk sheets from her elegant whorehouse. I'd had a considerable variety of girls since then, and a man or two—though the one of those that most sparked my fancy didn't seem to see me that way—but none could hold a candle to the joy of flying.

But my sky today was not limitless. On the fogbound earth Ho Ming and her crew waited for the signal to draw me back to the launching platform. I cut off the flow of coal gas to the burner, the air in the ballooning envelope of silk above being quite hot enough to keep at this altitude for some time. It was merely a tethered test ascent, the first since the *Prairie Lily* had been unfurled from winter storage; the view at three hundred feet would have to do. Fog still clung to the land, but sunlight flashed from wavelets in the bay, and the forested Oakland hills were in full sunlight. Directly northward the peak of Mt. Tamalpais stood clear and serene above veils of mist caressing its lower slopes.

I gripped the ropes connecting the gondola to the balloon, exulting in the freedom of my sky, my space; mine alone...

Until something denser than fog rose suddenly below, shattering my elation, very nearly stopping my heart. I pushed up the goggles and stared, unbelieving, as a great dark shape breached the mist like a whale surfacing from the ocean's depths. Once in the sunlight it was dark no longer, but glinted with a coppery sheen. Not a whale after all, I thought, in a daze born of panic, but a fish, with scales...or...no, those were meant to be overlapping feathers, decorative traceries inscribed into a skin that was, in fact, metal.

This was no monster or wild delusion, but a machine, some sort of flying device! A machine, however fantastical it seemed, was something I could understand. More to the urgent point, it had moved sideways enough that it would miss colliding with me as it rose. A flying machine that could be steered, and propelled! And with lift enough to cloak its gasbag with copper!

I didn't realize my breathing had stopped until it started up again. Then I gasped again, and cursed, as air currents stirred up by the intruder hit and made my gondola pitch and sway. It was all I could do to hang on and not be tumbled out, and the *Prairie Lily* above me thrashed about until I wasn't sure the tethers could hold her.

Observation of much about the flying machine rising past was impossible, except to note that the gasbag was oval in shape and so was the enclosed gondola tucked up close beneath it. But I did catch a glimpse of a face at a window, helmeted and goggled and hidden as well by a short black beard. I recognized that beard with its jagged silver streak on one side. To my shame, I'd even dreamed about that beard, in vividly improper ways, proceeding from stroking it with my fingers to feeling it against my skin in a very different region.

It was Miklos, that cursed lecturing fellow from the symposium!

When I managed to look again, his gondola was higher than mine, though scarcely a stone's throw away. I fervently wished I'd brought along a supply of just such ammunition.

He'd shut down his propelling devices, at least, so the air wasn't battering at me much. I glared across at him. He pushed up his goggles and looked nearly as panicky as I'd been, but when I let go of one rope to shake my fist at him, he flashed the broad smile that had also figured in my dreams, put a finger to his lips as though signaling a secret, and drifted away upward before restarting the propellers. From below I could see that both gasbag and gondola were colored a misty white on their undersides, the way some birds and fish try to blend in with the brightness above them. Then he set off toward the northeast, confident in his craft's ability to cross the Bay to its northern tip without depending on the whims of the wind.

I shook now not with fear but rage, and a burning envy. A directable airship! What was the word from that lecture? Dirigible? But he'd made it seem all theory and speculation, and wild speculation at that; nothing already possible, already built and fashioned with such attention to fanciful detail. Who could ever see that tracery of feather shapes on the top surface? Unless they were flying in another such airship—or a hot air balloon like the *Prairie Lily,* which he'd clearly regarded with a degree of condescension when we'd conversed after his lecture.

Later, though, when the old professor had brought him along to Ruby Lou's notorious parlor house, he'd appeared to take some interest in accounts of my uncle Thaddeus Brown, who'd flown surveillance airships with Colonel Lowe's aeronauts in Mr. Lincoln's war, and who had left the *Prairie Lily* to me when he died. I'd even begun to think this attractive young man had taken some interest in me, Maddy Brown, though it was clear I wasn't one of the girls for hire. But then the new French girl in a satin corset and not much else had attracted his interest enough to lead him upstairs, both of them babbling away in the French language. He came back every night for a week, and would converse with me about scientific matters and foreign countries and even my life in Wyoming, in quite a lively fashion, until some sort of inner reminder would strike him, and he'd go off with one girl or another. In all that time, he'd never mentioned flying a true dirigible airship.

So now that I *had* seen the reality of this airship, did he truly think I wouldn't tell? Well…I might not, at least not yet. The notion of a possible hold on him calmed me down somewhat and warmed me up a tolerable bit as well.

A light breeze was building from the west. I was pretty sure the air currents could be sufficient as the day progressed to take me all the way across to a landing in the East Bay, but without a paying passenger I couldn't afford enough fuel for such a flight. The air in the *Lily* was cooling already, and we were beginning to descend. I increased the gas flow just enough to keep from falling too fast. The crew would crank the tethers onto their giant spools as soon as they felt the slack.

Ho Ming's customary impassive expression was just a hair less impassive when I climbed out of the gondola. The flailing of the balloon must have been felt through the cables, but I was glad enough that she said nothing beyond the necessary, and neither did I. Once we had the *Prairie Lily* and gondola safely packed up in the wagon and were making our way back to Ruby Lou's I thought a time or two that she was about to ask, but it never quite came to that.

If I confided in anyone, it would be Ho Ming. We never talked much, but after two years we were as good friends as could be managed in the circumstances. We worked well together, both of us being women dressing like men, though Ho Ming could pass so well that even I thought of her as "he," while I made no pretense of being anything I wasn't. Those who call me "Ruby Lou's boy" do it with a grin and often a leer, showing they aren't deceived a bit by my trousers and shirt and short pale hair. I don't mind what they call me. I've always been nobody's but my own.

Miss Lily had given me a letter of introduction to Ruby Lou, who had taken me in and given me work as a sort of secretary and assistant. If I expressed my appreciation to her in other ways now and then, that was my own business. Ho Ming did more of the heavy chores and security work. She came from the north of

China and was bigger and taller than most Chinamen in California, and would toss a drunken troublemaker out the door with secret moves that nobody else could ever quite figure out. Just as Ruby Lou's influential notoriety protected me from insults that might have come my way, it shielded Ho Ming from much of the ill will against Chinese immigrants so widespread in the area.

That night the professor came to Ruby Lou's and headed right for me. I was keeping an eye on incoming patrons, making sure they weren't already too drunk. I didn't look around to see if that deceitful lecturer had come along; the way his dirigible had been heading, by now he'd landed somewhere in Sonoma.

"What was the name of that quack lecturer on flying machines?" I asked the professor. "Miklos...something? I never quite caught it."

"Maddy, my dear, would I take you to quack lectures?" he objected. "Never! Miklos Karvaly is no quack, but a man ahead of his time!"

I watched him sidelong, trying to figure whether he knew more than he let on. "Sounds foreign."

"Hungarian, yes," he said. "Though I believe he was raised in Los Angeles. Cousin to the Haraszthy family. They do think he's somewhat on the wild side, I will admit."

"Ah," I said. "The wine people. That would explain why he was heading up toward Sonoma."

The professor just looked puzzled at that and swiftly changed the subject to the upcoming event with Mr. Mark Twain at the Bohemian Club, which was so like him that I couldn't justifiably find it suspicious.

Some folks call me the professor's boy, instead of Ruby Lou's, with an extra snide round of leering, and I don't deny that he may entertain that fantasy himself at times. But he's been good to me, and if I repay him now and then with such mild pleasures as he's able to manage, that's my own business, too. My scant education has been expanded by his conversation and the books he's lent me and the lectures and symposiums we've attended together, often in places where no acknowledged woman would be admitted.

Just now, though, I didn't want any further conversation with him, for fear of saying too much. He drifted off to exchange some words with Ho Ming, as he often did to practice speaking the Mandarin Chinese language. The surprising part was that Ho Ming spoke back to him with uncharacteristic volubility.

Next morning was clear and fine. I took the wagon to purchase more tanks of coal gas for flying, and all the way from the Tenderloin to the coal plant at Potrero Point and back I was pondering what to do if Mr. Miklos-lying-Karvaly didn't come back soon to face up to my questions. The fact that my image of such an interrogation involved him being tied to a great cogwheel was just a bit of private entertainment.

I needn't have worried. Miklos was right there in front of Ruby Lou's stable, and as Ho Ming stepped up to unload a tank, he hefted one onto his own broad shoulder with no regard to his tailor-made coat. Ho Ming muttered something to him as he passed, and he muttered something back in Chinese, while I sat there in the wagon stewing in silent irritation that he knew both French and Chinese. Not that it mattered a whit, but I had a strong disinclination to feel at a disadvantage to him in any way.

With only two tanks left, Miklos came to stand by me. "Miss Brown...Maddy?...do you expect to be needing these to fly today? With such fine weather?"

I looked at him with what I hoped was a steely gaze. He did seem a bit embarrassed, or penitent, or maybe even shy.

He tried again. "I must apologize for our near-collision

yesterday. I had no notion you'd be flying in such fog, but I should have steered clear of your launch site from the start. I hope you weren't too greatly frightened."

"*Frightened?*" I paused to keep my voice from rising to a shrill squeal. "Not frightened, furious! Don't we have something more to discuss than your blundering? Something you hadn't seen fit to mention to a lowly balloon pilot who happens to be merely female?"

I saw I'd gone too far when he smothered a smile. "Ma'am, I would never think of a balloon pilot as lowly, or any woman as 'merely' female. Someone who can manage being both at once is truly awe inspiring."

That was something, however insincere, but not enough to win forgiveness. I pretended to ignore it. "As to making an ascent today, I wouldn't expect to find paying passengers this early in the season, and in midweek. On Sundays enough folks ride the streetcar out to the park to improve my chances, but we generally don't see weather this fine until May or June, and I don't count on it even then."

"But you'll have a paying passenger," Miklos said, "if you'll take me. And we'll have a chance then to discuss all those other matters."

I pretended to consider. "I suppose it wouldn't hurt to have the *Prairie Lily* on view, getting folks thinking about going up some other day. I'll take you up for half an hour or so."

"I was thinking more of a regular flight, right across the Bay to Oakland. I've even brought a luncheon to share." Miklos gestured toward a wicker hamper on the curbside. "But only if you think the wind's right for the trip."

I figured this was some sort of challenge, so I named him a high price, more than enough to cover bringing the *Prairie Lily* back over on the ferry, and he paid it right out. I resolved to save his cash and thrust it back at him some day for a flight in his far grander vessel.

Golden Gate Park had been only sand dunes before the city had greened it up. Through Ruby Lou's influence with city councilmen, I'd been granted a launch base near enough to the horticultural gardens that most folks would pass by at one time or another, and tethered rides in a hot air balloon became a fashionable enough adventure that what I could earn in good weather got me through the harsh times.

Miklos acted as crew along with Ho Ming and asked enough questions to nearly persuade me that his education in flight had skipped the finer points of hot air inflation. The look on his face when the *Prairie Lily* stood suddenly upright, inflated to positive buoyancy, reminded me of just the way I'd felt the first time I'd seen it happen. So did his expression as we rose gently from the ground.

"I won't be sure about the wind direction until we've got some altitude," I said, working the gas flow to keep a slow, steady ascent. "If I have any doubts I'll put us down along the Embarcadero." I kept a keen eye on the drift of smoke or steam from chimneys, the flight of seagulls, and, once we were high enough, the wave patterns on the surface of the bay. Air currents could be different at different elevations, and change as the sun heated land and water.

"We'll do it!" I called over the roar of the burner, as I poured enough heat into the air bag to take us abruptly higher. Miklos grinned like a schoolboy. I smiled back, glad to be sharing the joy of flight with someone who understood, and nearly forgot my grudge against him.

At my chosen altitude I turned down the burner. We soared along steadily in the near-silence that only comes with traveling with the wind instead of battling it. I leaned over the rim of the gondola to watch the waves immediately below us, then turned suddenly to ask Miklos some serious questions about the structure of his airship. It seemed best to get some solid information before raising the issue of secrecy.

"Do you use a single gasbag within a rigid framework?"

Miklos raised his head with a jerk. He'd been staring at me, not at my face, but well below.

"What is it?" I looked down to see if something was wrong. I'd dressed warmly, with long johns under my denim trousers, but it's true that Levi Strauss and Co. doesn't cut their work pants to fit the female form, and slim though I am they're a bit snug in the seat, especially when I lean over as I'd just done. "What? Have you got some complaint about my choice of clothing?" My tone made it clear that he'd danged well better not.

"No! Just the contrary!" His face above the beard reddened, and he looked flustered to an astonishing degree for someone generally so self-possessed. "But...oh, you were asking about the rigid framework. Yes, and in larger machines, we—"

I broke in coldly. "Let that wait. I'm the pilot in this craft, and I won't be made game of. Apologize for your rude staring, or explain yourself."

"I do apologize," he said sincerely. "I was just thinking... well, someone like you would naturally not be pleased to be admired in such a way, but I couldn't help thinking that if the ladies of this town only realized how becoming trousers can be on a woman, you would start a fashion craze."

His face had got even redder. It was hard to be angry at a full-grown man who could blush, and very tempting to see how long I could keep him that way.

"Why would I not be pleased to be admired?" I had a good notion what his misconception was, and thanked my stars I'd never had the tendency to blush myself. "I'm not some simpering damsel who denies having any parts below the waist."

"No, of course not! But it's known that your opinion of men is…is not quite that of most women."

Enough fumbling around the issue. "Plenty of women share my opinion that men are boring and overbearing and a bar to our freedom. That doesn't mean we can't appreciate them under the right circumstances. Just because I have some appetite for women doesn't mean I draw the line at men."

He brightened a good deal. "And what circumstances do you prefer?"

"Well," I said, to jolt him a bit, "back in Wyoming I made the ranch hands let me tie 'em to a fence post, and those who objected at first didn't seem to mind it much later." Just one ranch hand, a very young and shy one, but close enough to true.

"And all this time I thought I'd be better off to forget you if I could!" Miklos looked almost angry, until he flashed the smile that always sets off a spark in me. "So all I needed was a fence post to get tied to!" He pretended to look around our cramped space. "But you don't seem to have one handy, and I didn't think to bring any of my own." He spread his arms wide and gripped the ropes connecting the gondola to the balloon. "Would this do, if I promise to consider myself tied?"

This was both game and challenge, I saw, though I wasn't at all sure how one would judge the winner.

Miss Lily had stood just so, while I worked my way through her opulent delights…but with Miklos spread out at my mercy, all other visions faded. Miss Lily would have understood perfectly.

"We'll just see how long you can hold that position," I said, and took time to check our altitude and assess the balloon's state of inflation. When I finally moved close enough to press against him I could tell through his expensive broadcloth trousers that he was getting to a considerable state of inflation as well. So, in my way, was I, but it would be easier to keep control of the situation if I didn't let on.

"Consider your head tied, as well," I said sternly when he tried to duck his mouth toward me. "I'm the commander of this ship." Then I stood on tiptoes with my body rubbing against him, set my hands on his shoulders, and touched my lips very briefly to his before running them across his beard. It felt silky and rough both at once. The white streak covered a scar of some sort, more like a burn than a cut; I stroked it so lightly with my tongue that I could feel him shiver.

"Good god, Maddy, this is harder to bear without moving than a whipping would be!"

"Well, I didn't think to bring my whip, so you'll just have to put up with whatever I choose to do, but if you fancy something harsher I'll try to oblige." I slid my hands inside his jacket and around to his shoulder blades, and gripped hard, which thrust his chest against my breasts. He kept his hold on the ropes but wriggled against me, which I allowed until I was enjoying it very nearly too much for self-control, and leaned back.

"Enough of that! Stay still!" I ran my hands down his back, noting for future reference that he seemed a bit ticklish about the waist, and dug my fingers into his truly fine, firm buttocks. I'd admired those even when I was watching them travel up Ruby Lou's gilt staircase trailing that saucy French wench.

Miklos gasped at every savage squeeze, and jerked, and his trousers seemed fit to burst, but he held on. I worked one hand between his thighs from behind. His muffled groan sounded like the wail of a steam engine.

With both hands busy, I dropped to my knees and applied my teeth to the situation. Practice with women had made me an expert at buttons. It turned out that trousers and underdrawers had six each, and I needed to switch my grip to his thighs to keep him steady enough for me get them undone before there wouldn't be any more point to it.

Just before the final button I glared up at him. "Don't go thinking I'm kowtowing to you just because I'm down here. One wrong move"—I put some upward pressure on his thighs— "and I can topple you over the edge."

"You nearly have already," he gasped. "Maddy, for god's sake…"

"All in good time," I said, and stood, and turned to adjust the gas flow. We'd been drifting downward too far. I felt his presence behind me like heat from a burner, even though he hadn't moved, and at that point I wouldn't have minded if he'd lurched forward to press his urgent cock against me from behind and let it all go, but he held on.

So it was up to me to turn and come at him, ripping open that last button, grasping the ropes below his hands so I could pull myself upward and mount him. I gripped his hips with my knees, ground my still-clothed crotch against his hardness, and felt my pleasure surge until his rasping cries took me right over the edge with him. Then, at last, he let go, and we both crumpled to the floor of the gondola.

I recovered first, stood up, and looked out over the Bay. "So," I said, not wanting to assume anything serious about what we'd just enjoyed, "where's your preference for a landing? I may not be able to steer the *Prairie Lily* like your airships, but the air currents here are complex, and I can do tolerably well by moving from one level to another."

Miklos stood up, his clothing still in disarray. "Just land anyplace horizontal, and preferably private," he said, still out of breath. Then, looking down at his open trousers, he added hopefully, "I don't suppose you can do buttons up the same way they got undone, can you?"

"I can, but I won't." Then, as though it were an afterthought, I added, "Not this time, anyway. Now tell me about your dirigible airship."

"What would you think," Miklos said, feeling out his words carefully, "if next time happened to be up north in Sonoma? You could get all your answers there, and some of them on the way. And you might even decide to be part of something that's going to change our world."

"Miklos, tell me straight out what's going on. For starters, where did you come from when you nearly hit me?"

He sighed. "Down the coast, traveling mostly at night and early morning. I set down in Golden Gate Park overnight—there was just enough light from the moon and the gaslights along the edge—and was taking advantage of the morning fog to get as far north as I could without being seen. I'd been fetching some materials from Los Angeles for our main base in Sonoma."

I wasn't so much doubtful as puzzled. "If this is all such a big thing, and so secret, how can you be telling me all this?"

"It's about time! Maddy, you might as well know that you've been watched by one person or another ever since you came to San Francisco and we saw that we'd have to share the sky with you. I finally persuaded the leaders that you could be trusted; you didn't tell the professor you'd seen me, and you didn't tell Ho Ming, and there's no doubt that we need you. Good pilots are hard to come by. Most of us don't have half your skill at judging air currents."

My mind was whirling, but it grabbed on to one detail. "The professor and Ho Ming knew?"

"They knew." He saw my stormy face and rushed on. "Here's the thing in a nutshell, even if it won't make much sense at first. We're building airships, and some day not too far off the skies will be so filled with them that you and I might wish they'd never been built at all, but there's no holding back progress."

I must have looked interested, because he went on at a steadier pace. "The secrecy is partly because we don't want our methods copied, but even more because our chief inventors and engineers are Chinamen who left their country before they could be imprisoned or killed for the 'impiety' of trying to conquer the sky. My uncle got to know and respect some of them who were also stone workers, digging caves in Sonoma for the storage and aging of his wines. Most places, though, they're still in danger because of willful ignorance and bigotry against all immigrants from China. We'll get past that, once we get to selling aircraft to European countries where there's already considerable interest, but it will take time."

"Speaking of time," I said, "we'll be setting down along the Oakland piers in ten minutes." And I went about my pilot duties still pondering everything Miklos had told me. And not told me. It was clear enough that he'd flown with me today as a final check on my skills before letting me in on the secret, but I was quite sure my additional skills had come as a very welcome surprise. And just as sure that I wanted to be a part of whatever went on concerning flight.

He had certainly been prepared to find me suitable. Ho Ming had packed a change of clothing for me in the bottom of the ignored lunch hamper, and would bring along the rest of my gear herself. A private railroad car had been reserved to take us, and the *Prairie Lily* in a freight car, to Vallejo, and an airship hidden nearby would take us the rest of the way at night.

The gondola of the dirigible was overwhelmingly beautiful in both its engineering and its artistic design. I went from one wonder to another, not noticing the length of the flight, until Miklos drew me at last to the front window.

"I wanted to show you something, so we've taken a round-about way." He seemed nearly as nervous as when I'd caught him eyeing my derriere that morning. "You haven't flown before at night, have you?"

I hadn't. Now I looked out at a splendor of stars in the night sky, slightly dimmed by a full moon high and serene in the sky.

"*Sonoma* means 'valley of the moon' in the language of the Miwok tribe," Miklos said softly at my shoulder. "But to me the moon is nowhere more beautiful than at the edge of the valley where the mountains rise." He directed my gaze downward, and I saw that we were flying over a sea of low clouds flowing between a maze of higher mountain peaks, fog to those below but a white glory of reflected moonlight to we who watched from above.

"I...I want you to know, Maddy..." He hesitated. "Since I've known you, this moonlight vista always keeps me thinking of you. Not just your lovely short pale hair," and here he touched my head lightly, "but you, not brazenly gorgeous like the sun, but with a silver glow part mystery, part strength." He shook his head and turned away a little. "I'm sorry, I'm no poet and don't generally get so fanciful. I just want you to know that it's not just the work we can do together, or even the..." He paused, as flustered now as I'd ever seen him.

"The sex," I filled in for him. "Though that alone would be enough." I took his hand and gripped it hard. "Don't worry. I came for more than the work and even the sex, as well. Where we're going I can't be sure, but I'll take a chance on whatever currents are taking us there."

That was enough for now. That, and a bit of scientific exper-imentation as to what positions two eager bodies could achieve in an elegant gondola twenty times the size of the one belonging to my dear *Prairie Lily*.

THE UNDECIPHERED HEART

Christine d'Abo

Miranda raced down the darkened hallway as quickly as her skirts and exhaustion would allow. She knew her face was flushed, smudged with ink and dust, her eyes too bright, as she'd run from the basement War Room to arrive in an unladylike fashion. Harbacher waited in the foyer when she topped the stairway, the butler no doubt anticipating her spectacular arrival once word of their visitor reached her.

"Where is he?" She didn't have time for pleasantries. "The Blue Room?"

"Yes, mum. The captain looked less than pleased." Harbacher sniffed. "Shall I bring tea?"

Blood pounded with an uneven gait in her ears as it raced through her body. For three days and nights she'd stood before the wall of barometric tubes, circuits and conduits in the War Room, consolidating dates and readings, measuring wind speeds and temperatures. Her hair had long discarded the elaborate coils and braids her maid had created. Since then hairpins had been shoved this way and that to keep the auburn locks from covering her eyes and distracting her as she shifted through the cipher.

The pulling weight of the portable statistical computation device on her arm reminded her of its presence. She forcibly straightened her shoulders to stop from slipping into the lopsided droop her body naturally adopted. Strange. In her excitement at having finally broken the French code, and determining the perfect opportunity for an attack against their rising forces, Miranda had forgotten she wore it. The bloody thing was so much a part of her she'd long expected to be buried with it secured to her arm.

While she might have wished for a looking glass, her appearance no longer mattered. It wasn't as if she needed to impress him, the Captain of the Dead. He was here to receive his orders—she was to deliver them with brevity. There was no reason to adjust the neckline of her corset or card her fingers through the wild tangle of hair. Still, she released the bindings holding the device to her arm and handed it to Harbacher. The less machinelike she was, the easier it would be to remember her place and his.

"Tea won't be necessary, Harbacher. The captain won't be staying long enough to enjoy our comforts." Miranda took a step toward the Blue Room, but hesitated when Harbacher didn't move. "And we are not to be disturbed while I debrief him. Is that understood? This is the matter of utmost confidentiality."

"Of course, mum." His disapproving frown spoke volumes. He knew of their history. They all did.

The servants would be all aflap by nightfall, of that Miranda had no doubt. Still, she was following protocol, fulfilling her duty to king and country to the very letter. No one must know of this final push to drive the French from the skies over English soil if they were to win this war.

Miranda waited until Harbacher retreated to his post off the main hall, before resuming her journey to the room where the captain waited.

The large oak door was opened only a crack. Miranda couldn't see inside and was forced to pause and listen if she wanted to determine his state. A fire crackled in the hearth, but it didn't entirely mask a soft, steady ticking sound. She knew there was no clock within. Miranda swallowed—the unwavering rhythm broke her heart.

She threw her shoulders back and held her spine rigid. Miranda was chief analyst to the king's military advisor, not some green girl fresh from the schoolroom. She couldn't afford to show the cracks that permeated her soul.

Not to him.

Taking a cleansing breath, Miranda pushed the door wide and stepped inside, unseeing. "Captain Stromguard, thank you for coming on such short notice."

Only once she'd shut the door with a firm click did Miranda shift her full attention to the man standing before the hearth.

His black hair had grown unfashionably long, the strands curling around his ears. The sharp press of his uniform was accented by the pistol at his side and the air goggles around his neck. The scruff of a beard darkened his cheeks, making him look older than his thirty-three years. The captain held the appearance of a man ready to receive his orders, no matter what hell they might lead him toward.

Miranda laced her fingers together to hide her nervous tremor. "Would you care to sit?"

"No, mum." His voice was as ragged as her nerves, cold and impersonal. "I would like to begin the briefing, if you would.

My men will need time to prep the ships if we are to fly soon."

Her gaze drifted down to the brass buttons of his greatcoat accentuating the slight rise and fall of his even breaths. Miranda knew it was impossible to see the metal plate that surely covered a generous portion of his chest. Nor would it ever be likely for her to run her fingers around the hard ridge of skin that bound it to the muscle beneath.

"Lady Miranda."

Shaking her head, Miranda hoped her blush would be lost in the dim light of the room. Absently, she fingered where her computer had been moments earlier, missing her touchstone. "Of course, Captain. It's your preference."

Miranda wasn't sure she'd be able to get through the entire debriefing without her knees buckling. She quickly moved to the leather-back chair in the corner and perched on its edge. The deep seat threatened to swallow her, throwing her off guard as she slid back several inches across its smooth surface. The motion pulled at her skirts, tightening the corset across her sensitive breasts. Lord, she felt as if *she* was the spectacle in the room.

Clearing her throat, she met his gaze evenly and refused to give in to her own cowardice. "We finally cracked the French spy code and found a weakness in their defense grid. The Admiralty wishes to exploit their discovery as quickly as we are able, lest they discover what we have done. I have orders for you and your airfleet to bomb their fleet amassing on the coast of Le Havre. We plan to destroy the French landing strip, along with their ships. With one strategic attack, we can end this war."

The captain nodded once, his crystal blue eyes never once breaking contact. "Who broke the cipher?"

Of course he would ask that. Miranda fingered the lace around the waist of her skirts. "As you are well aware, His Majesty employs a team of analysts and spies who ferreted out the relevant information. It was simply a matter of—"

"Who?"

His eyes tracked down her length and back to her face, and Miranda looked away to glance into the fire. "I was the major contributor in breaking their code, as I'm sure you have already guessed."

The captain stared at her for several long moments, before he finally cleared his throat and frowned. "Then I have no doubt the details are all in order."

He held out his hand, waiting for the dossier he knew she had secured in the deep pocket hidden in her skirts. Miranda was a creature of habit—one he knew intimately. Ignoring the sudden burst of warmth on her face, she rose to her feet. Miranda pulled the folded leather pouch free from its hiding spot and squeezed its warm bulk before gently pressing it into his hands.

"You'll find all the details within." Miranda resisted the urge to bite her bottom lip when the captain brushed his finger down the length of hers.

He's dead. Dead and not mine anymore.

"Are you sure you don't wish me to review the details with you, Captain? You may have a suggestion for how to improve the—"

"Lady Miranda," he said in a voice so soft it would have been easy to miss it. "Of all His Majesty's analysts, his code breakers and spies, I only trust you."

Tears burned the back of her eyes as the steady ticking of his heart filled the silence. "You shouldn't."

"But I do." The captain stepped away and made a direct line for the door. "Please inform His Majesty the Second Battalion Airfleet will make English skies safe once more."

Miranda could hear the ticking of his heart long after he'd left.

* * *

The wind whipped up, sending her skirts flapping as she continued the steady climb up the steep stairway to the launch deck. Miranda pulled up the military points of her jacket in hopes of hiding her identity as long as possible. The French would love to get their hands on her, or more aptly, her brain, if given half an opportunity. Her ability to break down the tactical significance of each move the French had made to date was a thorn the opposing military force had been vocal in wanting to remove.

They'd only gotten close to her the once.

"Hey, yer not supposed to be up here!"

Miranda slowed, eyeing the shipman and the glint of the moonlight off his pistol, but did not stop her ascent. "Pray, what do you know of where I should or should not be?"

The thuds of her boots were swallowed up by the strong wind as she stepped fully onto the deck. The shipman on guard opened his mouth to say something, only to snap it shut and stumble back half a step.

"Sorry, mum. We didn't know you were coming." As an afterthought, he pulled his hat from his head and lifted his goggles to rest on his forehead. "The Ministry usually tells us when one of you dignitary sorts is on the way."

The shipman's left arm had been replaced with a metal prosthetic. Silver fingers curled around the worn woolen cap. Miranda could only imagine what other injuries the man had suffered in his service to the king—and yet he was now regarded as dead to all polite society.

Lifting her chin, Miranda pushed aside her doubts and fears. "Where is the captain? I must speak to him."

"Yes, of course, mum. The captain was on the command deck last time I saw. Wanted to personally check the attack route calculations and wind currents and such before we launch at dawn, he did. I can let him know yer on your—"

"Thank you, Shipman. I know the way."

The last thing she wanted was to give the captain any reason to avoid her. Miranda needed to do this: say her piece, offer him what few reassurances she could regarding the quality of her assessments. There would be no cause for errors, no chance she'd misread the signs or been fooled by a clever French ploy. Tucking a stray strand of her hair behind her ear, she strode across the deck to the still opened bay door.

The howling wind outside was silenced as she navigated her way through the narrow corridor to the control room. The crew was all gone, no doubt drinking or whoring before they would have to leave on their mission, and the hum of the engines and the hiss of steam through the piping were the only sounds. Miranda's stomach flopped as she approached the closed port-hole door. On the other side was the captain, *her* captain, the man she'd wronged more than any other. Flexing her fingers, she quickly rapped on the door before she lost her nerve.

"Come!"

The captain was bent over an air chart with a glass on the navigation area, muttering softly. He'd shed his military greatcoat and waist jacket, and he'd rolled up his shirtsleeves, exposing the pale skin and lean muscles of his forearms. The blue wool of his pants was pulled tight across his firm buttocks, leaving nothing to her imagination.

"Give your report, then leave. I don't need distractions this evening."

Miranda closed her eyes and let his voice wash over her. For the briefest of moments, she could picture things as they had been. The way he'd touch her cheek before pressing a kiss to her lips. How his large hands would cup the swell of her hips, pulling her closer than was proper. The fullness of his cock as he'd rut against her thigh.

The steady ticking of his heart jarred her from those pleasant memories, reminding her of all she'd lost because of her carelessness.

The captain growled as he turned to face her. "Shipman, I said to—"

"Hello, Frederick."

He froze—eyes wide. "Lady Miranda? What in blazes are you doing here?"

The remnants of her confidence disappeared. Her chin dropped and she found herself unable to look higher than the tops of his boots. "I needed to offer you my personal assurances that the mission data is correct. You have no need to worry for the safety of you or your crew. I don't care what the Ministry says, I wouldn't risk any of your lives."

When Frederick didn't speak, Miranda's nerves ratcheted higher. She forced herself to look up once more, this time stepping closer to where he stood. The top two buttons of his shirt were undone, exposing the hollow of his throat and revealing a few wisps of chest hair.

"I ran and reran the scenarios, making sure the formulae were correct. There is no doubt in my mind that the French will send at least thirteen airships and ten hoppers over the channel in two days time. We've caught glimpses of the ships on the coast, preparing for the attack."

"Lady Miranda—"

She wanted to press her hands to her ears to block out the ticking. It grew louder with each step closer she took, but she continued. "The weather patterns will be in their favor then, giving them the advantage of both wind and cloud cover."

"Lady *Miranda*—"

"We will only need seven ships, each carrying twenty tons of drop explosives to cripple their fleet. With the spy information about their landing field—"

"Mandy!"

She snapped her mouth shut. Frederick stood only a few inches away, his blue eyes flashing with anger and concern. "Yes?" she whispered.

"It wasn't your fault." Each word was said deliberately. They felt like screws being wound into her chest.

"Yes, it was. The calculations were all wrong, the timing was all wrong. I should have realized the intel I'd received was a ploy to pull the fleet and soldiers away. I hadn't anticipated them sending their assassins for *me*. Lord, how do they even know who I am?" She let out a shuddering sigh.

They'd made love that night for the first time. Her pussy had throbbed from the sweet torture his body had inflicted and her nipples ached from where his mouth had nipped and sucked her until she could take no more. She'd been pushed to the limits, exhausted by too many late hours bent over her calculations and reports. Their night of lovemaking had left her wrung dry, mind floating and body blissfully numb.

"Mandy, look at me." When she didn't move, he lifted her chin with the crook of his finger. "I'm still here."

"But you're *dead*." This time she couldn't stop the tears, didn't want to. A single stream rolled down her cheek to catch on the edge of her jaw. "You should never have been where you were. Dammit, why did you step in front of that bullet? Your heart..."

For the first time since Frederick's rebirth, Miranda reached out and pressed her hand to the metal plate that comprised half his chest, barely concealed by the thin fabric of his shirt. He covered her hand with his, pressing down so she could not escape.

"As we flew, we could barely make out the ships flying in formation with us. The fog made it impossible for us to see the ground. That was the only indication I had there was a problem, that the French had lured us away to go after a different prize. There was nothing wrong with your information or calculations."

"Why you?" *Why us* was what she really wanted to know, yet dared not vocalize. "It's not fair."

"The rules are there to keep our society sane." He reached up and brushed her hair from her forehead. "It would be chaos if people lived forever, built on parts that never wore out. There must be consequences for the gift. But never doubt that I would step in front of a thousand bullets to save your life. No hesitation."

Without warning, Frederick caught her by the back of her head and kissed her deeply. Their last kiss had been nearly two years earlier, three nights before he took a bullet to the chest to save her life.

Their teeth clacked as she fought to get closer, soak his warmth into her body and make it a part of her. Her pussy pulsed with need as she spread her legs, inviting him to press his thigh between.

"Ah, darling," he muttered against her lips.

"No!" Miranda gasped and backed away. She'd almost let herself go, carried away with her desire. *Lord, I must be mad!* She pressed her fingers to her lips. "I must go."

"Mandy, please."

"You're *reborn*. They will take your heart if they suspect you've resumed our relationship! I won't have your death on my conscience twice."

"Mandy—"

"I shouldn't have come here. I—I wanted to reassure you

about the plan, n-n-not...*this*. I shouldn't have come."

She jerked her hand free of his and managed three steps toward the door before his arm hooked her around her waist. Frederick lifted her off the floor, his grasp sure and unrelenting as she beat her fists on his arm.

"Let me go!"

"Not until you *listen* to me."

"No!"

Frederick pressed her into the pilot's chair, trapping her between the high control-laden armrests and the periscopic captain's viewer. He filled up every bit of free space, giving no quarter as she struggled to push past him. Before his body had been fitted with metal gears and fittings, Miranda would have been hard pressed to win a fight. Now, it was impossible.

He did nothing to stop her struggles. She kicked and punched, tears turning to outraged cries. When Miranda bashed her knuckles against the metal plate of his chest, pain bloomed, quelling her rage.

"I'm sorry," she whispered between hiccupped sobs. Frederick slid his hands up the length of her arms and along her shoulders until he cupped her cheeks.

The kiss was chaste, but the thrill was not lessened by that fact. Miranda didn't remember when her eyes had closed or when she'd stopped struggling. Her world shrank to the slide of his rough lips against her soft ones. After a moment, she parted hers to lick at the seam of his mouth. Growling, Frederick plunged his fingers into her hair and pulled her closer still.

The warmth building low in her belly spread out, making her clit press against her undergarments. Her corset constricted her breathing, as the boning rubbed against her hardened nipples. It wasn't enough. She needed his hands on her, touching and teasing her skin until she was begging for him to fuck her. The king's rules be *damned*. They'd both given so much for this war, to save their people, for once Miranda wanted to take for herself.

Pulling back with a jerk, she ignored his groan of protest, tearing at his pearl buttons, needing to see. "Off. Take this off now."

Frederick straightened out of her reach, taking on the task himself. When she began to pull at the ties of her corset, he gave his head a hard shake. "Don't."

He pulled the air goggles from his forehead and tossed them to her. Instead of dropping them to the floor, Miranda slid them on. The smell of his soap and sweat clung to the leather, marking them as his. It was odd seeing him through such a narrow view, making him seem more human than he had to her in years.

Frederick paused when he reached the end of the row. "Mandy, are you certain about this? I'm...this is not pleasant to see. There are nights when I can barely look at myself."

She leaned forward, the goggles sliding down her nose, and placed her hands on top of his. "Please."

Together they opened his shirt, revealing the smooth steel plate the doctors had shaped into a replica of his chest wall. They'd gone so far as to add a nipple, a match to its twin of flesh. Moving to the edge of her seat, she leaned in and circled the metal nub with her tongue. The cool taste of steel exploded on her tongue, sending a spike of arousal through her body. Frederick's breathing grew labored, but he didn't move or pull away, nothing to dissuade her exploration.

"I would lie awake at nights wondering what they'd done to you. What you looked like now." Her words echoed back to her from against the unrelenting steel. She shifted over so her nose brushed the seam of metal and flesh. Darting her tongue out to lick it she was surprised to note it tasted like sweat. "I wondered how they could possibly meld flesh and steel? How you must have hurt as you healed?"

"The pain meant nothing." He pulled several of her hairpins free and let the weight of her hair pull the mass to her shoulders. "As long as you were safe."

Miranda let Frederick move her back in the chair as he dropped to his knees. His fingers were steady as he popped the buttons of her jacket free of their cloth confines. Together they worked it off, along with her overskirt, leaving Miranda clad only in her corset and petticoat. Her heart pounded as he lifted the heavy material to her knees, exposing her calves.

His heart continued its steady beat. "I never got to do this before."

Leaning in, he hooked an arm beneath each of her knees and lifted her legs to rest on his shoulders. Miranda had to look away. She'd never been this exposed before, so open she knew there was nowhere she could hide. He spread the opening of the fabric, exposing the folds of her labia to him. With a soft growl, Frederick lowered his mouth and sucked her clit.

Intense pleasure arched through her, sending her hips bucking to chase the sensations. Frederick pulled her legs wider, as he suckled and licked her, teasing her opening with his tongue. Miranda panted, reaching out to cup her breasts and squeeze her nipples as he fell into a rhythm that matched the beating of his heart.

"Frederick." She moaned and canted her hips. "More."

The press of his finger into her pussy had her crying out. She'd played with herself many nights, imagining it was him, but the reality was much more. The pleasure rose and she knew she would reach her peak if he didn't relent. Pulling at his hair to stop him, she was lost when he swatted her hand away and increased the pressure with his mouth. When a second finger joined the first, Miranda conceded defeat.

Her cry of pleasure filled the room, overpowering every other noise. Frederick didn't stop, thrusting his fingers in and out of her at a pace so rapid, another wave of release rolled through her. Mercifully, he pulled away then.

"Look at me, Mandy." With effort, she forced herself to watch as he licked her come off his fingers. "You're amazing."

Then he pressed those same glistening fingers to her lips. The idea of tasting her release should have been repulsive, but the look of ecstasy on his face as she darted her tongue up the digits quashed any hesitation she had.

Biting the tip of his finger, Miranda smiled. "I want you."

His hands shook as he fumbled with the heavy belt, button and ties of his pants, only pushing them down far enough to free his hard cock. The tip glistened in the dim light, tempting her. She circled the head with her thumb, relishing the open-mouthed moan that fell from him.

"I won't last long, Mandy."

"I don't care."

They still fit together. Miranda hooked her legs on each of the chair's control arms, forcing her skirts to bunch at her thighs and giving him room to move closer. The press of his cockhead at her opening was at first only a tease. He didn't enter her immediately, instead taking the time to work the laces of her corset free. Her breasts pulled free of their confines, her nipples bared to the cold air.

Lifting her breast, Frederick suckled her nipple, much as he had her clit. The flick of his tongue over the tip matched the little pulses he gave with his hips. One moment, he teased her breast, the next he thrust his cock into her with a single push.

He swallowed her moan with another long kiss. Miranda

fought to pull him closer—scratched and clawed at his back and neck as she drove her tongue into his mouth. Only once she needed air did she pull back. Their lips still touching, the words she'd wanted to say for two years fell from her.

"I miss you every day. I hate seeing you and knowing I can't touch you. You can't be mine. I hate them and love them for saving you. You for saving me. Don't leave me again."

Miranda pressed her hand to his steel chest, arched her back and cried out as she came a final earth-shattering time. Frederick increased the strength of his thrusts until the chair moved. His arms wrapped beneath her shoulders, crushing her body to his. Thrusting twice more, he let loose a powerful roar as his come filled her body.

Finally he collapsed against her. The goggles she'd worn had slipped from her eyes and lay dangling around her neck. Her heart pounded so violently, the rhythm jostled the eyepieces against her chest.

"I love you," he said softly against her neck, pressing a kiss to the skin.

"I love you as well, Captain."

Frederick pulled back, cupped her cheek in his hand and pressed a kiss to her nose. "This is no place for a lady."

She chuckled. "Thankfully, I'm not much of a lady."

Regret filled her as he slowly got back to his feet. They righted their clothing without speaking, but Miranda caught his small smile as he watched her. When they were once more presentable, she moved to take the goggles from her neck. He stopped her with a hand to hers.

"Keep them. Give them back once I've returned."

She nodded. "See that you do return, Captain. All of you."

Miranda would never know what he was to say next. The shouts of men from the hallway drew both their attention.

When the door exploded inward, Miranda reacted on instinct. She was told later the assassin looked to be little more than a boy, a French spy who'd discovered their plans and reacted the only way he knew how. He needed to kill the captain of the enemy fleet to stop them from launching their attack.

All Miranda could see in that moment was the pistol pointing at Frederick. It was an easy matter to step in the path of the bullet. She could understand why Frederick had done the same thing all those months ago. Her life for his—a simple exchange, happily made.

The cries and screams could have been hers, or the assassin's as the pursuing shipman tackled him to the floor. Miranda didn't even try to fight the darkness as it overtook her. The last thing she was aware of was a soft voice by her ear.

"Oh Mandy, what have you done?"

Pain.

The weight of her eyelids was too much for her to attempt to lift them, so Miranda didn't bother. The throbbing of her head was matched only by the burning in her chest. She tried to shift and scratch at the discomfort, but something held her down. A strap? Hands?

"Don't move."

The name of the voice's owner escaped her, but she sought comfort in it all the same.

"You're going to make it worse, Mandy."

Frederick? She forced her eyes open and was met by the sight of her lover's smile. "Hello."

Swallowing, she tried to sit up once more. "What...?"

"You were shot. Stupid girl, you stepped in front of a bullet."

Screams and tears, hot blood and cold steel. "I died?"

Frederick pressed his hand to her newly formed metal breast, not yet covered by her corset. "Yes."

She shivered at the feeling of pressure, his hand where her heart used to be.

"We're a set now, love." He leaned in and pressed a kiss to her forehead.

Miranda closed her eyes and listened as their hearts beat in perfect sync.

MR. HARTLEY'S INFERNAL DEVICE

Charlotte Stein

It's quite a queer thing that he's created. I must confess, I've never seen the like of it—and judging by the faces of the small crowd he's gathered here in his front parlor, I'm quite certain they've never seen its kind either.

It is similar to Mr. Tortoff's traveling apparatus—the one so often seen galloping about the streets these days—and yet it has many differences. It is operated by steam valves, true, and a great turning maze of brass pipes and so forth, but it does not appear to have any movement about it.

There are no wheels, no giant legs that creak and shiver and make their way through alleyways and between houses. And though it has a prettiness about it—stained glass panels, glittering like eyes and such—there is an ugliness, too. A sadness, much like the sadness that hangs over Mr. Hartley.

Even now on the eve of this presentation—the final culmination of his work on this marvelous contraption—he looks mournful. *Miserly*, Kitty calls it, and a good deal of me agrees.

He lives by himself in this grand old townhouse and has never given so much as a lick of thought to marriage or anything like it.

Though in all honesty, I can hardly say why I associate marriage with a state of unselfish giving. Perhaps it is not that at all—perhaps it is simply that Mr. Hartley is possessed of a rather long face and a meanish mouth of the kind you often see on cruel, rakish men. And his mouth is always down-turned, too, as though he has a great deal to think of and none of it is pleasant.

However, I will not go with Kitty on all assessments of his character and appearance. It is my belief that his eyes save him from true condemnation, because although they are cold, there is also something compelling in them that draws a person in. His eyes tell the tale of a man who would invent a machine like this, for no other reason than the fact that he could, and wanted to.

I can't help wondering what it will do. It takes up one entire half of his parlor, but it remains impossible to tell what its purpose is. There is a box on one side of it, upon which are several gears and buttons and other gizmos, but none of them are labeled. I try not to peer the way the others are doing, as I feel certain he would never allow anyone to easily discern what the machine is about.

Only then I catch him looking at me as though I am doing the worst of the staring, and I feel quite out of sorts. I think an unkind thing: *I wish I'd never thought well of you, Mr. Hartley.* But then almost immediately I want to take it back. It's as though those cold eyes see everything, and for all I know they do. Perhaps that is what the device is for—to steal the thoughts right out of a person's mind, then use those thoughts against them.

For some unaccountable reason it makes me flush red, to think of all the thoughts Mr. Hartley could use against me. Why, I've never imagined a single indecent or strange thing in all my days! My mind is a veritable banquet of nothing, an empty space between my ears—and even more so in the presence of someone like Mr. Hartley. Everyone always tells me, "Elspeth, you rarely have an interesting thing to say," and it is true.

I'm sure Mr. Hartley would say the same, if he were to catch a glimpse of the pumping, churning swirl of emptiness inside my head.

And yet he continues to aim his gaze on me, as we sit on the little circle of chairs he has laid out. Of course I think of séances and other such wonders of the modern world, though to me they seem a lot less like wonders and a lot more like terrors.

If he calls forth a ghost, I don't know what I shall do. Kitty said that when she went to the House of Scientific Endeavors they did that very thing, right there in the viewing room with everyone crowding in, and that the ghost had no mouth but tried to speak anyway. Frankly, I can hardly think of anything worse. Trying to speak with no mouth!

How awful, how dreadful, oh, lord how I long to leave. Kitty is far braver than I. She is red faced and excited, and whispering to Mrs. Hollingdale about mechanical wings that make people fly, whereas I am quite lost about such things. I do not wish to fly. I do not want to see ghosts.

I do not want Mr. Hartley to stare at me, or use his infernal device on my personage.

And yet I sit quite still when it comes to my turn to have the apparatus attached to me. I watch him go around the circle with his handful of wires and the little thing on the end of each that looks as horrible as a spider does, and my heart beats wild and high in my chest. I'm sure at any moment I'm going to faint, but it is somewhat easier when I do not look at him directly.

That way, I don't have to think of his cold eyes or the miniature spider thing, and as it appears that one must have it attached to the nape of one's neck, there's actually very little to fret over. I barely even feel his fingers against my skin, as he attaches it. There's no sense of something biting or anything like it.

There's just a coolness and then a low strange feeling of regret. I wonder how he was able to do it so successfully, without actually touching me? He's very deft, I suppose. Very deft and very tight lipped. When Mrs. Hollingdale says, "Why Mr. Hartley, you must now tell us what it does!" he barely acknowledges her. And he has such a way about him that she goes immediately closemouthed, as though sensible of a great faux pas that she has made.

It occurs to me, then, that he could turn his device on and kill us all. I've heard of currents being passed through bodies and things of that nature. I am not completely oblivious to the wonders of the age.

So why, then, do I not stand? Why does no one stand? Do they all look in those great eyes like cold, blue moons, and feel they brook no refusal? Perhaps they all wish, as I do, that he had laid a hand on the nape of their necks. Just one comforting hand, just one hint of humanity beneath that gleaming exterior.

I remember once attending a ball that he was present at, and when Father and I had gone about the room to offer our good-byes, he had taken my hand. I hadn't asked it of him, or even offered, but he had taken it anyway. Sometimes, I am certain I imagined it happening. Sometimes I hardly wish to think of it at all, because it feels strange that I so often do.

"Now," he says. "If everyone might close their eyes."

It is funny how you can believe that you'll be reluctant to do something, and then when the time comes you do it faster than

anyone else. My eyes are closed before he has finished speaking.
I can see his parlor still painted across the backs of my eyelids,
all heavy mahogany and straight lines and darkness—the device
aside.

No, the device is rounded, golden, messy. Now that he has
started it I can smell the rich scent it gives off—of gaslight and
smoke and perfumes too complex to name. Strange, really,
that such thoughts and sensations conspire to remove my fear,
though it's true. They do. After a moment of listening to it creak
and *huussshh,* I feel quite at ease.

Relaxed, almost—then more than that. A syrupiness infuses
my limbs, though I'm sure the machine hasn't begun whatever
it is meant to begin. I have not felt the spider do a single thing,
and there is no current running into me.

It is almost a disappointment. I say almost, because just then
I have the strangest feeling. I suppose one might say it is like
dreaming while still being awake, though how such a thing
should come about I do not know. I cannot say whether I am
naming it right or not, and opening my eyes to ask seems like
the very worst thing to do.

Everyone will think I am a buffoon—the others are so quiet
and settled! And Mr. Hartley doesn't say a word, so this must
be what the device is intended for. To make you dream while
you're awake, on seas of such vivid color that I almost gasp.

I am in a great, green maze the likes of which I have never
actually witnessed, and all about me each leaf curls perfectly,
each twig or blade of grass stands out as bright as the sun. My
own mind has never conjured up such vitality—I'm quite aware
of that. And as I traverse this half-dreaming world, I see a sky
above me, of a different hue than it is naturally.

I see a hundred things that do not occur naturally and yet
seem so real and right that for a moment my breath is stopped.

There are trees at the heart of the maze, and they have veils for leaves, and at the very center of all of this is a gleaming spire that reaches up to the violet-shot sky.

I fervently hope that none of the others have opened their eyes. If they were to, I'm sure they would wonder why a tear has found its way down over my cheek. In truth, I am wondering why a tear has found its way down over my cheek too, because there is nothing all that wonderful about a spire and the trees with leaves flowing like air and my heart, oh my heart.

How dull the world seems, next to this dreaming place. I want more than anything to open my eyes and thank him, for creating something so lovely out of something so smoke driven and mechanical, but I fear I will make a fool of myself. Perhaps this is all only my imagination and not his device at all. Perhaps I am simply not thinking clearly, because then everything in the scene melts away like a painting running, and suddenly I am in a corridor made out of tapestries.

I walk through it all—the blood reds and the swirling greens and everything so lush, so lush, and at the very end all is darkness. I cannot see a thing. But then a match is struck, a single match, and I see Mr. Hartley standing there in this pitch-black alcove, his eyes burning so bright a blue it's like the heat at the center of a flame.

"What are you here for?" he asks, and oh, I have no clue. I cannot bear to know. He takes my hand just as he did all those years ago, and I feel it in the exact same way I did then. As though the electric current comes from him, not some steam-powered machine.

My body heats all the way through—all the way from my too-red face, right down to the tips of my toes. I can feel each finger he's touching exactly, and when he moves closer to me I do what I would never dare to in real life. I sway closer to him, as though we're magnets and metal. As though I cannot help it, and I suppose that is true.

I cannot. I want to edge closer to him, and feel every word he speaks with that mean mouth—because he says so little and yet I am certain he says so much. He is the ghost who tries to speak without a mouth, he is the center of my maze, the gleaming spire, oh, lord why am I thinking any of this?

Perhaps he is making me, I consider—yes, perhaps. It could be that the very purpose of his machine is to fit strange images and fantasies into a young woman's mind, then have his wicked way with her. And yet I do not believe so, I cannot believe so, it could not be true, could it? What, by god, would a man like him ever want with a woman like me?

And he would never imagine something so simpering and lovelorn, I know it. If this were real life, he would not say, "I know why you are here." He would not blow out the match and gather me up in his arms like he would a swooning maiden; he would not kiss my lips with such soft pressure that I am quite undone.

My heart beats slow and thick, now, as though the entirety of my insides have been coated in syrup. I cannot see where I begin or this waking dream ends, though I know I do things that I would never. I am practically a spinster now—these things are not for me. I should not let him unlace my nightgown and pull it from my shoulders, so that he might kiss each one.

And yet I do, I do. I tell my mind that is just a dream, and let the warm waves of whatever this is flow over me, one after the other. I think of kissing—oh, how I have always wondered what it would be like—and lo and behold, here it is. Here is how it would feel exactly, perfectly, not like a dream at all but rich with sensation. The fine shimmer of something touching my lips, the way it forms a web that spirals out through each muscle and nerve in my face, my throat, my body. The heady sensation of something slick against a part of myself and then the pouring knowledge that it is someone else, another person.

In all my days I have never experienced such a thing—this feeling of someone else longing for me and wishing to touch me. It heightens every little thing—even something as innocent as two hands on my bare shoulders.

Though I suppose such a thing is hardly innocent at all. It isn't innocent to be bare in front of a strange man—one you've barely uttered a word to. We've shared no more than three sentences in all the time we've moved in the same circles, and yet when he runs those fingers I so hoped for down my spine—the one that isn't mine but the machine's, *the machine's*—I tremble. My body aches in a way I am sure it has never done, and I feel my nipples stiffening beneath the softness of my chemise, the rough edge of my corset.

It is how this dream body feels and reacts to things, I know, but still I feel it in my real self, too. I sit on this little chair in his dark parlor and thrum with a new kind of heartbeat—one that beats hardest between my legs. It is something that I've only previously encountered privately, in some idle and obscure sort of way, but here it is strong and rich and oh, how shameful, in front of all these people.

How awful, that I want to press myself tightly against this mean little chair and have that sensation swell and blossom— though really I have no need of physical action. When his mouth touches my throat in this dream state, my whole body sings like a string that's been plucked. My sex grows slick and plump—I know it does. I know of these things and I hardly want to turn them away at all.

What other things could he do? I think, but the dream does not require logic or sense or questioning. Everything just happens

as though it is real, in a way I could never think of—as when he
puts that mean mouth to my breast and kisses me there, too.

I am quite sure that I would never think of such a thing. I
certainly don't know what it would feel like, until his lips part
over the bud of my nipple—so loosely covered by a flimsy nightgown—and then pluck and pull at it.

Like kissing, I think, only not on the mouth.

And it feels so...correct, too. I know it does. If one were to
kiss a lady in such a way, the material of her nightgown would
grow damp and every sensation would seem doubled, because
of the chafe of the material and the slow spread into slickness.

All of which I feel, even in this strange dream state. I can feel
the moisture and feel the heat of his mouth, and when he pushes
one hand between my legs I can feel that, too. Oh, he is wicked,
Mr. Hartley. So very wicked and quite improper—though really,
what does it matter, here?

I suppose I should feel even more ashamed now, with images
of him almost kneeling before me, his hand between my legs
and his mouth on my breast—and yet curiously I do not. With
each passing moment my shame slips away, and a new sort of
idea takes hold of me.

Go ahead, this new idea tells me. *Ask him to do more.*

And though I hardly think I can, my dream self grasps at the
opportunity well enough. My dream self lifts her nightgown
and implores him to continue, and when she does he looks up at
her with those cold eyes—only now they are very far from cold.
Now they seem bright and fierce with some strange, lost sort of
emotion, and that fire in him only intensifies when he slips his
fingers over my bare flesh.

I part my legs and he follows me exactly, probing my sex
in a tentative way, at first. But then after a moment I can see
he wants more of me, and in truth I want it too. I want to feel

what it is to have a man stroke through those slippery folds, and uncover my little hidden bead and the waiting hollow of my sex. I want to feel it and he does not deny me, rubbing over things I had long forgotten, parting and fondling and oh, dear, oh, dear, I cannot tell if I have gasped aloud in the dream, or in reality.

I strain to hear if anyone else is making a single sound, but it is far too complicated to experience one world while trying to know things in another. All my attention needs to be in this place, this place where I am kissed and loved and spread over the bed.

I believe I am naked, now, but the idea does not seem to concern me. Mr. Hartley is naked too, but that hardly concerns me, either. He is as strong and firm as I imagined him to be— broad shouldered and silky smooth in places I thought he might be coarsely furred. I run my hands down over his bare chest, and a great pang goes through me to think I will never know whether this is real or not.

I will never know the real Mr. Hartley. This is just a dream-demon, perfect in its feel and shape, passionate in his kisses that he lays on my throat, my breasts, my mouth. I kiss him back with as much ardor as I can muster, because there is one benefit of this dream state, if nothing else.

It does not matter what I do. All of it may not be real, *but it does not matter what I do.* I have real freedom here, for the first time in my life, and I use it to taste the hot, wet insides of his mouth, the curve of his shoulder, the firm smoothness of his chest—and to my delight, he gasps when I do. Mr. Hartley, who in life is as stoic as a block!

Oh, what an invention he has made here. What a delight! I kiss him and kiss him until he is quite wild with it, until—even better—he takes my hand in a kind of frantic clutch, and pushes it down between his own legs.

Ah, he is a wanton, I think, and love him for being so. I want to touch him as he touched me, and I do so with an abandon I don't actually possess. I circle my hand around that thick, stiff pole he has, and feel its exact shape and size. I feel how it gives beneath my touch—only slightly—and how he bucks into my grasp when I tighten it.

And then I thank Mr. Hartley, for letting me see and feel all of this. I could never have created it on my own, never. I would hardly know how to begin with something like this—even the smoothness of the shaft is a surprise to me. So many things about it are a shock to my own half-held imaginings, and most of it comes from Mr. Hartley panting that I should not stop.

When he looks at me with his suddenly heavy-lidded eyes, his body all strung tight like a bow and his mouth so close to my own, I am sure I would do anything for him. I do not know why he even feels the need to demand—in truth he does not need to.

I want to give him everything he wants. I tell him to.

"Take me," I say, and he covers my body with his own.

How great he seems, how heavy and all encompassing. I shrink beneath him, and yet it hardly takes anything to spread my legs around the hard push of his body. It is more difficult for me when he looks into my eyes and won't let me turn away, then asks me if I have ever known how much he has wanted me. How much he longs for me.

I cannot answer. It is splitting me in two, this lie inside myself. This *truth* inside myself—that I have always thought so much of him. That is, after all, what this device is for. I can see it clearly—it is intended to draw out the viewer's deepest fantasies. Their most closely held desires.

And here is mine, in all its slow, sad, rawness. My love for Mr. Hartley is like a hand, reaching out to clasp at nothing.

"I love you, darling Elspeth," he says, and I know that isn't true because Mr. Hartley would never say such a thing. Not ever—not even when naked and entwined with his lover.

Still, I feel it strongly when his stiff shaft slides through my folds and finally, finally pushes deep into that empty hollow inside me. I think I cry out, though this time I do not care if it is dream or reality—it feels so different and so lovely compared to the thing I had expected that I am sure no one would care.

My sister has spoken often of the pain, the pain, but there is no pain here. It feels instead like I have a fist tight around something, something that needed pressure and firmness in a way I had never thought about. And when he ruts against me, rough and completely shameless, great ripples of pleasure run through my body.

I can hardly believe it. I don't believe it. This is not real, I think, then cling to him anyway, rocking hard against that delicious sensation so that when I am old and gray I can remember it. I will have it always now, this thing, this memory of sex-that-isn't-quite-sex, and oh, Mr. Hartley I am so grateful to you for that! I do not care what your intentions are, I do not care what this machine was built for.

I only care that you have given me this, this feeling of someone hard and good in my arms, his mouth on my upturned throat and the sense of him inside me, rubbing against nerves that feel like stars, bursting.

"I love you," he tells me, over and over, and I cling to him as tight as I can. I try to absorb everything—the feel of his skin when my nails bite in, the taste of him, so salt-sweet. The climactic reaches of that final sensation as it pulses through me, and the sound of him groaning as he takes his own measure of it.

It is almost like being wrung out, to have to come back

to reality. In the background I can hear the machine winding down, but for a long moment I don't want to open my eyes. The images are gone, but I don't want to open them.

If I do, perhaps I will forget what all of that was like.

"Elspeth?"

Kitty has put a hand over mine, so I suppose I must look. One cannot remain with one's eyes closed forever—though it is even more of a disappointment than I had dared to think of, when I finally open them.

No one has even noticed what went on inside of me. They are all twittering amongst themselves about the elephant they saw in their heads, or the memory they had reenacted that they had believed was long forgotten.

And I suppose I should be grateful for that. I should be grateful that the device truly is about drawing forth a person's most secret wishes, and that I have not shamed myself in some way with strange noises or movements or any other such thing.

I should, but I am not. I stand quite reluctantly and then just stare at Mr. Hartley's turned back. He is fiddling with his machine, now, and hardly seems to register that people are leaving—though he asked them to, not a minute since.

Of course they all obey, because Mr. Hartley is a genius. Mr. Hartley is a cold, reclusive genius, and we must all put up with his odd ways if we want to be asked back.

Though when I think about it, something about that attitude seems very unkind. It is, after all, steeped in the assumption that I had of Mr. Hartley only a few short minutes ago—that he is cruel, and unkind, and worst of all...miserly.

And this thought gnaws at me so hard that I wait, I wait and wait until everyone has left his parlor and it is only him, standing by his machine. When he turns, I am fairly certain he believed everyone had gone—the look on his face says as much.

It is naked, briefly, and quite full of that same aching loneliness I had felt, upon realizing that I would never experience anything like that in reality.

"Is everything quite all right, Miss Havers?" he asks, and for a second I wonder if he knows. But then the second passes and that urge wells up in me again, that urge to correct my long assumptions about Mr. Hartley—even though he cannot know I have them.

"You are so very generous, Mr. Hartley," I say, because that is the truth. "You are so very generous to share an invention like that."

Of course I expect him to dismiss me in some way—or laugh, perhaps. But he does not. Instead he takes my hand quite suddenly and all the electricity in the world pours through him, to me. And then he says, with his eyes flashing fierce and bright—just as they had in my dream—

"I did it for you, Miss Havers. I made dreams come to life for you."

A
DEMONSTRATION
OF AFFECTION

Elizabeth Coldwell

I was deep in the heart of the windmill's mechanism, wrench in hand, when someone banged the knocker down hard on the front door.

"Get that, would you, Smithy?" the professor called, raising his voice above the faint hum of machinery. The fact that I must crawl out from a tightly confined space while all he had to do was step down from the low wooden platform on which he stood did not seem to occur to him. The professor never answered his own door, not when he had an assistant to act as a buffer between himself and the outside world.

I didn't complain, even as I scraped my knee against a jutting piece of metal in my haste. I had known about the man's many infuriating habits from the day we met, yet I was prepared to overlook them all for the honor of working alongside him.

The heavy iron knocker slammed against the door again, more insistently this time.

"Coming!" I yelled, speculating as I did on the possible identity of our unexpected caller.

We almost never received visitors. The professor had chosen to live in such a remote location deliberately to discourage anyone who might interfere with his work. Only those with the most urgent need to see him would trek down the rutted cart path that led to the windmill.

Or, I realized as I opened the front door, someone with a financial investment in the professor's many projects. Standing on the threshold, shaking drops of water from her heavy black umbrella, was his current benefactor.

"Lady Portway, how pleasant to see you. Do come in out of the rain."

"Thank you, Miss Smith."

As I ushered her inside and helped her to remove her overcoat, I felt as ungainly and awkward in her presence as I always had. Not only did I stand a head taller than her, even with her in dainty boots that laced to the knee, but there were smudges of engine grease on my face, grime under my fingernails and a button missing from the front of my overalls. Lady Portway, in contrast, despite the length of her journey from the metropolis, looked sweetly feminine and fresh as a daisy.

"Let me go and announce your presence to the professor," I said, once she had made herself at home in the big armchair before the parlor fire, the one warm and cozy place in the vast, drafty living space beneath the windmill.

The professor's irritation at being disturbed melted away when I informed him who was calling. "Make tea for us, would you, Smithy?" he asked, running a hand through his unruly black curls before going to greet his guest. "And see if we have any of those caraway biscuits left." His smile of dismissal was distracted, but still had the power to bring a sudden flush to my cheeks.

Waiting for the kettle to boil, I reflected that without the

assistance, albeit indirect, of Lady Portway, I would not be here
to bask in the glow of the professor's smiles. My initial dream,
when it had become obvious I was by far the brightest in my
class at school, had been to attend one of the great universities.
However, my mother had objected strongly. It was less a question of the money involved than her fear that further education
would render me barren and unsuitable for marriage. In her
eyes, Lady Portway had made the ideal career choice, using her
great beauty to acquire a much older husband in ailing health.
Within nine months of their wedding night, Lord Portway was
dead, which did not greatly surprise London society. What did
was his newly wealthy widow's decision to use some of her
fortune to help Professor John Braithwaite finance his experiments in mechanical motion. The professor's work had been
highly praised in the scientific journals I devoured on visits to
the town library, and I dreamed of being able to aid him in his
pursuits. How much could an eager, inquisitive mind learn from
time spent in his presence? I wrote and expressed my willingness
to work under his tutelage, but given his lack of money it had
seemed an impossible dream. That was until Lady Portway's
generous financial input had enabled him to take me on, almost
a year ago to the day.

I was grateful to her, naturally, but on walking into the parlor
carrying a laden tea tray, the emotion that gripped me most
strongly was one of jealousy. They made a handsome couple
as they stood by the bureau, her blonde, ringleted head barely
reaching his shoulder. She appeared to be hanging on his every
word as he showed her one of his newest creations, a bejeweled
clockwork songbird that hopped and trilled as prettily as any
linnet.

"Oh, John, it's beautiful," she murmured, her tone utterly
sincere. No one who saw the professor's creations could fail to

be impressed by the way they moved and acted, as though a strongly beating heart pumped life through their body, rather than an intricately designed mechanism. The songbird was, in truth, little more than an amusement, one of his first attempts to breathe vital essence into a mechanical being. The culmination of his work would be to create a similarly realistic mechanical man, the project on which he and I currently toiled.

I set the tray down with a clink of china, the sound causing the professor and Lady Portway to turn in my direction. Deftly, I poured tea for the pair of them, adding a generous splash of milk and two sugar lumps to the professor's cup. Lady Portway took hers without milk and rejected my offer of a biscuit. It took more discipline than I possessed to maintain her enviably slender figure, I thought, filching a couple of biscuits from the plate to munch as I worked.

"Do you need me for anything else?" I asked. "If not, I'll return to what I was doing."

"We're converting the windmill so it has the ability to be powered by steam," the professor explained to his guest. "We're hoping our work will enable mills to be built in areas where there isn't sufficient wind to power the sails." Turning his attention to me, he continued, "I would like you to stay for a moment, Smithy. What Bella has to say concerns both of us."

Placing her cup delicately in its saucer, Lady Portway regarded us with her wide blue eyes. "I'm holding a soirée next week, to mark the international symposium at the Royal College of Science. Some of the finest minds in the field are going to be there. Martin Parnell, whose theories on the future of clockwork automata are attracting significant attention in Boston, I believe. Gunther Strondheim, of the Berlin Institute..."

Though she dropped the name casually, she must have known the effect it would have on the professor. Strondheim's experiments in the field were well advanced; indeed, it was rumored that he had already publicly exhibited a fully functioning mechanical humanoid, though we had as yet seen no written record of such an event.

"People are naturally curious to know how your own work is progressing, John. They believe I should by now be expecting a return on my investment, to prove this is more than just an act of charity on my part. So I thought it might be—diverting—if you were to present a demonstration of your clockwork man at the soirée."

"Why, Bella, I'd be delighted to."

I was shocked by his answer. Only this morning, he had been complaining about the lack of progress he was making on the project; now here he was, agreeing to show the finished result to an invited audience in a week's time. Lady Portway's powers of persuasion were clearly considerable. Or perhaps he was simply prepared to do whatever it took to impress her, in the same way—if he only realized it—I sought to impress him.

"Very good. So I'll expect you next Friday evening at seven, then, John." She rose to leave. "Thank you for your hospitality, but as you'll appreciate, I need to be back in London before nightfall."

"Before you leave, Bella, I trust your invitation extends to Smithy, too? I'll need her help with the demonstration."

"Of course." Lady Portway's sweet smile masked the sting of her words. "But please be aware, Miss Smith, this will be a formal occasion, and both you and the professor will be expected to dress appropriately."

Her perfume, heady with the scent of jasmine, lingered mockingly in the air after she had gone. I could not help feeling that she expected us to pass her first challenge—to have our automaton ready for public exhibition within a week—but, having seen my disheveled appearance on numerous occasions before today, she firmly believed I would fail the second.

The next week passed in a frantic blaze of activity. All work on the windmill itself was forgotten. Instead, our whole attention was focused on the mechanical man. We barely slept, and if I hadn't broken off from my own labors to bring the professor a plate of bread and cheese every now and again, he would never have eaten. The air stank with the acrid aromas of soldered copper and woodsmoke. My back ached from bending over the workbench, assembling the delicate mechanisms that would enable our creation to blink and move its jaw in the closest approximation of human emotions we could contrive.

All too slowly, it seemed, the automaton took shape. The professor's initial design had featured a head-to-toe covering of skin, made from animal hide, but we knew there would not be time to produce that refinement. As it was, our mechanical man was only completed to our satisfaction on the morning we were due to travel to London. We packed his component parts into crates, to be transported on the train. It had been arranged that upon our arrival at Liverpool Street Station, Lady Portway would have a cab waiting to take us to her home in the heart of Bloomsbury. There we would assemble Abel, as we had come to know our creation. We would also be able to take a hot bath—the first either of us had found time for in over a week—and change into our formal wear.

I hugged the capacious reticule containing my evening dress to myself as we waited for the train to arrive. It had been a present from my mother on my twenty-first birthday, a subtle reminder that she still saw me moving in circles where I might attract a well-connected husband, and as yet I had never had an opportunity to wear it.

Despite the uncomfortable rattling motion of the train, I was so exhausted I slept for most of the journey to London. When I finally woke, we were traveling through the overcrowded slums of the East End, where the houses and their inhabitants alike seemed grimed with the same sooty, industrial patina. I knew the professor dreamed of a world where automatons would do most of the backbreaking, dangerous jobs that were regarded as the provenance of the poor, so children would no longer have to climb chimneys or work down mines. He even saw a place in society for female automata, who would cater to the basest needs of men and save hundreds, perhaps even thousands of women from a life of prostitution. I wondered whether he had ever shared these aspirations with Lady Portway. If so, did she admire him all the more, as I did, for wanting to use his inventions for the benefit of society as a whole, rather than simply to increase his standing among the scientific community?

A taciturn cabbie helped us stow the crates containing Abel into the back of his vehicle. The streets teemed with life, but I paid little attention to the people scurrying past on the pavement, still lost in my dream of a world where automata were a commonplace sight.

Almost before I knew it, the cab was pulling up at the rear entrance to Lady Portway's residence. Once a couple of her manservants had carried our precious cargo into one of the anterooms, we could begin the process of reconstructing Abel. Even without skin, he was an impressive sight. He stood as tall as I did, limbs and head perfectly in proportion to his artfully constructed metal torso. Glass eyes in a cool shade of blue were the focal point of his face, giving him a piercing, intelligent gaze. Having assembled him to our satisfaction, we were able to retire to bedrooms upstairs to change.

A maid had drawn me a slipper bath, and my dress and

underthings were laid out on the bed. As I sank into the water and lathered myself with rose-scented soap, I could understand why my mother wished me to live a permanently pampered life-style. That, though, would have required me to find some sense of achievement in being purely a wife and mother, and my time with the professor had made me believe I had more to offer.

Having a skilled pair of hands to lace me into my corset was a novelty. Not that I wore such a constricting garment on a daily basis, but tonight it gave me the perfect silhouette beneath my scarlet silk dress. My waist was pulled in tightly, and my modest breasts thrust upward to produce a gently swelling cleavage.

For once, I left my hair loose, falling in dark waves around my face and resting on my uncovered shoulders. I spent a while admiring myself in the mirror, reveling in the femininity I so rarely displayed, until I heard a sharp rapping on the door and the professor's voice calling, "Smithy, they're ready for us in the drawing room."

When I stepped out of the room, it was to see the professor dressed in an elegant evening suit, an adeptly tied bow tie at his throat, his black curls brushed into some semblance of order and slicked back with brilliantine. He looked truly magnificent, so different from the shabbily dressed genius to whom I had become accustomed. My breath caught in my throat for the briefest moment.

Trying to damp down the fire the sight of him had set raging in my body, I gestured to my own formal attire, asking, "Do you think Lady Portway will consider this appropriate?" His eyes dropped to the low neckline of my dress, then back up to meet my amused gaze. At that, he seemed to collect himself.

"You look...absolutely stunning," he murmured at last, leaving me glowing with the compliment.

Downstairs, Abel waited for us in the room adjoining the

reception, staring sightlessly ahead. The professor handed me the small brass key that was used to wind the automaton's mechanism. "I'll make the introduction, then you bring him in."

Once he left the room, I inserted the key gently at the point where a living man's navel would have been and started to wind. With the door ajar, I could hear snatches of the professor's speech. "...Years of research...among them some of you present tonight...great advances in the world of clockwork construction..."

With a series of gentle clicks and a noise eerily reminiscent of a human sigh, Abel stirred into life. The professor had been unable to complete the automaton's voice box to his satisfaction in the time we had, so for tonight his creation would remain mute. But he understood vocal commands perfectly, and when I said, "Good evening, Abel, I trust you are well?" his head, with those glittering blue eyes, turned toward me and he nodded.

"And now," the professor's voice rose in volume, "I would like to present to you my assistant, Miss Violet Smith, and her companion, Abel."

That was our cue. Arm in arm, cool metal against my warm, bare skin, Abel and I walked into the drawing room to a collective gasp of astonishment and admiration. I caught sight of faces I recognized: Gunther Strondheim, with his luxuriant mutton-chop whiskers; Martin Parnell, clutching the walking stick he had needed ever since escaping from a near-fatal airship accident at the Staten Island landing strip. Strondheim was the first to lead the applause, appreciating more than anyone else in the room the enormity of our efforts, but soon everyone was clapping and cheering.

When silence fell, it took me a moment to find my voice, I was so overwhelmed by the reaction to our appearance. At last, I stammered out, "Abel, shall we dance?"

The professor had asked Lady Portway to ensure he had access to a gramophone. He placed the needle on the cylinder and set the mechanism running. The strains of a Viennese waltz filled the air and, as we had practiced briefly among the clutter of the workshop in the small hours of the morning, Abel and I danced. He led, I followed, moving in a sure-footed rhythm across the drawing room floor. What little we'd heard of Strond-heim's creation suggested his movements were jerky, betraying his mechanical origins. Abel glided, an intricate network of precision mechanisms working to create the illusion that he lived and breathed.

Whatever the assembled guests had been expecting, it was surely not such a lighthearted display. The professor might envisage his automata as beasts of burden, fetching and carrying, but it did not mean they couldn't be companions, too.

The music came to a halt. Abel bowed and I curtseyed. Then we were enveloped in a crowd, Lady Portway's guests keen to learn more about how this marvelous creation worked. I managed to slip away, anxious to see the professor's reaction. He was still standing by the gramophone, and Lady Portway was with him, holding his big, calloused hands in her tiny ones. Raising herself on tiptoes, she said, "Oh, John, that was truly miraculous. I knew I was right to champion you all along...." She planted a kiss on his mouth, pressing her body closer against his in a fiercely intimate gesture.

Unable to watch any more, racked with a fierce jealousy, I gave a little cry and fled from the room. I thought I heard someone call after me. Ignoring them, and pushing past a surprised-looking servant, I ran down the hall in search of a way outside.

Turning a heavy door handle, I stepped into a small garden surrounded by high box hedges. The air was heavy with night-scented stock, and somewhere high above me a nightingale sang lustily. Tears stung my cheeks and I brushed them away, annoyed at the strength of my reaction.

Why should it surprise me that there was such a deep attraction between the professor and Lady Portway? She had known him longer than I had, and had so much more to offer him in terms of worldly experience.

"Smithy?" I turned at the sound of the professor's voice. "What are you doing out here? Is everything all right?"

"I'm fine," I replied, trying to convince myself I meant it. "But what about Abel? He's in there on his own, and his mechanism will be running down."

"He's not my concern at the moment. You are. I didn't realize being the center of attention would be so awkward for you, and I wanted to apologize."

"You think that's why I ran out here?" I almost laughed.

"Isn't it?"

"No. I—I left because I couldn't bear to see you kissing Lady Portway." I wrung the folds of my evening dress in my hands, not wanting to meet the professor's gaze. "It was stupid of me, I know. She's perfect for you, after all."

"Oh, Smithy..." The professor put his hands on my shoulders, pulling me close. "Look at me." When I did, he continued, "Let me assure you Bella is the last woman I would choose to be with. If you'd stayed a moment longer, you would have seen how quickly I broke that kiss. We were discussing Abel and—well, she only sees the commercial benefits of patenting him, of making others like him available for sale. It's all about money with Bella; it always has been. Yes, she's invested in my work, but only for the return she'll receive."

"Isn't that true of any investor?"

"There are philanthropists around, Smithy, I can assure

you of that. Parnell is lucky enough to have found one to back him. But there are very few people who see how automata can be useful for the whole of humanity, not just themselves." He brushed a stray lock of hair away from my face. "But that's not the only reason why I have no interest in Bella."

"Really?" Unsure whether I was prepared for further revelations, I waited as the professor took a deep breath.

"Tonight, seeing you in all your finery, so beautiful and so assured as you took the floor with Abel, I realized I could no longer deny feelings I've had for a long time now. You may think I only see Smithy, in her unflattering overalls and with dirt on her face, but I have always been aware that Violet is close to the surface, simply waiting to be—unleashed."

As he spoke, he brought his face down close to mine. There was a moment where myriad possibilities presented themselves, but there was no attempt on my part to choose any but the most desirable. Our lips met, the kiss deepening and growing sweeter as our bodies twined together. We each breathed in the other's essence, the vital spirit the professor sought to recreate with his experiments but which never burns so brightly as between a couple in the first, heady flush of love.

Forgetting where we were, and all the dignitaries who waited to congratulate us in Lady Portway's drawing room, we surrendered to the passion we could no longer deny.

The professor wrestled with the fastenings on the back of my dress, pulling them apart so the glorious silk confection slithered to the ground, leaving me in my stays and bloomers. The sudden exposure of so much of my flesh to the night air—and to the professor's appreciative stare—brought me sharply to my senses.

"Is this wise?" I asked, as he placed hot, urgent kisses on my bare shoulders. "What if someone comes looking for us?"

"They won't," he assured me. "For now, they are still far too interested in learning the secrets of Abel's construction. Trust me, Violet..."

His mouth moved lower, kissing the exposed tops of my breasts. My body was responding to his caresses, a pulse beating hard in time with my heart between my legs and my nether lips beginning to bloom with sweet moisture.

He pushed me up against a sturdy tree trunk. Even the nightingale had fallen silent now, as though there was no longer anything in the world but the two of us. The professor's hand burrowed between my legs, finding the opening in my bloomers and straying inside. For the first time, I felt a hand other than my own stroking the soft, haired-fringed lips, then pressing between them to find the whorled bud that held the key to my pleasure. So many nights I had lain on my bunk in the windmill, stroking these secret places and dreaming that one day the professor would do the same. Hopeless dreams they had seemed, even as my body had arched in fierce ecstasy beneath the bedcovers, but now he was touching me in a way I was sure would bring me to those same arching spasms in moments.

A second finger joined his explorations. This one pressed up, up into my tight channel, till it met a gentle resistance. A firmer push, and the barrier was breached. I hissed between my teeth.

"Hush, Violet," the professor soothed. "Now there is no impediment to our immediate union. At last, we can become one."

Fumbling with the fly of his evening trousers, he brought his cock out into the open. I gazed at it in wonder. The professor and I had talked at length about the possibility of fitting Abel with a similar organ. As I reached out to touch him, I realized what a feat of engineering this would be, to recreate the hydraulic action that enabled a cock to grow and swell as the professor's had done, to simulate that steely core within its soft sleeve of skin. Pulling that skin back and forth over the plum-shaped head, I heard the professor's breathing grow harsh.

"That is so good, but I need to be inside you."

He guided himself into position, and as I felt his cockhead nudging at me, I wondered how it would ever fit inside. Then he was pushing up into me slowly and insistently, never going farther than he sensed was comfortable for me, as my body grew used to the feel of this delicious intruder.

I had never imagined my first time would be anything like this, half-dressed and pressed against an elm tree in a secluded Bloomsbury garden, but as the professor began to rock his hips back and forth with a steady, almost mechanical motion, I was sure it could not have been engineered any other way. Sensations pulsed through me from tip to toe, sweeter and more intense than anything I had ever experienced. My hands caught in the professor's curls, bringing them closer to their usual disorder. His mouth nipped at my earlobes, my cheeks, the base of my throat, rousing me further.

Faster and harder he moved, the laces of my stays scraping against the tree with every thrust. My hands clasped his still-trousered buttocks, seeking to pull him even farther into me. His groan told me the moment of his crisis was almost upon him and could not be averted.

"Oh, oh, Violet," he sobbed, and spent himself within me.

We clasped each other tight, until the professor's hand moved to find my bud once more, rubbing until I was the one who shuddered against him. In the moment before it seemed as though my whole being dissolved into its component atoms, I caught sight of Abel over the professor's shoulder. I had no way of knowing how long he had been there, or how much he had seen, and he had no way of telling me. His eyes shone and his face bore an unmistakable expression of enjoyment, but by the time I was able to alert the professor to his presence, his mechanism had wound down to nothing and he stood inanimate once more.

"Do you think he saw us?" I asked.

"I should not worry if he did." The professor smiled. "He would only have seen how wonderful it can be when two lovers feel free to express their longing for each other. Now, let us hurry. Where Abel leads, Bella and her guests may not be far behind."

Indeed, barely had I scrambled back into my dress when Lady Portway appeared in the garden. I stood with my back to the tree, so she might not see that the fastenings were awry.

"There you are!" If she felt any ill will toward the professor following their earlier awkwardness, she did not show it. "Please, John, bring your fabulous creation back to the party so we might all admire him further."

As the professor wound Abel's mechanism once more, he shot me a look full of love and admiration. Whatever other miracles he had demonstrated tonight paled beside his unequivocal demonstration of his feelings for me, and I knew we would move toward the future together all the stronger for it.

UNDERGROUNDED: HANNAH HAWTHORNE AND THE STRANDED TIME SHIP

Vida Bailey

1 The Crash

The ship lurched and groaned as it hit the deserted building. There was a brief, ominous silence before it disappeared into the floor, leaving clouds of dust and debris behind it. Lights flickered on and heads poked out of windows, but to all outside, it must merely have seemed that one more roof in the dilapidated row had given up the ghost and collapsed on itself. Hopefully no one would believe that an air balloon had crashed through the laundry roof, then fallen through the floor to the subbasements below. Not many people lived round the crumbling old laundries anymore. This part of town was sliding into gradual decline.

After some moments the dust started to clear and the clink and chink of falling brickwork quieted. The door of the ship creaked open and a figure stepped out. The light revealed a slim woman, somewhere in her twenties, with wild copper hair that had been fought into a thick braid. She peered around the side of the airship, taking in the deflated silk of the balloon and the crumpled blades of the propeller. Her breath hissed when she saw the damage.

She was joined by a man with a far less restrained reaction. Clad in an undershirt and leather trousers, implements shining from his tool belt and others stuck in his high boots, he danced around the downed ship in frustration.

"Damn it! Damn the bloody thing to hell! Blast! Blasted buggering *arse!*"

He kicked a pile of rubble and stood fuming in the ensuing dust cloud. "Ah, Hannah."

She reached out to him, wrapped her fingers round his arm. "It's all right, Darien. The professor can fix it, I'm sure."

"Sweetheart, I'm sure he can, but we can't get to him. We're back in eighteen-twenty. We've no idea where he is."

"So we'll look for him, we'll find him, I'm sure. We're in London, aren't we?" He nodded, disconsolate. "We're resourceful. I'm sure we'll find a way."

The door of the ship resisted as it was forced open from within, and a dazed couple stumbled out. Hannah's mouth fell open as she saw what her companions were wearing. Will looked respectable enough in boots, trousers and undershirt, but Elana was evidently naked underneath her silk kimono, and her hair was wild and loose, thick black tresses falling in silk ropes to the base of her spine. Her lips were swollen and red, and she was bleeding a little from her temple. They had clearly been caught *in flagrante* by the accident.

Elana shook her head, and wrapped her arm around her lover's back.

"I thought otherwise before we got interrupted by the crash. But now I can clearly see that we're fucked."

2 *Grounded*

Hannah and Will had left Darien and Elana crouching by the ship, banging things and cursing, and gone out to forage for supplies. When they returned, laden with bread and cheese and wine, things looked pretty much the same, but the cursing was louder. Darien looked up at them.

"We ain't going nowhere without the professor, darlings. We're all out of power. Did you see any sign of him?"

Will shrugged.

"We went to his workshop. There's a faded sign on the door, doesn't look like anyone's been there in a while. Who knows where he is? Or when..."

"It looks like we'll be here for a while, then," Hannah said calmly. "Hey, Elly, I got some silks and things—if we're going to be here for a while, we may as well make ourselves more comfortable."

Darien looked up. "Eh, hang on, I had a thought. We might be a bit less conspicuous one level down—I know we're fairly hidden, but this place seems to be on top of old London, there're lots of undiscovered layers. I was thinking if we just got a bit of strategically placed explosive, we could pop the whole ship through the floor and be even more out of the way." He raised an eyebrow at Will and their eyes gleamed with shared manly zeal at the prospect of an explosion. Elana looked quite excited too, so Hannah knew there was no point protesting.

"All right, you boys get on it, and I will sit here and drink and watch you singe your eyebrows." She perched on a beam, boots swinging, their buckles glinting, and pulled a gadget from her pocket. Unfolding its workings, she wrapped it round the bottle top, pushed, pulled, and uncorked the bottle with a pop. Elana cheered and came to sit beside her, letting her passion for daytime red wine override her interest in explosives. She twined

Hannah's bronze curls in her fingers absently as they watched, cheering as the floor gave way and the ship bumped another level down without discernable damage. The men appeared triumphantly from the dust cloud. Applauding, Hannah and Elana passed the bottle on to them and went down to investigate.

A couple of hours later, the ship was made secure, a ladder was rigged up to the hole in the ceiling, and the underground room had been transformed with silks and cushions and candles. Hannah lay back on her bed piled with eiderdowns and cushions, full of soft bread and creamy cheese. Darien tripped his fingers over the straps of her corset, tugging at the buckles and stroking the leather. Elana got up and pulled Will into the ship by the wrist, sliding the door closed with a whoosh and a snap.

"Hmmm." Darien began to pop Hannah's buckles and moved up to kiss her wine-stained lips. "I could grow to like this desert tent arrangement. Gimme some velvet." She kissed him again. He rolled over on his back, pulling her with him. She sat astride him and he loosened one more buckle. "I love this, Hannie, the way your bubs spill out over this tight leather." He palmed them, one hand holding her cinched-in waist. "My girl."

Hannah moved slowly on top of him, feeling his erection growing against her, pressing her clit to it, harder as it hardened.

"You seem relaxed down here," she said. "I thought you'd be climbing the walls to get out and find a way back." He shrugged.

"We'll see. For now, it's nice to have a break from all the breaking and entering. Maybe just focus on the entering for a while." He flipped up her skirts and ran his hands up her thighs. She raised herself so that he could undo his trousers, but he grabbed her silky buttocks and moved her forward until her sex hovered over his mouth. Hannah pushed her fingers into his hair and felt his tongue opening her up and teasing her, dipping in and out of her and sliding around her slit. He moved underneath her and she knew he had taken out his cock and was stroking it as he licked her. Darien was so good at this. He had once seduced her with a flying machine and time travel, but if she ever considered straying, it would be his clever tongue that kept her there.

She slipped back down and straddled him again, smoothly pressing him inside. They moved slowly together, until Hannah realized she could hear cries coming from inside the ship. Sharing a small space together had made the two couples matter-of-fact about their lovemaking, and now, knowing Will and Elana were about to climax too made Hannah all the more excited. And Darien loved that it did. He moved his hand from round her waist to her clit and rubbed, making her buck and press him harder against her spot. Hannah couldn't hold back the breathy moans that signaled her release was close, and Darien thrust harder, ready for it, ready to join her. She came hard, her hands on his chest, pelvis pushing against his as her aftershocks stilled.

"Lover."

"Lover."

3 The Underground Children

"Wotcha, Mister, Missus!"

Hannah jerked up with a shriek, causing Darien to gasp too. He peered around Hannah, who was rearranging her clothing and reaching for the little pistol that she kept in her garter. Darien fumbled his trousers shut and laughed.

"It's all right, love, I think we're safe enough."

Hannah looked around and saw a small crowd of grimy faces staring at her. Children of various ages, clad in hats and boots, coats and goggles and fingerless gloves. You could tell the girls by their hair and flounced skirts, but that was about it.

"I see it's a gruesome horde," Hannah observed, but kindly. Growing up in an orphanage had left her with tender feelings toward street kids. Or underground kids; none of these pale little waifs looked like they saw sunlight too often. She handed them the rest of the bread and cheese and they tore into it like a wolf pack.

"What's that, Mister, that big boat thing? Does it fly?" One of the older boys had noticed the ship.

"Not right now it doesn't, lads," Darien answered. "It needs fixing. We're grounded for the moment."

"I bet we could fix it, Mister! Or at least Doc could."

Darien laughed.

"Maybe not this one, kids. Here, go buy some more." He flicked pennies in the air, which they caught and were gone, all in a flash. All except one, a small child who lurked behind and stared at the ship with a gleam in his eye.

"Are you Doc, by any chance? Do you live down here?" Hannah tried to strike up conversation but only got nods in return. She assumed they'd blasted down into an old tunnel network, who knew how big or far reaching. She tried to imagine living in the dark indefinitely. Right now she felt safe here, but she knew she'd miss the sunlight soon enough. "Would you not be better off somewhere where you get fed? In an orphanage? Something?"

"Or the workhouse?" The child shook his head. "Nah, Miss, never. We likes our freedom. We make do." He winked at her knowingly, and she realized she had just met a small school of cutpurses. Kindred spirits, in other words. She and her friends made their living from clever *private acquisitions* and negotiation of the timeline and antique markets, in various eras. And here was the rub: being a time bandit was no good to you unless you could access your money. And as they lived off interest from future savings, there wasn't much to be had back in 1820.

4 Settling In Too Comfortably

Further searching for signs of the professor had proved fruitless. He didn't seem to be in London at this time, and subtle inquiries at other workshops had not suggested any other time mechanics were working in London then. Elana had even spent some happy hours in a high-end whorehouse, reminiscing with some old toffer acquaintances of hers, and making careful inquiries. She and Will came home with nothing more useful than the smiles on their faces.

They all spent more and more time with little bespectacled Doc, who was transfixed by the ship. He absorbed knowledge like a sponge and it wasn't long before they found out why. One day, in fun, Elana pulled off Doc's hat. A great mass of dirty blonde hair tumbled out around the little grubby face, and Elana gasped. Not only was Doc a girl, but underneath the spectacles that had come askew gleamed a prosthetic lens. It fixed invisibly onto the child's smooth skin, gold frames held in place without hint of scar or stitch. It was a work of beauty, that prosthesis, but alarming too, against the child's face it inhabited. A sudden hush fell.

"Where'd you get the eyepiece, Doc?" Darien asked.

"From a friend." The girl looked fearful, as if guarding a secret. Will held up his right hand, to reveal a silver and gold pinkie finger. He wriggled his fingers and the metal finger moved in synch.

"I think your friend might be our friend too, Doc. Can you tell us where to find him?"

Doc relaxed, visibly. "Nah, he's gone away. Long trip. Said

he'd be back sometime, but he didn't know when. I fink 'e went to Africa or summink." Ah. The friends looked at each other. The Egypt trip. That's where the professor was then. They'd been gone for a good six months that time.

And so for now, that end was dead.

Yet Darien seemed happy to be stranded. Hannah had spotted him standing on a street corner, chatting with a rat-faced individual who couldn't have been more shifty if he'd been hopping from foot to foot. She was mildly alarmed to learn later that Rat Face was a new contact of Darien's, a fence.

"Darien, did you run a job today?"

"Just a little one, my dearest, only a little one. But it means we have steak pie and ale tonight!" And he opened a small sack and trickled a rain of coins into her hands, which had been outstretched in appeal, not for rewards. Hannah put the coins back in the bag without speaking. She looked at her man leaning back on their makeshift bed, content with his small-time robbery, and she felt a pang of worry tug at her chest.

"We can't get away, if they catch you," she warned in a hushed voice. "No escape off the roof this time."

"Oh, Hannah. Why would you worry about that? You know I'm bullet proof." He winked and left her even less convinced. The broken ship, the dark of their home, the scurrying past of the children. It was all expanding into a ball of disquiet and she felt that some action was necessary to dispel it. Perhaps that was why she'd gone to see her parents.

5 The Fight

Hannah's nightdress swirled around her as she paced. She'd been listening for footsteps, and finally they came, too fast. Darien and Elana burst into the room, breathless and laughing. The laugh faded in his voice as he looked up and saw what she was wearing. Midnight blue silk clung to her breasts and fell in waves toward the floor. He could see her toes peeping out, a rare sight of them, so often boot-clad. The pink and white vulnerability of her naked feet made Darien all the more conscious of the softness of her stomach, freed of its usual bindings. Her breasts were looser than usual also, and the wider valley between them was captivating. Hannah caught his eye, let him know what she could read in his gaze. Her hair spread out like fire around her, crackling with static from the brushing it had recently received.

Hannah whispered in Darien's ear, "I found something today."

"You found this? I like it."

"No, Darien. I had an idea. I've been talking to my parents."

"What?"

Darien reared away from her, a familiar, stung expression on his face. "Why? You said you didn't need to do that, not anymore!" Hannah shook her head, put her hand on his arm.

"Darien. Listen, a minute, calm. I haven't changed my mind about telling her where to find me. I know the same rules hold true. I stayed with you. But I've been meeting my mother."

"What are you *doing*? You know if she finds you, we're all over, all changed."

"I promised you! Will you listen to what I have to say?" Hannah fought down the familiar frustration as it rose at the sight of her lover's compressed lips. Stubborn, unlistening man. "I'm not going to tell her who I am. She thinks I'm two, remember? I don't want to send the poor woman doolally. I know I can't help her find me." Hannah's eyes misted. Her heart was full of lost children and grieving parents. Darien's insistence that she stay away seemed more unreasonable every day.

"Let's give them Doc. Give her a chance. Help them too."

It was the perfect solution, she thought. A safe home for Doc and someone to fill her mother's empty arms. She had seen the heartbreak in the eyes of the woman who was so like her, whose arms she longed to fall into. *If I could just fix this*, she thought.

Darien frowned. "She's all right down here. She doesn't want people telling her what to do, whipping her arse for not minding her *P*s and *Q*s. It's not so bad. She'd hate it the other way."

"Darien, are you serious? She's filthy and lousy, half starved and desperate for some light and stimulus! Don't you want to see her warm and fed? What future does she have down here?" Her voice rose. Darien looked at her chest flush with the passion of her speech.

"She does all right," he muttered and turned and stalked into the ship. She followed.

"What is wrong with you? You cannot for a minute think this is all right? For children? This pitiful existence?"

"It was fine for me!" Darien's aggrieved roar startled her. "I came out of it all right! And you—you said it was good enough when we met. And now you're running to Mama and Papa and their money the minute my coffers dry up! So, great, go, good luck!" He turned and stalked into their cabin, slamming the door behind him.

"Darien!"

But no answer came.

Will and Elana found her rooted to the spot, staring at the door to her cabin. They cooed and shushed and pushed and pulled until she was out of her nightgown and corseted and booted again.

"Elana, have you been doing jobs with Darien again?" Hanna's voice was quiet. Elana's fingertips lingered over the buckles at Hannah's breasts until Hannah gripped them affectionately and held them at her side.

"Oh, well, a little bit. You know how I like to keep myself entertained, darling. And Darien likes to feel useful."

"What's he so angry about? He was like this when I wanted to go find them before. But there was more at stake then. And he knows which way I chose. Why is he being so, so..."

"Fear, Hannah, fear makes arseholes out of the best men, sometimes. There's things he hasn't told you yet, and your nobby background brings it out in him. You're trying to bring the kids out of here, into your parents' world, and he hasn't had the nutmegs to tell you that's where he..."

"Elana!" Will broke in. "Leave it to Darien, surely."

Elana ducked her head, but said no more. Will gestured to the outsized copper tank in the corner.

"Help us, I have a project in mind."

Elana handed Hannah a spanner, picked up the metal-saw and pulled her goggles down. The rest of the night passed in noisy hard work and quiet advice, and the door to the ship stayed resolutely closed.

6 Hannah Defiant

In a very different area of London, tall houses bordered a leafy park. Birds sang, and the flowerbeds were bright and well tended. Hannah looked back at the shining red door to Doc's new home. She walked into the park and stepped onto the grass, seeking out the refuge of the trees before she crouched down, a hand pressed to her breast, the other to her mouth. She gasped back tears, breathed in the smell of soil and spring. She looked up to see Darien leaning against a tree, a torn expression on his face.

"You did it anyway."

She nodded, hand still held to her chest.

"You wish it was you."

"Well, who wouldn't? For god's sake, Darien! I thought you knew enough to understand this isn't about you! Look at me! I'm right here!" She gouged out a handful of the damp loam they stood on and threw it at his feet in frustration.

"Nice, Hannah, nice form. I can hear someone coming, you'd better stop throwing things at me and start acting like a normal woman again." Bristling, Hannah brushed off her hands and strode out of the park. Darien started to follow her, but turned and walked in the other direction.

7 *The Art of Bathing*

The tub was a sight to behold. A giant copper tank, it was big enough for a child to swim in. Portholes gleamed on its scrubbed and buffed sides. Round wheels turned on jets of steamy hot water and nozzles bubbled foam into the center of the bath. The heating mechanism sent streams of bubbles fizzing through the tub.

Hannah's mouth fell open. She'd helped build it, but she hadn't seen it at work. The air was full of steam and candlelight. She could hear the gush and hiss of the steam heater that ran the bathtub. The smell of perfume hung in the moist air. Elana encouraged her forward.

"You need to relax, darling, relieve some tension." She pulled the pins from Hannah's hair, pulled at her dressing gown and unlaced her corset. "It's terribly uncomfortable, playing the lady, isn't it?" She smiled charmingly, making Hannah suspicious. The lure of the bath called her, though, and she rubbed at the red marks left by the whalebone on her white skin.

"Thanks, Elana." A titter came in response.

"You can thank me later!"

Hannah left her dressing gown where it lay and a trail of hairpins and underthings in her wake and nimbly scaled the ladder to the tank. She stepped down the rungs on the other side into a dim world of steam and bubbles. The hot water embraced her, she slipped up to her neck in it, felt the day's tensions beginning to ebb. Will and Elana were so clever, she thought idly. Perhaps they could fix her conflict with Darien too.

A grinding shrieking noise made her jump and splash and she turned to see the ladder disappear from the high sides of the tub. Will and Elana's faces appeared at a gleaming copper porthole, sporting gleeful grins.

"Enjoy, you silly children! We'll let you out when you've made up. Resolved your differences. There's plenty of hot water, don't worry!"

The steam cleared and revealed her lover at the other end of the tank, looking sheepish.

"Were you in on this?"

He held up his hands and shook his head. "No, this is all their doing, and I plan to have my sweet revenge at a later date. But I don't see them letting us out of here unless we make amends. So maybe you should come down to my end of the bath and we should talk, before my whirligigs get pruney."

Hannah rolled her eyes. "Whirligigs, is it? We may be naked and captive in a giant bathtub, but I'm not so sure it's time for talk of your whirligigs just yet. I don't know who you were, in that park today. Watching my pain and walking away from it. They offered me a job, Darien! And the way things are going, yes, I'm this close to taking it. If that's how you want to push me." She splashed water at him in frustration and turned away.

Darien dipped under the water and surfaced at her shoulder. His voice was rough when he spoke in her ear.

"I'm sorry. Can I...? I need to touch you." She sighed, and

without turning round, leaned back against him. He sank his forehead into the crook of her shoulder. He was quiet for a moment, lips still on her neck. When he spoke, his answer was so low she had to turn to hear.

"I'm not part of that world, the one your parents move in. And you could be, if you chose. I was scared I'd lose you. That I'm not good enough, and once you're out of the bubble of the ship, and the three of us misfits, you might see that." Hannah shook her head, mystified.

"I didn't grow up in that world either. I'm Miss Lowly Background too—an orphanage and a seamstress apprenticeship. That's me."

"Yeah, but Hannah, you didn't grow up down here. If the professor hadn't saved me the way he did Doc, I'd be...I don't know what I'd be right now."

"Oh. I didn't know. You could have told me about that, Darien. You know that."

"I wish I could offer you more. More than theft and moving and running away all the time. You never asked if we could take Doc with us. Maybe you think this is no life we live either."

Hannah turned to him then.

"I love our life, Darien, when we do it properly. I just don't feel safe right now, especially when you're not on my side. And my parents...that was something I needed to do. I thought you'd understand. I thought you'd support me." She finished in a whisper. He ducked his head and nodded into her breasts.

"I'm sorry," he whispered into her chest. "I wanted to. I'm sorry I wasn't there. It hurt to see you so upset." He gently put his mouth to her skin, placed kisses along the slope of her breast as it floated in front of him. Bravely, he started nuzzling her nipples, distracting her.

"Shh." She petted his tightly shorn hair, ran her fingers down his neck as he suckled her. The water lifted her, let her wind her legs around his hips and hold him as he licked her stiff nipples as they peeped out of the foamy water. Steam wreathed them, the pipes groaned and clanked, the water bubbled.

"You gave me a whole new life, Darien. Don't mess it up. Don't get arrested, or bring the police here, or slip away from me into the company of some rodent-man. I need you here, with me."

"Rodent-man?" He laughed. "Oh, you saw me with Clive! Ah, Hannah, it was just a little business; he doesn't have much to offer me. Not like you do, you give me so much."

"I can give you more." It had been a long separation for them, and they were naked together in the hot water and steam. Water beaded Darien's shoulders and lips, and she longed for the feeling of his body against hers again. She slipped from his grasp and dived in, her hair spreading around her like a heavy cloud. Its seaweed wreathing worked the tension from her sore neck and scalp.

In front of her was Darien's cock, standing proud, and she took its slippery length into her mouth and moved up and down it until she ran out of air. She surfaced for breath and a glimpse of his transported face before returning to the task, letting the heat of the water in her mouth do much of the work, then sucking him until his knees buckled and he pulled her back onto him. Darien turned her so her back was resting against the wall of the tank and eased her legs around his waist again. He crushed his erection against her clit and thrust and she bucked and moaned and pushed back at him. The pressure was always a sweet, delicious pain that she loved. He tipped her mouth up toward his, and kissed her, deep and intense, claiming her again. At the same time, his cock worked to unfurl her labia, nudging its way in. Hannah felt herself slip onto him, hot and slick, different from the heat of the bath. Darien's thrusts were slow and deep and she felt dreamy, floating on his cock and held up by the water. His hands found her breasts again, reached for her nipples, slippery in the water. Everything was heated and swollen, every touch magnified. She squeezed him closer and he groaned and pumped harder, sliding his hand between them to press and circle her clit.

"Oh, velvet, Hannah."

She lay her head back against the warm metal and shifted her hips, clenching down hard, making him gasp.

"Oh, easy, girl, easy.

Might as well go easy, she thought. *We've nowhere to go for the moment, and Will says there's plenty of hot water.* Darien lifted a hank of her wet hair in his hand and leaned his face into it.

"You're my mermaid in the water, Hannah. I'm sorry, Hannie, I'm so sorry, I'm a fool, I didn't mean to hurt you. I'm sorry I let you go alone. Angel girl."

He rubbed her harder, thrust faster, and she leaned in and bit his nipple as the shudders broke though her.

"Augh, I love you," he coughed out, and came, leaning down to bury his head in her shoulder.

"I like it in here," Hannah said, when their breathing had cooled, and Darien had slipped out of her. "Maybe we shouldn't tell them we're okay." She laughed, lifting her wrinkled fingertips to his mouth to kiss. "Though we must consider your whirligigs."

8 Airborne Again, A Moonlit Ending

With a clank, the ladder splashed back into the tank and Elana's smiling face peered over.

"I hope your rapprochement is complete in there, there's something you need to see."

They climbed out, gingerly. Before the ship stood a beaming Doc, clad in a new dress and a smear of grease and holding a multi-tool. A *whum* and a whir emanated from the ship. Will was looking stunned.

"It seems to be working. Doc, did you work with the professor?"

"Yeah, I was his 'prentice. He said I had raw potential."

Darien frowned.

"He never made *me* his apprentice."

"I think your raw potential was in a different area, old man," said Will calmly. "Here, put some clothes on."

"Told you I could fix it."

Some nights later, in the small hours, a ship rose into the night sky, hoisted by a glowing green and gold balloon. At the helm stood Hannah and Darien, airborne again, united once more, hands entwined and steering for the moon.

SPARKS

Anna Meadows

I would have been the first to concede how much better things were for me back when I behaved myself. Back when I rarely went out, when I only saw friends whose politics my father had approved beforehand; we were only allowed to sit in the salon and drink the hibiscus and rose-hip tea that made me so drowsy I no longer parted the curtains to catch a glimpse of the outside world. Back when my parents spoke of betrothing me to men whose company I could comfortably stand, and when I wasn't in love with a twenty-one-year-old boy who always had crescent moons of soot and ash under his fingernails.

Back when the clockwork corsos didn't stalk me like a pasture rabbit.

I had only moments until their brass teeth would tear into me. My thoughts, which I knew might be my last, strayed to Ezra; instead of longing for the neat linens of the bedroom where I had slept until I was eighteen, I wanted nothing more than the touch of the boy who had first led me away from the safety of my parents' walled gardens. The boy who had first

taught me the landscape of the black market liquor trade that
had flourished since the Ban. I wanted his hands up under my
skirt, tearing my slip in his haste to reach the warmth and
wetness beneath my crinoline.

But he wasn't there, and knowing I would never again feel
the heat of his breath against the hollow of my neck filled me
with more dread than my approaching hunters.

I had none of the liqueur on me. But I had three-dozen
autumn damask roses and two pounds of Parma violets under
my coat. They were tucked neatly inside the red satin of the
lining, but the corsos could still smell them, so I ran, holding
my coat shut and trying not to let my heels call out my steps on
the wet cobblestone.

Thanks in no small part to Ezra and me, roses and violets
had been banned, and gardeners grudgingly filled their flowerbeds with clove-pink carnations and peonies, whose fluffy frills I
loved, but the more reserved groundskeepers found garish.

Each of the clockwork corsos had a large, sturdy shape and
a dark gleam, distinctive of the dog breed that was their name-
sake. As a child, I had once seen a month-old canine corso—a
real one of course, since the clockwork corsos were always built
full size. The puppy had a sad but determined face and a coat
so shiny it looked like damp coffee grounds. It had belonged to
the daughter of an Italian businessman who visited my father
whenever he was in the country. The puppy's little body had
been so warm on my lap; now I could find no resemblance to
the brass and wrought iron creatures policing the streets and
country roads, searching out contraband blooms.

I had chosen tonight because I had heard that the worst of the
clockwork corsos were in the shop for repairs. But I recognized
the growl of their gears from blocks away, the sound echoing off
the brick buildings. They had been fixed and released from the

shop early. If they cornered me, they would tear me to pieces. I had seen it happen to a man who had tried to smuggle a dozen bottles of juniper-berry gin into the city. Ezra and I had been walking home when we saw a crowd gathered, and he pulled me into him and whispered, "Don't look." Before Ezra shielded my gaze, I saw that a corso's tooth had come loose in the struggle, the triangle of brass glinting in the dead man's neck.

Whenever the corsos killed a man, the authorities termed it a mechanical failure, an accident. They recalled the involved dogs for inspection only to release them hours later. But they knew what their hounds were doing; they had designed them for it.

I ran toward darkness, down the alley between E. P. Logan's Clothier and the hat shop that always smelled like chamomile. There was no use calling for help. Even if the businesses hadn't been shut for the night, no one would have helped me for fear of looking guilty. I pressed my back against the damp brick, willing myself to disappear into the wall. But the corsos weren't searching for me by sight. Even I could smell the violets and roses. My clothes and hair were soaked in their perfume.

The corsos paused at the corner, the metal of their bodies creaking as they sniffed the air. In no hurry, they turned their heads toward the dark where I hid. The gas-flame blue of their eyes grew brighter as their iron joints creaked, readying their bodies to lunge.

They would make no sound as they tore my throat open. They had not been built to bark or snarl like living dogs. Only my screams and the grating of metal on metal would cut through the silence on the empty street.

A few more points of light joined the glow of their eyes. At first I thought more had come. But the new lights were too low to the ground, and instead of gas blue, they were tinged with violet, like iolite. Even the corsos stopped to watch them glide over the cobblestones. The biggest among them lowered his head to sniff one. Electricity arced through the iron and brass of his frame, lighting it up pale purple, and he clattered to the ground. The others drew back, skittering away from the remaining little lights. But one by one, they too glowed with the same violet sparks and then fell, eyes vanishing as their brass lids snapped shut.

I couldn't move. I had lost my night vision to the hounds' eyes and the little wisteria-colored lights. The corsos blocked my path out of the alley. They had been stunned, but they could shock back into life at any moment.

The last little point of glowing violet rolled toward me. It was nothing but a clear glass marble, with a tiny lavender spark captured inside. But I didn't have enough breath to run from it, and it came to rest against the side of my boot. Its heat and electricity shimmered through my body. My head fell back against the brick, and my bangs cleared from my eyes, letting me see the blur of the stars and the thumbnail slice of moon.

I saw him running toward me. Though I could only see his silhouette, I knew his shape better than mine, because I had touched his body more than I had touched my own. My hands had learned him in every second they'd spent on his back and thighs. But he couldn't have been there. He had emerged from my fever dream. If I wanted it enough, he would push me up against the wall and take my weight on his hips.

The warmth in my temples made me dizzy. He held me and put his lips to my ear, whispering my name as the stars and moon went dark.

I dreamed of him in the sweet, damp haze of touch and bayberry candle glow.

Hours later, I surfaced from sleep to the feeling of chambray cotton sheets, worn soft by years of washing. The scent of violets and roses mixed with the soft spice of ashes and cloves.

Cambric and ash: it identified him as well as a fingerprint.

"Ezra?" I said before I was awake enough to open my eyes.

I could feel his weight on the bed as he sat near me and stroked my hair. "It's all right," he said, and stood up again. "You're all right."

I shut my eyes tighter and then let them relax open. It was still night, but through the space between the shades I found a thin line of pink that traced the hills and *mesas* along the horizon. In an hour or so, it would be morning.

"How did you find me?" I asked.

He shrugged, his back to me. "We still run similar routes."

"I haven't seen you."

"I haven't wanted you to." He turned up the lamp, the same pressed-lead glass we'd made love by a year earlier. He looked almost as young as the last time I saw him; a faint shadow of stubble along his jawline made him look barely older. Locks of his hair fell in his eyes, and the lamp lit up the red strands that hid within the brown like stray threads. His trousers had the same pinstripes I remembered, and over his collared shirt he wore a waistcoat he had inherited from his father. It used to be big on him, and now it fit; even though he had a little more muscle to him now, he must have had it taken in.

My coat hung on a hook near the bureau, with my crinoline next to it. I had on only the velvet of my dress over the cream-white of my slip. I hadn't been this naked in front of a man since the last time I saw him.

He'd loosened the lacing on my corset. I could breathe. I sat up, and my hair fell around my shoulders. He'd freed it from its pinned curls.

I combed it with my fingers. "Were you planning to take advantage of me?"

"If I were, I wouldn't have left your dress on." He filled with water two chipped vases that had belonged to his late grand-mother. "You wouldn't have been able to sleep in your coat."

I recognized things from where he had last lived, where I had lived with him for a few months. The railroad pocket watch his grandfather had given him was on the bureau. The lamp gave off an apricot glow I knew by heart. I remembered the rose-wood table where he set the vases. But this was somewhere else. It was far enough out in the country to see the *mesas*, instead of right in the city.

He slipped the Parma violets and damask roses from the lining of my coat into the water. "You've got to stop wearing your corset so tight. You'll crack a rib."

I wore it that way without thinking. My mother used to tell me, "Better in pain than unkempt."

"It's a habit," I told Ezra.

"It's a bad one." He checked the flowers for crushed petals. "Who's your grower?"

I sat on the edge of the bed, letting the toes of my stockings catch dust from the floor. "I am."

"Where?" he asked.

"My sister rents me a half acre on her land."

"Luisa?" He almost laughed. "She never wanted you involved in the first place."

Luisa, like my mother, had never wanted a Reyes woman like me involved with a *gringo* like Ezra.

"Her new husband is a businessman at heart," I said. It wasn't exactly the truth. I had stayed with them for a few weeks after I left Ezra. Within a month of seeing me leave my bed only to help Luisa with the housework, my brother-in-law suggested that starting a garden might help my mood. He turned a blind eye when he realized the flowers I grew helped produce spirits rather than lift them.

Ezra's mouth was the exact color I remembered it. Once when he was sleeping, I had matched it to the outer petals of a blush moss. I wanted to kiss him so badly it stung between my legs.

We had worked together once, taking flowers to the distillery Samuel Arlings had concealed in his barn, and then smuggling the product away. Ezra had worked in the city as a chimney sweep since he was eight years old, so no one thought anything of his going in and out of houses, where he brought the quarter-liter bottles. Our regular buyers furnished him with keys and allowed him in when they weren't home; he hid the contraband bottles inside the masonry of their unused chimneys, where they would find them, but the authorities wouldn't.

Our friends had asked why we never opened our own operation, but there was an art to making violet and rose liqueur. It took more time and skill than the bathtub-faucet alcohol that had come into vogue since the Ban, so dreadful it needed three parts cream or orange juice to salvage it. Parma and rose liqueur, if made well, could be sipped pure, but the flowers were so delicate they had to be distilled with water instead of steam.

Ezra still wouldn't look at me. He kept his back to me. I slid off the bed and put my hand on his shoulder. How hurt he looked made me unsteady, and I braced my other hand on the rosewood table. I'd always thought he'd fall in love with the next girl who carried roses inside her coat.

"I thought you left me to go back to your parents," he said, checking the flowers again.

I slid my hand down over his shoulder blade and said nothing.

"If you were going to keep working, why did you leave?" he asked.

"Because I knew you'd get yourself killed," I said.

"I know how to stay alive."

"Not with me around." I took his face in my hands to make him look at me, and I felt the soft bristle that had grown in since he last shaved. "I drew too much attention to you. I thought that whenever we got caught, at least I'd have my family's reputation behind me. The name Reyes means something. I had that. You didn't."

"Your family's name." He pulled away from me. "Hell of a lot of good that did you last night."

I grabbed his hand before it left the table. His fingernails still had soot under them, but he had cleaned them recently, so the whites were silvery gray. "Thank you," I said. "For saving my life."

He smiled the smile I'd first fallen in love with, uneven because he'd lost some of the feeling in one side of his face to a childhood illness. "You had a lot of good petals up under your dress," he said. "Would've been a shame to see them ruined."

My hand traveled up his arm to his neck, and my mouth found his. I caught the taste of spiced wood on his tongue; he hadn't broken the habit of holding a dried clove between his back teeth when he was working. He gripped my waist like he always had, trying to feel my body under my corset and slip.

His mouth broke from mine, but he still stayed so close we kept our eyes shut. "Is that really why you left?"

"Yes," I said, giving up the truth before I could think to lie.

"You didn't go back to your parents?" he asked.

"I couldn't." Not after being with him. Not after making love at midnight and watching the sun rise over the *mesas* when we were still drunk from it.

His thumbs grazed my cheeks, his forehead resting against mine. His hands bore patches of calloused skin, but his touch was so gentle that the roughness on his palms felt as soft as lilac leaves. He held aside a loose curl and kissed my forehead;

I tried not to think of how he used to say my hair reminded him of black magic roses. I was so sure this was a good-bye that I gripped handfuls of his waistcoat fabric; I would not let him go.

He moved his head so his eyelashes brushed my temple. He was taking in the scent of my hair. "Marry me," he said.

I opened my eyes.

"You may have been worried about me," he said.

"I still am," I interrupted, pulling away enough to look at him.

"And now I'm worried about you." He shrugged one shoulder. "Think of it as strategic business. If we're married, no one will ask questions when we're together."

I tried to tickle him through his waistcoat and shirt. "Who said I'd work with you again?"

"You already are. You just didn't know it." He kissed me again, once. "Are you going to answer my question?"

"You first," I said. "I want to know how you saved me last night."

He smiled again, like full dawn after rain. He knelt near his bureau and pulled up a board from the floor, unveiling a faint violet glow.

"Lightning marbles." He offered his hand to help me to the floor. "Sam gets so many strikes out on his farm, we thought we'd do something with them."

"You still work for Sam?" I knelt next to him. "Why haven't I seen you?"

"I didn't want you to," he said. "He's teaching me to distill."

I cleared a slash of hair from in front of his eye. "Good." Sam's wife had wanted him to retire for years.

Ezra looked down at the floor. "He figures I know how to

handle flowers by now. Even the delicate ones." He pushed the board out of the way.

Beneath the floor, an old jewelry box held a dozen or so marbles, blown-glass and all different sizes. Within each, tiny veins of electricity sparked and pulsed.

"How do you catch it in there?" I asked.

"You'll have to marry me to find that out," he said.

I tried not to smile. "How do they work?"

With a pair of porcelain tongs, he lifted one of the bigger ones to the light. It shimmered like raw amethyst.

"When it makes contact with a conductor, the lightning tries so hard to get out that it melts the glass away, just leaving the electricity."

"So you can shock police guards and former lovers?" I asked.

He cringed. "I didn't mean that to happen. I thought you'd run. Didn't your mother ever tell you not to touch something if you don't know what it is?"

"My mother told me never to touch anything," I said. "Especially you."

He lowered his head so his hair would shadow his blush.

"What if you accidentally shock yourself?" I asked.

He laughed. "It hurts."

"Then why did I..."

"Because you're smaller than I am. And I'm used to it."

I wondered how he pulled the electricity from my body enough to take me home, if my skin let off little shocks when it met his, if the charge passed through the petals in the lining of my coat as he held me. I wondered if it was still inside me, if sparks still spread heat through my body.

"They're dangerous," I said. "You shouldn't be carrying them."

He set the marble back in the wooden jewelry box. "They're the only way to stall the corsos."

"You'll hurt yourself."

"I won't." He lifted out another with the clay tongs, cupping his other hand to receive it.

"Ezra, no!" I said.

It landed in the hollow of his palm. A halo of violet glowed around his arm, and he fell back against the floor.

"Ezra." I cleared his hair from his face and felt little shocks on my fingertips. "Ezra."

He laughed, his eyes still closed. "I told you. It hurts, but that's all."

I shoved his shoulder. "Don't do that." I took his hand and kissed the faint burn in the center of his palm.

"Don't worry," he said. "It'll fade. It always does."

I climbed onto him and kissed him. I could almost feel the remnant lightning on his tongue.

He opened his eyes. He was trying not to breathe hard, and his lips were trembling for it. His pupils dilated and constricted with the slow rhythm of a lighthouse.

We grabbed at each other's clothes. I unbuttoned his waist-coat and shirt. He unfastened my dress and slip. Too impatient to strip him naked, I undid his trousers and slipped my hand inside. He was already hard. Later, when we were lying in bed together, I'd tease him for it, but now I couldn't wait, even for the few seconds of a passing flirtation.

He wanted to look at all of me; he was so hungry to see me naked I could feel it in the way he took hold of my lingerie, like it bound me and kept me from him. He pulled away my bloomers and freed me from my corset. He kissed the under-sides of my breasts like he was thirsty and they would turn to water against his mouth. While he followed the lower curves, his fingers explored the rings of brownish-pink at the tips of my breasts, like he was learning to draw them.

I straddled him, my knees on either side of his hips, and guided his erection inside me. He bit his lower lip to stop its trembling. His hands moved so easily from my breasts to between my thighs that I did not realize they were there until his strokes drew out more of my wetness. The tiniest sparks, so small I couldn't know if they were real or imagined, leapt between his fingers and the pearl that held my deepest lust.

I put all my weight onto him, and it both heightened his pleasure and maddened him, because he barely had the freedom to thrust into me. But he knew the way inside me, as no other man did, and I opened to him so he could reach that last trace of electricity that his amethyst lightning had left the night before. When he found it, his own seed of newer lightning, still in his body, shuddered through his hardness and met the spark I held within my darkest place, just as dawn soaked the room in rose-gold light.

He said my name. I answered with his, my palms mapping the contours of his chest. He said mine a second time. "Yes," I said as I kissed him, an answer I would give again to any question he asked. "Yes," I said, as involuntarily as the noises I made when he touched me between my legs. "Yes." A response to the question he'd asked but that I'd left suspended between us, unanswered, in lantern light. "Yes." A cry for more of everything: his mouth on my neck, his hands on my breasts, his erection growing harder as he moved inside me.

Yes, things were better for me when I behaved myself. But I preferred the desperate heat we held between our bodies, and the sweet, slight pain of our shared lightning.

GREEN CHEESE

Lisabet Sarai

O h, I do beg your pardon! Are you hurt? Please, allow me to assist you…"

Caroline Fortescue-Smythe scowled up from the ground where she sat in a crumpled heap of skirts and petticoats. The tropical glare behind him made it difficult for her to see his features. Nevertheless, despite his impeccable English, the man who had slammed into her was clearly Siamese. He extended his hand to help her to her feet. His other hand clutched some bulky contraption of leather and brass, embedded with lenses that glittered in the sun.

"You should pay attention to where you are going," she grumbled, brushing the dust from her heavy clothing. Perspiration trickled down her spine and her stays dug into her ribs, adding to her foul mood. "I'm not injured, but I might easily have been. You were barreling along like a locomotive."

"I am so sorry," the young man repeated. "I was trying to capture images of the race." He pointed to the strange mechanism he carried. A cheer rose up from the crowd as some stallion or other crossed the finish line. "I was so focused on the horses, I didn't see you."

Caroline snapped open her parasol. In its welcome shade she felt fractionally cooler. "What is it?" Aside from the lenses, it did not look like any camera she'd ever seen.

"My latest invention," her companion replied, pride evident in his voice. "A moving picture recorder and player."

"Like the Lumières' projector?" The French ambassador had been boasting about this marvel of Gallic technology at some official function only last week.

"You are familiar with their work?" He favored her with such a warm smile that it melted a good deal of her annoyance. "My videographic device is similar in function, but much faster and more versatile. The same machine can both capture and display moving images. You see, here, I can show you the last race..." The stranger drew her closer and indicated an oval-shaped glass panel built into the side of the recorder. He pressed a button. Sleek equine shapes galloped across the glass surface, the motion so smooth and natural that Caroline was astonished.

"Of course, the images can also be projected externally, for public viewing," he continued. "I am working at the moment on the problems of color and sound."

The enthusiasm in the young man's voice banished the last of Caroline's anger. He stood far closer to her than would normally be proper, his bare hand clutching her gloved one. When she took a shallow breath (the only sort permitted by her corset), she caught hints of cloves and jasmine. The scent, in combination with the pitiless sun, made her briefly dizzy.

She examined him more closely. Although he was dressed in Siamese costume, silk pantaloons and a formfitting white jacket with brass buttons, he wore his coal-black hair cut in Western style rather than bound into a topknot. His complexion was the color of antique ivory. Behind his wire-rimmed spectacles, his eyes were like pools of melted chocolate. His beardless features looked boyish but his broad shoulders and narrow waist suggested he was at least as old as her own twenty-three years.

"Quite impressive," she said, finally. "My father will be interested to hear about this."

"Your father? Oh dear, please forgive me once more. I get so involved with my little projects that I completely forget my manners." He drew himself up to his full height, a few inches taller than Caroline's petite stature. "Allow me to introduce myself. I am Ruangkornpongpipat Suriyarasamee. Please, don't even try to pronounce it! My friends call me Pete." He squeezed her hand and gazed boldly into her eyes. "I hope that I shall be able to count you among them."

Caroline felt hot blood climb into her cheeks. "Suriyarasamee—I've heard that name, I think."

"My father is one of the wealthiest merchants in Bangkok—quite fortunately for me, since he has ample resources to support my investigations. I am surprised that a foreigner would be aware of him, though. Who are you, if I might ask?"

"Caroline Fortescue-Smythe, at your service," she replied, still embarrassed by her earlier rudeness. "The daughter of Thomas Fortescue-Smythe, Her Majesty Queen Victoria's ambassador to Siam."

"Ah, that explains it. My father frequently attends diplomatic parties. You may even have met him." He released her, reluctantly it seemed. "Well, Miss Caroline—I do hope you will allow me to use your given name according to our custom, since Fortescue-Smythe is almost as much of a mouthful as my own moniker—I am truly delighted to meet you. And I apologize most sincerely for my clumsiness."

"There was no harm done." Caroline realized that she was still blushing. Meanwhile, her heart danced a hornpipe under her tight bodice. "I—um—I should get back to our box. My father will be concerned. Please excuse me..."

"Wait!" He snagged her hand once more and heat shimmered through her. "Do not go yet."

"I must. I'm sorry..."

"It's such a pleasure to converse with you. It's not often I meet a woman, Siamese or European, with any interest in technology. Look, are you engaged this evening?"

"Tonight?"

"I've arranged a little performance at my house, for some of my friends. Another one of my creations. I'd love for you to come see it. With your father, of course."

"Well..."

"I'll send an invitation with the details to the ambassadorial residence this afternoon. I hope I will see you this evening. Until then, Miss Caroline." Pete raised her hand to his lips as though to kiss it, but appeared confused by her glove. Finally, he turned her hand palm up and pressed his lips against her bare wrist. He lingered there for an endless moment. The wet tip of his tongue flicked across her pulse point. Electricity arced up her spine.

He smiled into her eyes, nodded, and moved on, pointing his recording device once again at the horses thundering down the track. The strip of naked skin between her glove and her sleeve tingled long after he'd disappeared into the crowd. It was several minutes before she recovered.

Caroline threaded her way through the spectators pressed against the rail, wondering at her reactions to the charming, unconventional young man. Normally she was quite immune to masculine attention. Freddy had been flabbergasted when she refused his offer of marriage, especially after the scene in his uncle's library. She'd been curious, that was all. True, she'd enjoyed the experience, but it was not after all so different from pleasures she could administer to herself. Why would she want to submit to a husband? In any case, her father needed her.

She reached the diplomatic boxes. Mrs. Vandervoordt smiled and waved as Caroline passed, her apple cheeks pink in the heat. Her husband, the Dutch ambassador, yelled at the top of his lungs as the horses swept by, his stovepipe hat practically toppling off his bald head. The Lázaro-Batistas and the Ortegas called out friendly greetings. Monsieur Charbonnet, however, gave her the briefest of nods, his mouth puckered as though he'd eaten an unripe plum. She returned the minimum acknowledgment custom permitted.

Wedged between British Burma and French Cochin, Siam was neutral territory. Up on the moon, though, Britain and France were fighting a bitter war.

"Caroline!" Her father stood so that she could settle her voluminous skirts into her seat. "Where have you been? I was worried."

"Sorry, Papa. I met someone—a rather clever Siamese gentleman, though not, I think, all that accustomed to Western women. We've been invited to his house this evening for some sort of entertainment."

"Really, my dear, we can't go charging off to some stranger's place, especially a Siamese..."

"He's quite rich, Papa." Caroline pulled off her glove and reached for the iced lemon juice waiting next to her chair. "I believe you know his father—the name's Suree-something." As she raised the glass to her lips, she caught a whiff of cloves—Pete's distinctive scent, clinging to her skin. The heat was suddenly unbearable, despite the awning arching over their box.

The tangy liquid slid down her throat but did nothing to quench her fever.

"I don't know..."

"There's also the possibility he could be of some concrete assistance," Caroline argued. "He's a talented inventor. He might be able to help with the war effort."

"All right, all right!" Her father threw up his hands. "We'll go, if that's what you want. Now hand me the program. Which horse do you favor in the next race?"

Their carriage drove at a sedate pace along Wireless Road. Dusk had brought a hush and a hint of coolness to the city. Starlings twittered in the trees that arched over them. Frogs boomed in the canal paralleling the road. Night-blooming flowers perfumed the air.

Caroline heard a low buzz, coming from behind. As the sound grew closer, the pitch climbed to a whine, as though a massive mosquito were pursuing them. A shape emerged from the semi-darkness, something like a giant metallic cigar. It hurtled past their coach, disappearing into the tree-hung shadows ahead. The wind of its passing ruffled the curls on Caroline's forehead. The horses shook their harness and whinnied in fear.

"Bloody French bastard," her father swore. "Showing off. What a waste of viridium!"

"It might be one of the Siamese nobles," Caroline countered. "I heard that several of them have acquired these vehicles."

"I'm sure it was Charbonnet. He was trying to run us down."

"Papa, there's no way he could have known we were in the carriage. I've heard that visibility is extremely limited inside those things."

"Hmph. He has his spies. He probably knows exactly what we're doing tonight."

Caroline allowed the subject to drop. Her normally phleg-matic father had a sensitive spot when it came to the French.

Viridium. That was the cause of it all. Discovery of the rare, energy-rich element in 1872 had turned the world upside down. Gold and silver became near-worthless as viridium prospecting grew to a frenzy. A few fortunes were made. Many were lost. Alliances shifted and conflicts erupted as countries struggled to maintain control over their viridium resources and acquire new ones.

Powered by viridium, airships could circle the globe in two days. Ships could dive beneath the seas. Viridium sent rockets to the moon. Britain had arrived first, France a few months later. On that barren satellite, Major Stanley T. Harkness had found vast deposits of the crumbly green substance, coating the floors of lunar craters like algae at the bottom of dried-up ponds: a practically unlimited supply of viridium. Three years later, the rival nations were locked in a battle that had claimed thousands of lives and come close to bankrupting both economies.

The carriage pulled up before a stone wall two stories high. Caroline's father announced their names to the liveried guard. The carved wooden gate swung open, revealing a lush, torchlit garden, through which the coach proceeded. They halted in front of a substantial dwelling. A familiar figure emerged onto the veranda.

"Miss Caroline! I am delighted that you were able to join us. And you must be Ambassador Fortescue-Smythe."

Pete was dressed less formally than he'd been at the Turf Club, in loose white trousers and a matching tunic. The snow-white costume emphasized his athletic build. His complexion appeared dark in contrast. His feet were bare. He looked incred-ibly exotic.

He clasped her hand in both of his. The scent of clove and

jasmine swirled around them like incense.

Caroline swallowed hard, struggling to control her reactions. "Ah—um—Papa, this is Ruangkornpongpipat Suriyarasamee."

"Bravo! You have an exceptional memory!" Pete practically danced over to shake her father's hand. "Sir, I'm honored to welcome you to my humble abode. But do call me Pete. Please, come inside. The others have already arrived."

After removing their shoes, they followed their host into a spacious, high-ceilinged room floored with polished teak. Roughly a dozen men and women lounged on cushions around the periphery. Low tables set before them were crowded with food and drink.

The musical babble of the Siamese language faded as Pete entered. Their host introduced each of his jet-haired, doe-eyed friends. Their one-syllable nicknames fled from Caroline's memory as soon as she heard them.

"Please, make yourself comfortable," Pete urged, indicating a pile of unoccupied cushions. Then he noticed the ambassador's discomfort. "Or would you rather have a chair, sir?"

"That would be excellent, thank you." Caroline's father sounded deeply relieved.

"And you, Miss Caroline?" She thought she caught a hint of laughter in Pete's voice.

"The cushions are fine, thank you." With some difficulty, she lowered herself to the floor. The full skirts of her evening frock definitely hampered her movements. Pete beamed.

He settled himself on the pillows next to Caroline, so close that his sleeve brushed against her bare arm. She considered whether she should attempt to put more space between them. Ultimately she decided that doing so would be obvious and thus impolite. Pete grinned at her, as though he knew what was passing through her mind.

"Well, then. I think we're ready to begin. Kai?"

One of the women brought out some sort of musical instrument, a flat, triangular box with metal strings stretched from one edge to the other. She cradled the box in her lap and struck the strings with tiny hammers. A cascade of silvery notes shimmered in the night air. They coalesced into a strange but haunting melody.

The music continued for several measures. The anticipation was palpable. A humid breeze floated in through the open windows. Did the smell of jasmine come from the garden outside or the man beside her? Caroline could not tell.

In a curtained doorway opposite them, something stirred. A long-fingered hand pulled back the drapery. A dainty foot shone on the dark wood floor. A lovely face appeared from behind the velvet hangings.

A doll about half human height, costumed in brocade and crowned with gold filigree, stood before them. Placing its palms together, it raised the fingertips to its forehead and bowed to the audience in a gesture of respect. Then it began to dance.

Caroline had seen performances of the Siamese classical forms by some of the court masters. This automaton appeared no less skilled. Her movements (the doll exuded such a feminine quality that it was impossible to use the designation "it") were as precise as one would expect from a mechanism, but they conveyed emotion as well. When the music became languorous and sad, the robotic dancer's limbs seemed weighted with sorrow. When the tempo quickened, joy and laughter animated her gestures. The aesthetic effect and the technical achievement were equally astonishing.

"She's incredible," Caroline murmured to her companion. "Truly amazing." Pete captured her hand, without taking his eyes off his creation. The coolness of his skin against hers made

Caroline wonder if she was running a fever.

The music reached its end at last. The dancer bowed once more and retreated behind the curtain. The guests broke into excited chatter.

"Excuse me for a moment, Miss Caroline." Pete rose to his feet in a single, fluid movement. "I must go accept the congratulations of my friends. I will return shortly."

Caroline also stood, with more effort and less grace, and made her way to her father's side.

"We've got to get hold of that," the ambassador whispered. "Automatons like that would allow us to win the war."

"What? Dancing dolls?"

"Soldiers, girl! If you can teach a robot to dance, you can teach it to fight. Think of our poor boys, lumbering around up there in those cumbersome spacesuits, carrying a portable atmosphere around on their backs! Clockwork soldiers don't need air, or food or water... It's the break we've been waiting for, if we can only convince this young genius to work for us."

"But Siam is officially neutral, Papa. How are we going to convince him?"

Thomas Fortescue-Smythe fixed his daughter with his shrewd eyes. "I thought you might have some ideas, Caroline."

So it was that Caroline found herself alone with Pete, the last of the guests to leave. She would have been angry at her father for sacrificing her virtue (as he imagined) to political expediency had this not coincided so completely with her own desires.

"I regret that your father became indisposed," said Pete, pouring her another glass of excellent French wine.

"Spicy food frequently disagrees with him." Caroline settled back into the cushions, closer to Pete. To her disappointment, he sighed and sat up straight.

"It's well past midnight. I suppose that I should call for the carriage."

She laid a hand on his shoulder. "That's not really necessary, is it?"

He started, then allowed her to pull him down to her level. "Caroline? What...?"

She removed his spectacles, stowing them on a convenient shelf behind them, and gazed into his eyes. She watched the emotions chase each other through those velvet depths: surprise, disbelief and finally understanding. Still, he hesitated. Tired of being patient, Caroline leaned forward and kissed him.

As though the touch of her lips had freed him from constraints, he grew suddenly bold, pulling her to his chest and thrusting his tongue into her half-open mouth. He tasted spicy and unfamiliar, utterly delicious. Although she had begun the kiss, he soon assumed control. Freddy had been annoyingly tentative, but Pete clearly knew what he was doing. His hands engaged in wanton exploration, molding her silk-sheathed breast, thumbing the nipple, then slipping under her skirts. She gasped when he brushed the bare skin on the inside of her thigh. Sparks flared wherever his fingers traveled. Her quim felt soaked and swollen, aching for his attention. Her many-layered garments were a sweltering prison.

She stroked his lean thigh through his trousers, then allowed her hand to creep upward. Pete groaned into her mouth as she cupped the substantial bulge she discovered in his groin. He wore no undergarments. The bulb nestled in her palm, quivering and damp, while she ran her thumb around the ridge. He tensed, thrusting into her fist. Under the fabric, his prick felt hard and smooth as polished river stones. It was long and slender, as exotic as the rest of him.

His lips slid away from hers to nuzzle the sensitive skin

below her ear. Her heart fluttered against her stays. Her cunny throbbed, wet and hungry. His cat tongue swirled across her throat while underneath his hand groped blindly, seeking a way into her knickers.

"Oh, Caroline," he breathed, rocking against her hand while fumbling with her petticoats. "That's marvelous! But these bloody skirts..."

"Shall we retire to your room, then? I should very much like to remove them."

"Indeed, a capital notion..." With some difficulty, they untangled themselves. After retrieving his spectacles, Pete assisted her in rising to her feet. The white tent at his groin made her think of a schooner's sail. "This way, please."

Seizing her hand, he pulled her through a shadowy corridor to a room near the back of the house. Compared to a European bedroom, it was rather bare: a mattress arranged upon a pedestal, a carved teak wardrobe, a low table circled by bright-hued cushions. Several oil lamps shed a golden glow on the scene.

Without preliminaries, the Siamese man untied his sash and pulled his tunic over his head, then pushed his trousers to his ankles and kicked them into a corner. Caroline found herself transfixed by the alien beauty of his smooth, hairless body. Aside from the curly black nest surrounding his rampant cock, he might have been fashioned of marble, like Michelangelo's *David*. Still wearing his glasses, he settled himself onto the mattress with a broad grin on his handsome face. Now he reminded her of some classical satyr, his rigid prick rearing up from his loins, taunting and tempting her.

"Well?" He raised an eyebrow. "I thought you said you'd like to remove your clothing."

"Indeed, though I fear it will take me somewhat longer than

you." Despite her earlier boldness, Caroline's cheeks grew hot under his scrutiny. She reached behind her, struggling to release the long line of buttons that fastened the tight silk bodice.

"Might I offer you some assistance?" Laughter lurked under his politeness.

"No, no, I can manage." The notion of a man undressing her was simultaneously shocking and arousing. Her hurried coupling with Freddy had been mostly clothed.

The bodice fell loose. She slipped it off her shoulders and set it on the table. One layer at a time she peeled off the ruffled *tablier,* the overskirt, the underskirt and several sets of petticoats. Finally she stood before him wearing only her corset, chemise and drawers.

She strained to reach the back lacing, without success. Pete's eyes were glued to her near-naked form. She'd never had to deal with a corset without her maid. When she was breathless from trying, she swallowed hard and beckoned to her audience.

"Please, if you don't mind..." She offered him her back. He was on his feet in an instant, his deft fingers plucking at the laces. She filled her lungs with a grateful breath when the corset released its iron grip on her torso.

"Oh, thank you...oh!" Pete had slipped his hands into the loosened garment and captured her breasts. He cradled their fullness, kneading softly. Waves of pleasure rippled through her. She relaxed against him, delightfully aware of his cock prodding at her bum. The scent of cloves tickled her nostrils.

"Caroline," he murmured, burying his face in her blonde ringlets. "You are so very lovely." He rolled her taut nipple between the fingers of one hand while slipping the other into her damp knickers. Her cunny ached for him but all he did was brush his fingertips across her pubic fur. Lightning sizzled through her. Her sex clenched and wept.

"Oh...please..."

"Yes? What can I do for you?" His fingers tapped gently on her mons, driving her wild, but still he did not enter her.

Caroline whirled around and pressed her barely clad body against him. "You know what I'm talking about!" His hard prick poked at her belly. She seized it and delivered a desperate squeeze. "Take me. Please, I need you inside me."

One slender finger slithered into her soaked cleft. "You mean, like this?" He flicked his tongue across her earlobe.

"Yes! No! I mean, more! Please!" Caroline pumped his erection. A second finger slid into her, grazing her clit and making her writhe. "I want you—this—oh, god, please!"

She danced on his hand, pleasure coiling tighter with each breath. Then he did something—touched something—deep inside her, and everything exploded. Sensation drenched her, sharp, sweet and wet. It was glorious, intense, almost unbearable.

She would have collapsed had her partner not supported her. While she still shuddered, rivulets of delight trickling through her senses, he swept her into his arms and bore her to the bed. Her few remaining articles of clothing disappeared as if by magic.

"You astonish me," Pete told her, kneeling between her spread thighs. "I had been led to believe that European women were cold creatures who cared more for propriety than the joys of the flesh."

"Most are, I suppose...oh! Oh, my! What are you doing?" The question was rhetorical. Caroline understood, intellectually, that Pete was licking her cunny—she just couldn't believe it. His lips fastened on her clit and sucked until she thought her hot little bead would burst. His velvet tongue delved into her, while she squirmed and moaned and begged for his cock.

Finally, when she thought she could bear no more, Pete relented. He crawled up her body, his flawless skin like satin against her heated flesh. He pressed his lips to hers. He tasted like raw oysters—like her quim, she realized. Meanwhile, his prick slid into her lubricious folds without the slightest effort, as though that was where it belonged.

With Freddy, there'd been some pain at first. Pete's cock was pure delight. He filled her empty places, places she hadn't known existed. His thrusts were fluid, unhurried, giving her time to appreciate each instant of contact. When he buried himself in her body, she felt complete. When he drew back, sweet friction across her clit tempered the loss—along with the knowledge that in a moment she'd be full once more.

She wrapped her legs around his waist, trying to pull him deeper. He plunged into her, again and again, smooth and regular as a well-oiled machine. His face, hovering above hers, showed every nuance of feeling. He hid nothing from her. Lust, gratitude, joy, it was all there for her to read. His full attention focused on her. She understood, suddenly, that she was equally transparent. He knew her. He saw her hunger, understood her unconventional ways and did not judge her.

Little by little he picked up the pace. The climb toward release was so gradual that her climax took her by surprise, stealing her breath, welling up from her core and spilling over. When the pulse of pleasure finally died away, she opened her eyes to his smile.

"*Ti rak*," he said. "Would you be willing to turn over?"

Caroline rolled onto her stomach. "Like this?"

"On your hands and knees," he urged, grasping her hips to pull her into the desired position. With her naked bum in the air, Caroline felt deliciously lewd. He reached around to pinch her nipples. The tiny pain woke echoes of her climax.

"Sweet, you're the answer to my every dream," Pete murmured. Then he rammed his cock into her so hard she thought he'd split her open.

"Oh…!"

"Too much?" He paused, his bulk stretching her to the limit.

"No, no! I love it," Caroline cried. She was not lying. "Argh!"

He drove into her again, forcing the breath from her lungs. Sharper pleasure bloomed in her depths. "Oh! Oh! Oh…!"

In their new position, he could penetrate to the very root of her. He jerked behind her, grinding his pelvis against her buttocks, his rhythm wild and irregular. Gone was the grace, the control, he'd exhibited before. He fucked her like a savage, like an animal. Caroline adored it.

She still felt connected to him, despite his frenzied lust. She sensed the growing tension in his body. She was aware of every detail. When the hot cylinder of flesh drilling into her swelled, burst, and flooded her, she rejoiced. Focused on her partner, she did not expect the whirlwind climax that swept her away.

Some time later, she regained her senses. Pete lay beside her, apparently asleep. His pale, oval face was the picture of peace. The corners of his mouth turned up in a half smile. She smiled herself, recalling their shared passion.

All at once, she remembered her mission. A pang of guilt shot through her. She hated to bring up the topic of the automaton. What if Pete thought that she didn't care? She couldn't bear to have him believe that her motives were merely political, that she'd tried to buy his cooperation with her body. For one thing, it wasn't true. Right now, Caroline didn't give a damn about the war. All she wanted was more time in Pete's company.

"What are you thinking about, *ti rak*?" Pete put his arm

around her shoulder and drew her close. "You look so serious. Do you regret...giving yourself to me?"

"Oh, no!" Caroline raised her chin to catch the kiss Pete bestowed. "Not at all. It was wonderful."

"You'd consider doing it again?" He circled a nipple with his forefinger, making her squirm.

"Do you doubt it?" She stroked his penis, which stirred at her touch. "No, I'm just concerned about my father, and the war. It's not going well. If the French were to gain control of all the viridium on the moon..."

"Viridium?" Pete laughed. "That's just so much green cheese! Who needs viridium?"

"You're jesting, right?" Caroline's voice was sharper than she intended. "I would think that a brilliant inventor like you would realize the importance..."

"I've discovered a new energy source, something better than viridium." Pete tangled his fingers in her soaked pubic hair, pulling lightly. Caroline moaned. "A sort of bio-fuel. It doesn't emit toxic vapors the way viridium does. It doesn't need to be mined. We can grow a more or less unlimited supply—anyone can, not just wealthy countries like France and Great Britain."

"Truly? You've tested it?" Caroline wasn't sure how much of her excitement was intellectual and how much was sexual.

"What do you think powers my dancing girl? And my videography device? Of course they use tiny amounts, but I'm quite confident that my capsicum-based fuel could power airships in sufficient quantity."

"Oh...capsicum? Ah—what's that?" Caroline rocked back and forth on the fingers that impaled her.

"Chili peppers. Siam grows the hottest in the world, you know." Pete grinned. "I've discovered how to turn that heat into usable energy."

"Oh...oh, god...Pete... You can stop the war. You can save the world... When are you going to announce this?" Under Pete's expert ministrations, Caroline was quickly losing the capability of coherent thought.

"Soon," said Pete, as he found that special spot and launched her into ecstasy once more. "Rocket fuel is all very well, but right now, I want to get the video device and capture the way you look when you climax. I believe that's the real wave of the future."

Trembling with residual pleasure, blushing at the naughty implications, Caroline couldn't help but agree.

LOST SOULS

Andrea Dale

B enedict crashed his way into my workshop, not bothering to knock, as usual.

I'd become attuned to the sound of his key in the front door upstairs, though, so my hands remained steady as I soldered a terribly thin, delicate piece of copper wire to a switch plate. Only then did I turn.

He looked impeccable as always, square jawed and strikingly handsome with his dark hair curling neatly at the edges of his collar, his waistcoat straight and his cravat perfectly tied.

I, on the other hand, had on a dirty leather apron over my simple white blouse and everyday skirt, my bun was no doubt askew and my hands were rough and calloused from my work.

I was utterly besotted with him, with his thick-lashed blue eyes and his crooked rakish grin and his simmering energy, but if he were aware of that fact, he kept it well to himself. I preferred to think he wasn't, to spare myself the humiliation.

He was determined to wed an heiress to up his standing in

the world, as only a third son could be. I was determined to make as much money from our venture as possible, because the time would come when our partnership would end and I'd be on my own.

I didn't want to think about that right now, so I firmly pushed those thoughts aside.

I removed my magnifying spectacles and set them down, carefully away from the soldering iron.

"How is your latest incarnation of the table mechanism coming along?" he asked. He saved pleasantries for those he tried to impress.

"It's nice to see you, too, and it's nearly there," I said. "Why?"

He rubbed his hands together. "We have a commission," he said. "In the Lake District. A holiday in the country—won't that be lovely?"

The prospect of a week away from my workshop failed to thrill me, but the prospect of a lucrative appointment went a long way towards piquing my interest.

Thanks to Benedict's connections, my mechanical skills and the current rage of spiritualism, we had a most excellent scheme afoot. I posed as a medium, rigging the table and indeed the entire parlor with gadgets Benedict and I could control. Knocking, table shaking, a cold mist—and now, if my calculations were correct (and they usually were), an actual appearance of an apparition. Benedict apprised me ahead of time of the details I should know about the client and the dearly departed loved one they wished to contact—he was usually in their circle, after all—and we made a tidy sum.

And on the side, Benedict usually managed to pocket a few trinkets and baubles we could fence on the London market.

I didn't really approve of the latter; that was common

thievery. Our deception, on the other hand…well, if Benedict's friends with too much money and not enough sense were gullible enough to believe I was a Gypsy, then they deserved to be swindled.

I mean, me, a Gypsy? My father was Indian, to be sure, but my mother was Scottish through and through, and just because there was a dusky hue to my skin, it didn't make me a Roma.

It didn't make me a delicate English rose, either, just the disinherited granddaughter of a laird, without any prospects other than the ones I make for myself.

Benedict took my face in his long-fingered hands, and a delicious thrill ran through me.

"You are a wonder," he said, kissing my forehead, and I closed my eyes and allowed myself to imagine him kissing my lips, my breasts and that sweet spot between my thighs.

And then I thought about another item I'd fashioned, one shaped like a man that hummed and buzzed, and how I'd put it to good use tonight, thinking of him.

The train journey to the Lake District passed without incident; Benedict slumbered and I wiled away the time alternately reading a scientific journal, sketching plans for a more efficient telegraph and fantasizing about hiking up my skirts and settling myself on Benedict's lap after freeing his member and…

I jolted awake and cursed reality.

The house was large and rambling, right on the stony shores of a dark lake, the kind you could imagine harbored a kelpie in its depths (if you believed in that sort of thing). My mind wandered to thoughts of a contrivance that would allow you to travel underwater and quest for such creatures.

Something to ponder.

Everyone else was off on a ramble through the hills (and, no doubt, down to the local pub), the housekeeper informed us, which was fine because it gave us uninterrupted time to set up the equipment.

As we did, Benedict provided more details about our client.

"You remember Jessamine, yes?" he asked as he held the green brocade curtains aside for me so I could attach the bits to make them sway just a bit, as if in a strong breeze.

I did remember her, a fair girl with pearls woven into her masses of red-gold curls—an artist and model, as many of his other friends were. Not the society ones, but the bohemian ones.

"Well, Thomas, our host, took a shine to her and married her right up, even though he's nearly forty! But she died of consumption less than two years later."

I glanced over at him then, hearing a change in his voice. His face showed no emotion—which in itself was unusual.

I'd wondered what had happened to Jessamine, it was true. "Not a match I'd expected for her."

"Oh, it wasn't for money," Benedict said. He took one of the sensory devices and reached up to tuck it behind the picture rail. As he did, he brushed against me, and despite layers of clothes, I felt the heat of him, sizzling to my core.

Thank goodness I'd tucked my special device amidst the other clockwork in my luggage....

"It was a love match for both of them," Benedict went on. "They were besotted with each other. It's said"—and here his voice dropped conspiratorially, giving me another shiver because that's how I imagined he'd sound in my bed—"they had quite a passionate connection as well."

My fingers fumbled on the connections that would allow me to make the parlor table judder when I pressed a remote hidden in my shoe.

"I see," I said, and had to clear my throat. "Is that something I should be bringing up during the séance, then?"

Now it was Benedict's turn to pause. "If you think you can do it convincingly," he said finally.

My breasts swelled beneath the confines of my corset, tender and tantalizing. I ached for him.

But at the same time, I hid a smile. Could I be convincing? There were things Benedict didn't know about me, and I suspected he would be the most shocked of them all to find out.

Thomas was a handsome man, and I could understand why Jessamine had been attracted to him. His eyes were shadowed and there were lines of sadness around his mouth, and I felt a pang of conscience.

Usually our clients wanted the salacious aspects of a séance—wanted to believe there were spirits and we could contact them and here were the delightful shocks of doing so. Or they wanted to know where Aunt Henrietta had hidden her diamond brooch or ancient Chinese vase or other expensive item.

Rarely was it ever about true loss, deep emotion.

Even if I couldn't contact Thomas's wife from beyond the grave, I could at least try to give him some peace.

The rest of the assembled group were bohemian friends of Benedict, half-stoned on absinthe and who knew what else, their fingers stained with paint and ink. Some had attended a séance or two before.

"May I present the amazing Philippa," Benedict said to the assembled group. "In her native land she was called Vadoma, which means *the knowing one*," and here he paused to let that information settle, "but to ease her acceptance into society, she has chosen a proper English name."

I mentally rolled my eyes at the ridiculous spiel I had heard

many times before. We'd decided early on to use my real name
so that I didn't forget to answer to something else.

We didn't have the required twelve in attendance, but since
this was at a remote location rather than a London townhome, I
had said we could waive that detail. "You will all have to ensure
your focus is especially strong to make up for our reduced
number," I said.

Benedict never participated in the actual séance. His job was
to remotely operate his own controls as well as to discreetly step
in if an effect wasn't working properly. He claimed he was an
impartial observer—that if I was found to be a fraud, it was his
reputation that would be harmed.

I told them to clear their thoughts and be of like mind, and
then we joined hands, Thomas at my left and a foreign lad
named François on my right (although I suspected he was about
as French as I was Romani).

I had remotes in each of my shoes and one between my knees.
Benedict had one as well, since the fashion of the day allowed
him to slouch indolently against the marble mantelpiece with
one hand casually in his pocket. His heavy-lidded blue eyes
missed nothing.

I wished, as I so often did, that he was raking his gaze appre-
ciatively over my naked form as I reached for his hard, quivering
prick...

No. I had to focus my attention here, now.

"We seek an audience with the spirit world," I intoned,
pressing down with my big toe. The curtains shivered. At the
same time, Benedict eased the flue closed, causing the flames to
lessen. The room would become slightly cooler, and the vision
of the curtains' movement would make people believe they felt
a breath of chill air.

"Come, grace us with your presence. In particular, we wish

to make contact with Jessamine Blackstone, beloved wife of Thomas, who passed too early. Jessamine, your husband mourns your loss and wishes to know you are in a better place."

I eased my legs together, triggering the remote between my knees. The ceramic vase we'd placed in the center of the table—one of Thomas's own, with a rose for Jessamine—began to gently seep steam, thanks to the device I'd set inside.

A woman gasped.

Squeezing my thighs made me more aware of the heaviness I felt there, of the wetness that dampened my split drawers.

The things I was about to say wouldn't help matters any.

"I sense a presence," I said. "I believe it is indeed Jessamine."

"Are you sure?" It was Thomas who asked, his voice breaking with emotion.

"She has a message for you," I said. "She says she misses you dearly, especially the nights when you would crouch between her legs and worship her most intimate places."

Pretty much everyone gasped at that, and out of the corner of my eye I saw Benedict stand up straight. I didn't dare look at him.

Thomas laughed once, half sobbing, but with a relieved happiness as well. His hand clenched mine. "Oh, that sounds like my Jessamine! I miss you, my darling, desperately so."

"She says there are erotic joys in the afterlife, too," I went on, choosing my words carefully. "Tonight, she says, you should pleasure yourself, and she will know, and share in your delight."

I would have been more direct and bawdy had I known the group better, but I didn't want to shock anyone too much—or embarrass Thomas.

And I also wanted him to find peace.

"Every time you find your release, she says, she will be with you—even when you find another woman to share your bed. She wishes you to have that paradise again."

"I could never—" Thomas said.

I coughed, Benedict's cue. The round table we sat around jumped once, then shook. One of the women across from me—Livia, I recalled—squeaked and pushed back her chair, but the people on either side of her kept a tight hold on her hands so she couldn't break the circle and flee.

"She says yes, when it is time, this is what she wishes for you, more than anything," I said. "She desires your happiness, Thomas. I feel it, I truly do."

The table stopped shuddering. Everyone, even the men, breathed out heavily, a whoosh of released air.

"I just...I just miss her so much." Thomas's voice broke.

"There may be a way to see her again," I said carefully.

His head shot up. "Really?"

"I'll make no guarantees," I said. "It's a new device I've developed. If my calculations are correct, the energy raised will allow a spirit—your lost wife—to manifest for a few moments. You won't be able to touch her, though," I warned. I paused. "Would you like me to try?"

Without hesitation, Thomas breathed "Yes."

And so Benedict wheeled my new invention into the room and dramatically flung off the sheet that covered it.

It was a thing of beauty, if I say so myself: brass and burnished wood and gears and levers, and two intricate coils between which strands of stunning blue electricity would arc like lovers reaching across time itself.

The image that would appear (and I had practiced on the thing, so I was reasonably confident it would) wouldn't be a spirit at all, but a projection. For a moment I felt guilty, but then I decided it was what Thomas truly wanted—he *needed* to believe.

I let Benedict handle this one, because the controls were more complex and the rules of a proper séance said that you mustn't release each other's hands until the ceremony had finished.

Behind me, the machine hummed and sang, and then crackled as the energy whipped between the coils.

When everyone's eyes widened—and Thomas's glistened with tears—I dared not turn and look behind me. Instead, I looked at Benedict.

He wasn't staring at the apparition. His eyes were on me, and his expression was curious, one I'd never seen before.

It made the breath catch in my suddenly tight throat.

When he caught my gaze, however, he looked away, as if I'd come upon him, red-handed, looking at something salacious.

"I'm sorry," I said, "but her force is weakening. She cannot stay."

I expected Thomas to argue, or bargain, or question. Instead, he said in a small, choked voice, "Be well, my love."

It was Benedict's cue to cause the apparition to fade, then turn off the contraption. Masked by the noise of chairs sliding back and everyone rising and stretching, he eased open the chimney flue again. The flames shot greedily upward toward the fresh air.

"The spirits have left us," I said.

I took my leave of them, claiming exhaustion (and indeed, the stress of the evening had been great). Thomas followed me out into the hall, took my hands in his, and thanked me profusely. Embarrassed, I escaped as gently as I could.

But not before sneaking a decanter of sherry to take with me.

* * *

As I loosened my corset, wishing it were Benedict tugging free the ties, I found myself envying Thomas and Jessamine. I'd taken a lover when I first went to university, and another soon after, but since entering the business partnership with Benedict, I'd had no one.

Which was silly. I had to stop pining for him and get on with my life.

But the séance had made me a bit maudlin and the sherry I sipped while I removed my layers and slipped into my night-clothes made me decide to indulge in my fantasies one last time.

I lay back on the pillows, my fingers plucking at the budded peaks of my breasts beneath my white nightdress. The pressure of the corset always made them sensitive. I cupped the heaviness of my breasts, stroking the tips with my thumbs, wishing it were Benedict's slender fingers performing the task.

I imagined him leaning over me, murmuring in that low voice about how they pressed, reddened, against the cotton. I licked my thumbs and repeated the motions while in my mind's eye Benedict was bending to suckle the buds through the fabric, his mouth warm and then the air cooler when he pulled away.

I pushed my nightdress up and reached for the device I'd set near to hand on the nightstand.

The space between my thighs felt thick, needy, and the scent of my own arousal drifted to my nostrils, spicy-sweet. My hips shifted restlessly on the bed, as if of their own accord, as I fumbled with the brass dial, trying to get the infernal thing to—

The knock at my door startled me so badly I nearly shrieked. I muffled it down to a squeak and managed to call out in a mostly normal voice, "Who is it?"

"It's me, of course." Benedict, sounding brisk to the edge of impatience, as usual.

My heart leapt for a different reason, my desire- and fantasy-fogged brain allowing me to believe that he was there to see *me*, finally.

I scrambled off the bed, staring at the device in my hand. I couldn't just set it back on the bedside table! There was no other easy hiding place, so I shoved it under my pillow and grabbed my robe, belting it around my waist just before I pulled the door open.

Benedict shoved his way in and closed the door behind him, then turned. Whatever he was going to say died on his lips, and for a moment he simply stared at me.

Benedict had seen me in my nightclothes before, due to the nature of our late-night excursions, but perhaps it was that my hair was unbound and loose around my shoulders. Or was I flushed? It took everything in my power not to raise a hand to feel if my cheeks were hot.

Then he shook his head and said, "Everyone's getting drunk downstairs. I slipped away saying I had to relieve myself, so they might eventually notice I'm gone. We have a little time. There's a room behind the library—I'm sure Thomas has something interesting in there—you did remember to bring your lock-picker?"

Ah. Oh. I'd once watched the landing and deflation of a hot air balloon, and now I understood how it felt.

I folded my arms across my chest, suddenly feeling exposed without my corset. "Really, Benedict? You'd pilfer from the man after seeing his grief this evening?"

He had the good grace to look abashed, I'll give him that. "I just want to *see*," he said, sounding like a little boy eager to peek on Christmas morning. "We won't touch anything today. Just so I know for next time."

I sighed. The fact was, we were in this together, and I'd never had much strength to deny him. I slid my feet into slippers and found the pouch that contained my lock-picker. If we were caught out, as we had been once before, our story was that I was sleepwalking and Benedict was seeing me back to my room. People already thought I was curious and odd, given that I channeled spirits and all.

Early on I'd devised a little automaton that could thwart any lock, but this one was so simple, I could've done it myself. The hidden room was more a deterrent to prying eyes than a vault to prevent valuables from being stolen.

In other words, we were greeted with a room full of salacious writings and artwork: photographs of women wearing stockings and shoes and pearls and little else; photographs of women with men in the act of love; paintings, etchings, sketches.

There were small statues from the Orient, which at first glance looked like two lovers in a chaste embrace, but when you turned them over, you saw in clear detail that beneath their robes, they were copulating.

I saw books—titles I recognized and, I confess, some of which I had read—describing all manner of perverse things.

Although all these things were considered ungentlemanly and, indeed, outwardly shunned by society, they were available to people of mature age and respected morals...which meant the wealthy.

"Good lord," Benedict said. "Philippa, avert your eyes. This obviously isn't what we're looking for—"

"Don't be ridiculous," I snapped. The moment I'd seen the room, I had felt a fresh flood of desire, and it made me unaccountably tetchy. "I'm not innocent about these things."

Benedict stared at me. "But...a lady..."

I snorted. "When have I ever been a lady? My parents felt a woman should be educated in the ways of pleasure. And I'm no innocent, Benedict. My bed has been shared."

He shook his head, a stunned expression in his dark eyes. "I had no idea."

"Well, now you do." I wanted to leave—or I wanted to stay and have him leave.

Now he gazed around the room, arms crossed over his chest. Although I didn't know why, I waited. Finally, inexplicably, he said, "You did the right thing, telling Thomas it was time to move on. Three years is too long."

"Two years," I corrected automatically. What was he on about?

And then it all made sense: his expressions, his demeanor, his willingness tonight to walk away from easy money.

The dull, delicious ache between my thighs was joined by a curious churning sensation in my stomach.

"Too long," he repeated, as if he hadn't heard me. His eyes were on my lips. "I believe," he said slowly, "that I have been a right fool."

"Benedict?" I whispered, not daring to hope.

"Pippa," he said. "I've long respected you—though I fear I've never said as much—but I thought after I'd lost in love that I would never find another love match. That I should be practical and strive only for a relationship of convenience...yes, one of money."

"Benedict."

He took my hands. Was it the first time he'd done so? I believe it was, and I thrilled to the simple touch.

"I think now that I've loved you longer than I can imagine," he said. "I just didn't believe—"

If romantic stories, and even the books in this room, were to be believed, it was appropriate that he should initiate a kiss.

I have never put much stock in *appropriate.*

He held my hands. It was a simple enough matter to yank him toward me so he was within range for me to press my lips against his.

I half feared he'd pull away. But to his credit, after a moment's surprise, he responded in kind—better, even, in that he released my hands and cupped my face in his in order to draw me in closer.

I allowed myself to be drawn under by the kiss, which reignited the fires in my breasts and loins, better than I could have ever imagined. His touch, his tongue—oh, sweet mercy, the way his tongue stroked against mine! I only hoped he was skilled in the ways of performing that motion elsewhere.

If he wasn't, I could assuredly teach him.

Also unlike the penny dreadfuls, this was no gentle coming together, with no sweet music swelling. This was unleashed passion, desperate groping, and the only sound was the blood in my ears and perhaps Chinese fireworks.

The swelling, I suspected, was in Benedict's trousers.

We broke apart, chests heaving, gasping for air, and as much as I wanted him to take me right there, amidst the explicit depictions of lovemaking, I said "No. This is a shrine to his lost love. It wouldn't be right."

"I agree," Benedict said, surprising me once again.

Thank the heavens for my automaton, because my hands shook too hard for me to have locked the room up again on my own. Then we were racing upstairs, uncaring of who might spy us.

Once back in my room, he made short work of the laces of my robe, then stood back to admire me, shaking his head, before taking my face in his and kissing me again with a ferocity that left me shaking. With trembling hands I plucked at his clothing—he was still fully dressed so it took longer to strip him bare than it did me.

Finally we were on the high, soft bed; lips to lips, flesh to flesh. Benedict's hands roamed my body, stroking, petting, sensitizing. He followed with kisses and, when he discovered I enjoyed them, gentle nips.

He worshipped my breasts, suckling and pinching, murmuring his awe and delight over them as I squirmed and moaned.

My need for him was ferocious, but I also wanted to explore his body as he had mine. We rolled as one, and as I straddled him to press my lips to his chest, he restlessly drew his hands up beneath his head beneath the pillow.

"Hallo, what's this?" He drew out my personal pleasuring device.

At any other time I might have been mortified. But his reaction emboldened me: understanding dawned on his face as he sussed what the man-shaped object was for, and an enormous smile lit his face as he looked at me. His member surged against my thigh. "Pippa, you little minx! Did you invent this thing?"

"I did," I said, plucking it from his hand. I showed him how it operated, with dials to select the intensity at which it hummed.

He reached for it, but I held it away. As randy as he'd made me, it was still my turn to play. I slid farther down on the bed. His cock was red, oozing clear fluid. I rubbed my thumb along the head of him, making him groan, and then tasted the sticky sweetness.

Although my device was shaped like him—made for pleasuring a woman—the vibrating surface proved to be highly pleasing when I ran it over his prick and balls.

Even as I thrilled to see how it excited him, I couldn't help but ponder how I might fashion a similar device designed specifically for men. So I was startled when Benedict encircled my wrist with his long fingers and drew me down beside him.

"Ordinarily I love the way you're always working out the

next bit of engineering," he said, "but right now my goal is to make you stop thinking about everything. Everything except me, and how you feel when I do this—"

He crouched between my legs and ran his fingers along my most intimate folds, slipping in my wetness. I tried to cry out his name, but it caught in my throat.

"—and this—"

Now his tongue stroked and swirled on my pearl—he needed no instruction, to be sure—and the noise I made was incoherent. Thought indeed fled as my need reached a dizzying height.

"—and especially *this*."

He slid his fingers inside me, coaxing and thrusting, and continued his sweet assault on my pearl, and I shrieked and writhed as sweet ecstasy consumed me.

At which point, he pulled me atop him and encouraged me to sink down on his stiff prick, which sent me over the edge yet again. Gripping my hips, he shouted my name as he joined me.

There would be time later to speak of past loves, healing hearts and future dreams. Right now, all souls were at peace.

GOLDEN MOMENT

Lynn Townsend

Eliza St. Vincent tapped her toe impatiently. She never had been particularly good at waiting. There were times when this unfashionable habit served her well. She never hesitated to go after anything she wanted, and that ambition had been much to her advantage in the world beyond London. Strange archaeological digs held no terrors for her, nor was she the type to mind getting dirty or climbing into cobwebbed catacombs.

In London, however, that world of soft feminine hands that poured tea instead of wielding a shovel; where flabby female backsides idly sat in parlors instead of straddling a horse racing across gritty deserts; where painted lips spoke only of the weather and the latest fashions instead of reading ancient texts or puzzling over mathematical equations; in that paper and lace world, her impatience was no asset. Already she had gained several telling glances. She raised her eyes to look at the street and immediately those good, gentle people, who had, really, nothing better to do, quickly went about their business, pretending with their icy dignity that they had not been staring at the woman standing on the doorstep of one of the city's most eccentric inventors. Eliza was certain that, once they were out of her sight, there would be much gossiping behind elegantly gloved hands.

Eliza had been waiting, with as much grace as she could manage, on Justin Clayworth's front porch for almost an hour—without knocking, without going in, and only occasionally looking down at the timepiece fitted on a gold chain around her waist. To be honest, she was astonished that no one had yet inquired as to her business. Unmarried ladies did not, as a matter of habit, visit a bachelor's home without proper escort and invitation; if they did so at all, they did so with the utmost discretion and concern for their reputations.

To pass the time, Eliza removed the letter from Doctor Clayworth from her pocket. It was well creased, smudged with dirt, spotted with tears, and showed all evidence of having been read nearly to tatters. She had long ago memorized the contents, but reading the words her beloved mentor wrote to her—his last, parting wishes—it was almost as if she could hear his voice again. The style was completely his own, and he wrote exactly as he spoke.

There are men who, when adversity or failure strikes in their lives, handle it with aplomb. They become more focused, learning from their mistakes, handling the matter with graciousness, dignity. They persist until they overcome, or they direct their intellect and energy to other matters where they have more success. Above all, they behave with honor and discretion, demonstrating to the world that they are gentlemanly.

My son is not such a man.

Eliza smiled again over these words. From any other, the love behind such a criticism might not have been obvious, but

Doctor Clayworth treasured the unusual, the unique, and above all, the spirit of creation, the lust for knowledge, and the drive to succeed that imbued each of his associates and students and could not have failed from reaching his only child.

Eliza tilted the parasol to shade her hand and opened up the auspiciometer. Sunlight—and it was an oddly bright, sunny day, quite unusual for London's spring—interfered with the device's function. From a distance, the device looked like nothing so much as a slightly oversized man's watch. It was only by looking at the face that any would see it was more, much more. Several sweeping hands passed over the surface. One indicated the direction, another counted down toward the Golden Moment: the moment when luck and action combined to bring about the best possible results. She could only have wished it was more accurate as to the timing. The immediacy of this Golden Moment had wavered back and forth for the last two hours.

Most people were fortunate if they'd struck more than a half-dozen of the perfect moments. The opportunity passed them by before they even realized what path their lives might have taken if they'd just said a word, met the glance or made the decision. With the auspiciometer, Eliza had only missed a scant handful. She'd placed the right bets, met the right patrons, stumbled across the find of a century more than once, and invested in the right businesses.

With a little luck, she thought, smiling to herself, everything was possible.

The auspiciometer's hands ticked up to matching another Golden Moment.

Eliza rapped on the door.

Mere seconds later, a sudden, violent explosion rocked the house. Eliza squeaked in surprise and staggered backward, forgetting the narrow incline of steps behind her. She was teetering on the edge when her arm was firmly grasped by the man opening the door. She blinked and looked up at her savior.

Justin Clayworth was not at all what she expected. His father, the doctor, was an excitable genius, a scrawny, aging man with the barest remains of his hair clinging to his scalp and enormously bushy eyebrows that seemed determined to make up the lack. The son, on the other hand, was tall and broad shouldered. His hair, which stuck all up in the front as if he was constantly running a hand through it while thinking, was thick and a rich golden brown, the exact shade of honey being dripped from a spoon. He had moss-green eyes and a smudge of ash along one narrow cheek.

"And you are?"

"Eliza St. Vincent?" She introduced herself hesitantly. "Professor Clayworth?" Surely this handsome, very masculine man couldn't be the scientist she had intended to meet.

"Well, which one is it? Because I assure you, if you don't know who you are, I'm quite unable to assist you. Although I'm fairly certain that *I'm* Professor Clayworth. So perhaps you are Eliza St. Vincent?" He took her hand in his, and even through the thin leather of her gloves, she could feel the heat of his skin, warming her in places she hadn't even known she was cold. "In which case, you are about two hours late. Your letters gave me reason to expect you somewhat *before* I blew up my lab."

"And here I thought I was right on time," Eliza responded pertly.

Justin bowed her into the house, eyes lingering on her as she passed. Eliza wondered what he must see when he gazed at her. Women's fashions were meant to contain and constrain everything about her, from the narrow skirts that hampered her vigorous stride to the constricting corsets that inhibited her breathing. Her long legs pulled taut against the material of her tight skirt, giving evidence to the fact that she spent more time in the field wearing trousers than mincing along in ballrooms. Her curly, unfashionably red hair was swept up and pinned relentlessly in place and still copper coils had pulled free and bounced against her throat. A sprinkling of cinnamon freckles adorned her nose, cheeks and the tops of her shoulders. She was a horror in the sight of every well-mannered woman in London. And yet, when she met his gaze, just before he set about opening the door to the laboratory, he seemed anything but offended.

Describing the lab as an unmitigated disaster was an insult to actual disasters everywhere. The mess was contained to one small corner of a vast laboratory and was constrained to a black smudge against one wall and a pile of ashes that were scattered across the floor. "It doesn't look like much," Justin shrugged, "but I assure you, your knock probably saved my life. If I had been standing there, there wouldn't be much of me left to have a conversation."

"See?" Eliza jiggled the auspiciometer at the end of its chain. "I'm quite timely."

"As usual," Justin nodded. "My father mentioned you had a knack for being in the right place at the right time."

"The auspiciometer was a gift from my father. He invented it. I could use it to help you with—what were you doing before it exploded?" Eliza was intensely curious. "I've never had an experiment fail—"

"Quite so dramatically?" Justin interrupted. He scrubbed one hand across his chin, leaving a charcoal smear.

"At all."

"Never?"

Eliza nodded absently. "Is it terribly depressing for you?" Of course she'd never failed, not with the auspiciometer directing her decisions.

"Why should it be? Even a spectacular failure is an opportunity to learn. Some of the greatest inventions in history were accidental."

"And what have you learned from this?" Eliza swept a hand derisively over the dust heap.

"Nothing, yet. That's the beauty of it. I get to reconstruct my experiment, and my notes, and discover exactly what occurred. And thanks to you, I'm alive to do it."

"Well, let us get to it, then," she said. Eliza pulled out the auspiciometer and was stopped suddenly by a warm hand on her wrist.

"Why not try it the ordinary way?" Justin shrugged. "I'm not in a hurry."

"Why would you want to do that? Do you like failure?" Eliza was astounded. Who would deliberately throw away an opportunity to get something exactly perfect?

"Did you have something better to do?" Justin smiled at her, his intense eyes melting her resistance. Truth be told, she didn't have anything particular planned. And there was something appealing about spending time with him.

"Your father said you didn't deal with failure well," Eliza hesitated. "He asked me to bring some letters to you, and his journals. It was his dying request." She reached into her satchel to fetch them out.

"My father," Justin said, gently entwining his fingers with hers, "had not been in London to know much of me, one way or another, for several years. Whatever he had to say to me has waited this long. It can continue to wait. His letters to me described you as being the foremost mathematical mind on the planet. Humor me for a short while. Then I'll read his remaining letters and you can go back to your adventures, duty done."

"I agree." By every measure of polite society, she should refuse. And yet, it was difficult to refuse him anything when he held her fingers so intimately, when his gaze was so compelling.

"Excellent." Justin handed her the broom. "You can start by sweeping the floor."

Several hours of work later, Eliza had to admit there was something satisfying in a job done completely on intellect and muscle. The cleaning had been somewhat onerous, but the mathematical equations she then delved into had been so problematical and tricky that she would have welcomed the chance to wash the walls, instead. Her brain ached from a constant degree of concentration that she had not maintained in years. She sank gratefully into the soft cushions of the sofa, tilting her head back against the crushed velvet. Her gown was stained, and probably torn, but she felt as satisfied as those hot days in Cairo, overseeing the dig. The only difference was a strange, tingling sensation that took her a while to identify: anticipation. She had no idea what to expect next, nor when. Even in Cairo, as exciting as that had been, she knew success was within her grasp.

"So, how does it work?" Justin asked. "Your clockwork?"

"The auspiciometer," Eliza said, pulling it out from her pocket. "You hold it, clearing your mind of everything, save for your goal. The auspiciometer then detects the concentration of karmic particles coalescing around your every decision and will indicate the best time and place to act. It is part timing, part luck. This dial here indicates the intensity of karmic particles, this monitors the exact time left until the action is to be performed. The compass indicates direction if there is a person you must meet, or an object you require. With some practice, you can learn to read it easily, and know exactly when to make your move. And you have to keep it out of the sunlight."

"You're kidding," Justin snorted. "It's nocturnal?"

"Not precisely. But sunlight has an adverse effect on its accuracy. My father thought…well, he theorized that because people tend to *feel better* in sunlight, they give off a false kismetic reading. I'm not certain. I haven't tested it thoroughly. But the evidence my father accumulated suggested that the readings were inaccurate in sunlight."

"May I?" Justin held out one work-roughed hand. Eliza hesitated and then nodded, sliding the device into his palm.

Justin closed his eyes for just a moment and then gazed down at the whirling dials. "Excellent."

Eliza shifted closer to him; the auspiciometer was upside down to her view. Already, the karmic indicator was green, the dial rapidly ticking down. Less than a minute remained.

"What were you looking for?" There was nothing in this room that seemed incredible or lucky to her. Justin returned the auspiciometer to her pocket, leaning across her to do so. She shivered as his fingers brushed against her hip.

"I was wondering"—he was closer to her than was proper, his breath soft on her face—"when would be the perfect moment to kiss you."

His mouth covered hers with warm supplication, tongue flickering gently over her bottom lip, tickling. Feeling the warmth of his breath against her mouth, she wrapped her arms around his neck, melding her body against his with sudden desire. With a strangled groan in the back of his throat, Justin pulled her closer, nearly crushing her in his fervor. "Ah, Eliza." His voice was rough, shaking. He kissed her again, his mouth warm on hers, his tongue parting her lips. She surrendered to his kisses, one hand sliding restlessly over his back, feeling the heat of his skin through his shirt and vest. He covered her face with kisses, tasting each cinnamon freckle.

Justin caressed her back, her hip, the side of her ribs, the swell of her breast. Even through the fabric of her gown, her nipple puckered in response and she arched under his hand. He lowered his head to kiss her neck, tracing a line of warmth across her collarbone.

With a soft grunt of effort, he lifted Eliza into his arms, cradling her against his chest, continuing to nuzzle at her neck as he carried her up the stairs and down the hall to his bedchamber. Lightly, Justin set her back onto her feet, and then turned her gently, his fingers reaching for the row of buttons down her back. She was breathless with wanting, one hand pressed to her flaming cheeks, the other holding up her dress as it loosened. Working the laces out of her stays, he kissed her again. Each time the lace slipped another notch, her stays loosening, she shivered.

"Are you cold?" Justin asked, a sly grin playing over his full lips.

"Not with you here to warm me," she responded, daring. Eliza had taken lovers before, of course—an adjunct professor during her years at university, and the lead of her archeological team—but those experiences had been nearly wordless grappling in darkened tents and abandoned classrooms, not brazen trysts in the middle of the afternoon with a man she knew mainly from letters. It was difficult, and then impossible, to be shocked with herself, however, when he nibbled lightly at the ends of her fingers, driving all thought and reason from her mind. Justin deposited a kiss in the palm of her hand and then tugged her chemise down.

Eliza stepped forward, her bare breasts pressing against his vest, as she untied his cravat, adding to the pile of clothing on the floor. Justin trembled under her touch, his skin rippling with gooseflesh. He lightly slid warm fingers down her shoulder and enclosed her breasts, his palms teasing her erect nipples. She panted, leaning her head back, her fingers twining in his hair. He groaned, licking at her neck, leaving a trail of searing kisses. Slowly, teasing, he continued tracing a line of kisses down her neck and across her chest, his mouth seeking her breast. Finding it, he suckled, his tongue a wet lash of sensation. She mewled with need, her back arching, straining up on tiptoes to pull him closer.

Justin kicked off his boots and shucked the rest of his clothing, eager to have her pressed against his skin, feeling the lush warmth of her body. He backed up, sitting on the bed and pulling her to him. His hands encircled her waist and his mouth sought her breasts, licking one nipple, then the other. She folded her arms around his neck, holding his head to her as she abandoned herself under his questing tongue. He left her breasts, his tongue moving down her stomach, his hands sliding down her hips and across her thighs to tease her stockings down.

"Eliza," he breathed her name. "So beautiful."

She laughed softly. "I'm not beautiful, Justin."

He stood then, turning her in his arms toward the full-length dressing mirror. "I beg to differ. Look." He met her gaze in their reflection, his eyes glowing with desire. He stood behind her, holding her gaze, as his hands slid down her body, his fingers bringing her nipples erect again. Eliza gasped and blushed, embarrassed and fascinated by the view in the mirror. She watched Justin's reflection intently as he kissed her neck again, one hand tormenting her breast, the other sliding lower, over her stomach, along her hip. She quivered, unable to look away.

"Look how luscious you are, so soft, the curves perfect,"

Justin whispered in her ear, his hands tracing every inch of her. Softly, nipping at her earlobe, sending delicious shivers down her spine, he spoke, "You've always sought after golden moments...shall I give you one, my dear?"

She quivered under his skilled mouth. "Oh, yes. I want you."

He nipped her neck, teeth grazing her skin. Her knees buckled as he ran his tongue down her spine, and then nuzzled at the small of her back, his fingers encircling her waist, teasing her hips, brushing across her belly. She couldn't look away from her reflection, watching the heat of passion paint a rosy pink blush across her cheeks and chest, her nipples hard, her breasts proud and upright. Eliza felt both vulnerable and powerful to see a handsome, strong man on his knees, his mouth worshipping her body. His tongue traced lower, licking just over one hip, and she nearly fell, clutching at his shoulders to remain upright.

"My turn." She regained her balance, and then hauled him up, muscles lean and strong from months of archeological digs coming to her aid as she nudged him onto the bed. He spread out, gazing up at her as she bent her head, kissing down his chest and stomach until her tongue reached his navel. Justin groaned and twisted under her tongue, his hands plunging into the wealth of her copper hair, spilling her curls free of pins. With sudden, urgent need, he pulled her over him, his tongue thrusting into her mouth. One hand trailed up her thigh to reach for her sex. She moaned into his mouth, trembling, and parted her legs to his hand. He pulled back from the kiss, watching her face, his fingers exploring gently, tracing over each feminine fold.

His fingers moved over her clit, circling slowly, his breathing ragged as she shivered over him. Her body writhed with need. She moaned, whispering encouragement and direction. "Y-yes, oh, Justin. Yes, there...oh!" Her fingernails bit into his shoulders, her cries rose until she was nearly breathless. She arched backward, stiff and shaking, each muscle straining, her skin glowing and overheated. She shattered into a million joyous shards. Eliza collapsed against his chest, her racing heart thunderous in her ears. For a long, golden moment, she lay there, secure in his arms. Perfect.

When the world slowed its mad spinning, she shifted, rolling to one side. Eliza leaned on one elbow, gazing down at his body. She traced long, slow lines of exploration down his chest, marveling at the sprinkling of crinkly hair, the silken feel of his skin, the firm ridges of muscle underneath. She locked him with her gaze, watching the play and twist of emotion and sensation along his strong features. The quiver of his stomach as her fingers grazed lightly over his flesh urged her onward. She paused, heightening the anticipation, before allowing her hand to drift lower, wrapping her fingers firmly over his shaft. Justin groaned, his hips lifting off the bed to meet her.

Eliza stroked him, running her curled hand along the length of his cock, a breathless smile painting her lips as he gasped and strained in harmony with her movements. She lowered her mouth to him, peering up at him from under her lashes, waiting. He captured a handful of her hair, twisting it against her neck, not quite pushing where he wanted her, but urging her on, nonetheless. She relented, letting the warmth of her mouth enclose him.

"God," Justin murmured, voice rough. "That's so good."

"Justin," she cried, urging him on top of her, "love me."

He shuddered at her words, kneeling between her legs, then covered her body with his own, his cock seeking her warm depths, his arms curling under her back, pulling her up to meet him. Hesitantly, as if afraid of hurting her, he thrust into her with slow strokes, clenching his jaw as he struggled for control. She was slick, her muscles still trembling from her climax, the voluptuous shudder that gripped him urging him forward and faster. He took her mouth with his, tongue echoing each rapid thrust, pulling the breath out of her and taking it into himself.

Eliza gasped, her hips rising to meet his strokes, hands clenching his shoulders. Gleaming sweat broke out along his skin as he panted for breath, thrusting into her, losing his sense of self in the wonder of it. Eliza stirred under him, her legs wrapping around his hips, pulling him into her. Justin surrendered to his need, gave one final, hard stroke, holding her tightly, until he released, nearly screaming her name.

With an effort, Justin rolled off her. Instantly, Eliza cuddled up to his side, twining one hand with his, draping his arm over her hip. "A golden moment," she said.

"I concur."

Eliza reached over the side of the bed for her shift and suddenly gasped.

"What?" Justin lifted her hair and planted a kiss between her shoulder blades.

"The auspiciometer." She was breathless with shock. "It fell. When we were... It's broken."

"I'm so sorry, Eliza," Justin said. "I know how much it meant to you. Maybe we can repair it?"

Eliza rolled over onto her side to face him. She curled into the heat of his body. "It is all right. Maybe I don't need it anymore."

LIBERATED

Mary Borsellino

As often happens, there was already a customer waiting
outside the wide double doors of the workshop when we
arrived in the morning. It was a man, maybe twenty-five or
thirty years old, with sandy hair and leather flying gloves that
had clearly seen considerable wear in their life.

He pulled off one of the leather gloves before holding out
the revealed hand to shake one of my own. I left my own, much
daintier glove—plum lambskin, that day, with pewter buttons
at the wrists—on as I took his hand and shook. Most people
whom I greet in this way assume I must be haughty, a grubby
little cog-spinner (a particularly ridiculous insult often aimed at
mechanics and metal-crafters) with delusions of grandeur. But
truly, I'm nothing of the sort. I love my work, I love my workshop, and I love the girls who study there. It's just that I don't
like my skin to touch the skin of others.

I was originally designed to work for a seamstress, and so
my fingertips have fine, hair-trigger senses. One brush of a

hand against mine and I know that person's body fat ratio, her general health levels, standard posture, likely activity levels. All this information can make a gown hang just that tiny bit more perfectly on its owner, move a vital fraction more elegantly. Applied correctly, the physics of fabric and flesh can look like talent and art.

Although the fact that I am an automaton is not exactly a secret, I don't advertise it either. Keeping my hands concealed, as well as protecting me from a deluge of information about each person I meet, hides the small screws and joins visible at the hinge of each knuckle. The tinted eyeglasses I wear serve the same purpose for the matte nickel color of my irises. My long dark hair hides the keyhole at the nape of my neck.

"Sam Tucker," the young man introduced himself as we shook hands.

"Kara Knight," I replied, gesturing that he should follow the girls and me inside the workshop. "What's the problem, Mr. Tucker?"

"Call me Sam, please. My word, this place is beautiful!"

I smiled at his exclamation. I'm always pleased when people properly appreciate the workshop. Most of the roof is made of panes of clean, clear glass, to let in the largest amount of light possible. I don't want any of the girls to destroy their eyesight by working in dim conditions.

The glass roof also gives anyone inside the workshop an excellent view of the traffic overhead, sky-ships and balloons and dirigibles made of oilskin sailcloth in emerald greens and ruby reds and sapphire blues: a jewel-box among the clouds.

The workbenches are lined up in three long rows, topped with high-quality green felt, against which even the smallest cogs and springs are clearly visible.

The girls began setting up for the day, laying out their tools and magnifying monocles. They each had their own project to work on—broken pocket watches, warped telescopes, things like that. Stephanie, who had the most experience of the current bunch, was trying to repair one of the small clockwork woodpeckers that had recently become the rage for sending and receiving telegraph messages. A household cat had pounced on the poor thing, ruining most of its little brass feathers. Repairing the damage without upsetting the internal mechanism would be difficult work, but the reputation of the Knight Workshop is well deserved.

"Marvelous," Sam said in wonderment, still gazing at his surroundings. Stephanie caught my eye and smirked suggestively. I ignored her. If the girls had their way, every sky-sailor and trader of diamond chips and aristocrat with a broken clockwork bird who came through the workshop's doors would end up between my legs. I need sexual congress often, but not *that* often. The modifications that the Liberationists made after stealing me from the tailor's didn't turn me into a nymphomaniac.

"What can we help you with?" I asked.

"Oh!" Sam fumbled with the pouch on his hip, remembering the reason for his visit. "My compass. The casing's been damaged and I can't get a sky-worthy certificate for trading in this province without it. The inspector said you were the best person to see."

"Hmm," I answered noncommittally, certain that whatever grudging recommendation the inspector had given me, the word *person* had not been uttered. Automatons, even apparently self-owned ones (I don't pass around the fact that I am stolen goods) are not well liked by most public servants. We need very little regulating; it makes them redundant. Nobody appreciates the new technology that renders him obsolete.

I took the broken compass in my gloved hands, turning it

over a few times to gauge a full sense of the damage. There was nothing too severe required; the apparent ruination was largely cosmetic and the job was well within the skills of any of the girls.

"Annabella, can you come look at this?" I asked, beckoning her to come join us. Annabella was one of the newest additions to the workshop team, a skinny little strawberry blonde with the hard, scrappy look they almost always have to them when they first arrive.

I handed her the compass, taking a moment to appreciate the difference between her hand and mine. Annabella's was the hand of a quintessential cog-spinner: shiny pink burns on the fingertips from the touch of hot brass and soldering pens, ragged nails, delicate movement. Girls with her skin tone usually have a dusting of cinnamon freckles all up the blue milk of their forearms, but not Annabella. My guess was that she'd spent her early days down in the deep tunnels of a diamond mine somewhere, far removed from the sun and its kisses.

"Think you can handle that?" I asked her, moving my gloved hand away from her living, hard-knocked one.

She made a soft scoffing sound in the back of her throat. "Easy. But I was supposed to go to the market today. I need a new click for the mainspring ratchet assembly on the Pearson-Smythe automatic alarm."

"I'll go get that. You do this," I offered.

"But you should stay here and get to know our new customer better," Stephanie put in with another of her wicked smirks. Impertinent child. If she wasn't astonishingly talented at reassembling difficult mechanisms I'd have found her suitable employment outside the workshop long ago.

"I'll come along," Sam spoke up. "Make sure you get a good price on parts. I'm something of a dab hand at bargaining at this point—can't stay aloft without a fortune unless you learn to haggle."

"All right," I agreed with a nod. A couple of girls in the back row laughed quietly together. I ignored them.

"You—and please don't be offended by this, because I don't mean it to be so—you're an automaton, aren't you?"

"Why would I be offended?" I asked, genuinely puzzled. "Something is true or it's untrue; your suspicions can make no difference either way."

"Now I'm sure of it," Sam said, looking amused at my brusque response. "And you could be offended because of how clearly you want to pass as human. I doubt I'd have been able to spot the difference except that when I was a boy one of my tutors was an automaton. I notice the tells."

"Was he Liberated?"

"Pardon?"

"Your tutor. Was he still standard issue, or had the Liberators got to him?"

"Oh." Sam shook his head. "No. The town where I grew up was quite isolated. I doubt any of the Liberation Front has ever set foot there. My tutor's settings were standard through and through. He was excellent at his work. Taught me geography. Made me want to go out and see the world."

We walked together without speaking for a few minutes, through the throngs of market shoppers, the uneven beat of hundreds of footsteps in arrhythmic counterpoint to one another.

"Sometimes I miss it terribly," I admitted. "Being standard-settings. Things are so straightforward and simple. You're built for a task, and you do that task. No doubts, no difficult decisions. Just...clarity."

I sighed. "And then the Liberators looted the couturiers

where I worked, took us, and...well, they said they gave us souls. Maybe that's true. I never had a sense of myself as...as a person, I suppose. Not the way I did after I was Liberated."

"What exactly do they change?"

"I'm matter-of-fact about most things, but there are some experiences, some secrets of myself, that I do prefer to keep private."

"Oh, I didn't mean to—"

"Let me finish, please. There are many aspects of what happened that I won't talk about, but I can tell you some of it. I was given the ability to make plans for myself and to decide preferences beyond what was most logical for my station." I smoothed my hands over my skirt, not looking at Sam as I spoke. "Perhaps the most obvious change to an outside observer would be the fact that the Liberator's changes leave automatons with a rather powerful sex drive. They say it's to give us more agency in our choice of lovers, but really that's only true for those who were created for pleasure and companion tasks in the first place. For models like me it's just one more new complication to worry about."

Sam didn't have a chance to respond immediately, because as I finished speaking we arrived at the section of the market that offered a huge variety of scavenged and spare parts for mechanisms such as the ones the girls at the workshop were busied with.

He proved to be an extremely adept negotiator, bargaining prices with such an aptitude that I felt it only fair to compliment him on it as we began our walk back to the workshop, the new purchases stowed in a calico bag at my hip.

"With a silver tongue like that, you should have been a politician," I teased. Sam laughed.

"I don't like the current state of the world nearly well enough to want to go into politics. I can effect far more damage and change as a quasi-legal smuggler, I think."

I had to smile at that. "You're probably right, yes."

"To return to earlier topics for a moment," Sam said. "I'm going to be in the city for quite some time—if I can get approved for a permit, that is, though I have every confidence in your girls—and it would suit me very well to have a regular lover I respected and liked talking to. Do you think that would—?"

"It would suit me very well, too," I told him, with another smile. He was pleasant, with just a hint of the rogue about him, and I found his conversation pleasing. Of course he'd be welcome in my bed. I may be a robot, but I'm not stupid.

He grinned. "Good. Very good. How long until your, um, increased sex drive next needs—"

"Tonight, if you aren't busy. Meet me at the workshop after nightfall," I told him. I wasn't in dire need yet, and wouldn't be for another day or so, but there was no logical reason to delay coupling with a willing partner.

"It's a date." Sam grinned. Our conversation paused for several more minutes after that, as we pushed and darted our way through the shove of the crowd. The city is sometimes so full of life it scarcely seems able to contain it.

"How did you come to have the workshop?" Sam asked when we were next able to converse easily, the crowds thinning as we reached the outskirts of the market. "Why was that the ambition that took root after your Liberation?"

"Have you heard the saying about the watch in the desert?"

"I think so," Sam told me with a nod. "That's the one about how, if you found a watch in the desert, you'd assume there's a watchmaker. That it didn't just appear there. That you can say the same about the world, that there must have been someone who created it; it didn't just appear."

"Yes, that's it," I confirmed. "The religious aspect of the metaphor is irrelevant to me, because I know without question where I come from and who created me. But I'm sure you can see why the idea of the world as a watch would appeal to a cog-spinner. Especially as the world is in need of so much repair—who better to mend it?"

"The girls," Sam said, clearly understanding. "I wondered, but now it makes sense. Teaching them a trade is your way of fixing the watch."

I nodded, and that was going to be all the answer I offered. He seemed to comprehend the situation well enough for it to be sufficient. But after a few seconds I began to speak anyway. There are few subjects I feel strong passions about, but my girls are foremost among my cares.

"In the earlier days, when I first started, they came from coal mines. Now, thanks to new technology, it's diamond mines. The health of the children who work down in the earth doesn't decline as rapidly mining diamonds as it did mining coal, but their lives are still short and unhappy ones.

"Poorhouses and orphanages are constantly overcrowded and underfunded. It's not that the overseers and matrons are particularly cruel, it's simply that selling some of their wards to the mining companies is a solution to both of their chronic problems at once.

"The lives and futures of children are just a commodity to be bought and traded, as if the meat of their flesh was no more precious than the cogs and springs of an un-Liberated automaton.

"I couldn't stand it, seeing a world so broken. A watch in need of so much repair. So now I run the workshop, to teach them the ways of fixing broken things."

It was close to nine in the evening when Sam returned to the workshop, and the sky above the translucent ceiling was deep blue, starlit and scattered with late traffic.

"Makes you grateful for diamond-based steam engines, doesn't it?" I remarked. "No coal smog to obscure the heavens."

"It's miraculous," Sam said, and I thought he was talking about the view until he kept speaking. "How on earth does it survive hailstorms, or snow?"

"It's far stronger than it looks," I told him.

He was looking at me when he answered, in a thoughtful voice, "Yes, I believe you're right."

I resisted the urge to roll my eyes at his awkward attempt at sentiment. He meant well, after all. "You seem to appreciate innovative engineering feats."

"I'm here, aren't I?" Sam answered with a cocky smile.

"Just so long as you don't try to couple with my roof when we're done," I countered, deadpan. "I don't mind if you gaze at it adoringly while I ride you, though."

Sam blinked in surprise. "Here?"

I shrugged. "It's the only place that's mine."

"But where do you go at night?"

I shrugged. "Sometimes I stay here. There's always more work to do. Sometimes I walk—this city is so full of beauty and strangeness and wild dreams. Iridescent little aluminum dragonflies that hum songs from the radio so passersby hear them and want to buy them on phonograph. Flashbulb fireworks in the sky to help the sailors see the tower-tops without sun.

"Sometimes I go to see the seamstress. The one who...my owner, before. She had good insurance. After the robbery she was able to buy new automatons. I visit her, and I visit them. I help with the sewing sometimes. They remind me of...a long time ago."

"Visiting Mama and the little sisters back home. You're more like us humans than even the Liberators think."

"Help me with this?" I began undoing the buttons down the front of my dress, tiny pearl nubs beginning at the high collar of my dark bodice and leading down to the nipped waist. The long skirt was embroidered with constellations of the zodiac in bronze and cherry-red thread against the crisp black of the linen. It was a modern, frivolous design. I'd commissioned it at the girls' insistence—if my workshop crew had their way, I'd be a fashion plate who spent every waking moment looking for her next lover.

They'd all be delighted, if they knew Sam's deft, tanned fingers were working each of the silly buttons on the silly dress open one by one. Too bad for the girls that I've never been the kind to gossip.

All that kept Sam's skin and mine from touching as he carefully opened the front of my dress was the whisper-thin muslin of my slip and the long dusty-rose velvet ribbon around my neck, with my key threaded on it.

"No corset?" His tone was appreciative. Only a few buttons left until he'd be finished. I started work on the worn-in olive tweed waistcoat Sam wore, the fabric imbued with the scents of the wind.

"The way I'm built, I don't need one," I told him. He smirked.

"That's true enough," he replied, resting one of his hands against the flat of my belly, over the remaining pearl buttons. Frustrated, I pushed his hands away and finished the job myself.

"You don't need to flirt like that," I told him in a curt voice. "You don't need to joke."

"May I?" he asked, gesturing to the key lying against my

skin just above the swell of my breasts. After a moment's delib-
eration, I nodded. I wouldn't need winding for several more
weeks, at least, but I'm not ignorant about the erotic aspects of
the act.

I slipped the slim ribbon up over my head and dropped it into
his palm, lifting my hair away from the back of my neck and
turning so he could easily see the keyhole. He slotted the key in
place carefully and gave it three slow, careful turns.

I could feel the coils and springs in my belly tighten with
each movement of the key, the tension making me more aware
of every part of myself, of every sensor and artificial nerve in my
skin. I pulled off my lambskin gloves, turning to face Sam and
taking his face in my hands as I leaned in to kiss him.

Knowledge of his body filled my mind—the aroused racing
of his heart, the flush of want under his skin. The slight sunburn
on the back of his neck, the good quality of his knee-high leather
boots and the good posture they gave him.

"Your compass is in working order again, by the way," I told
him when we broke apart from the kiss.

"When I have my permits, I'll show you and your girls the
skies," he promised me.

As we removed the rest of our clothes Sam found and
worshipped each small part of me, the neatly stitched seams
hidden at the joints of my thighs, the exposed hinges of my
fingers. I tasted each of his scars, the little marks and survived
wounds of a well-lived young human life.

I could taste his pulse, the electricity of his existence, on my
tongue again when I sucked at his neck. My thighs were straddling his lap, and I knew that I'd be able to follow his heartbeat
while I sucked his cock later, when he'd caught his breath and
was ready for another round. Automatons don't have the same
problems with exhaustion as humans do.

For now I needed him inside of me more than anything. I
ached with it, every refashioned ratchet wheel and suspension
spring inside me wound so tight I felt as if I'd shatter if I went
another moment without being touched.

I arched in closer, urging his face down toward my breast.
The flat, thin edge of his teeth grazed the nipple, barely a touch,
and I felt so open and ready for him that I think I moaned aloud.
He shifted his hips, lifting me up and then down, and then we
were locked together, parts in perfect mechanism.

I was going to fly apart, like an incomplete clockwork
knocked off the edge of a table, sending gleaming pieces in all
directions. I couldn't cope with something so good, not unless
I had something solid to grasp and ride through it. I rocked up,
experimentally, letting him almost slip free as I clenched and
held him in. The push back down made his length stroke the
upper wall inside me, and I felt a wave of sensation shudder
through me.

"You feel like silk," Sam whispered, his breath hitching in
damp gasps against my throat. I brought myself up again and
then down.

"You feel like life," I answered, as we moved together under
the jewel colors of the sky beyond the workshop. A smuggler and
a clockwork girl, in a glass room built to fix a broken world.

MAKE YOUR OWN MIRACLES

Nikki Magennis

Violet takes a steamcab to the dirty end of town. She suspects the driver is taking her on a tortuous, inventive route, but she doesn't mind as much as she should. She likes these dark, narrow streets, the pockets of decrepit and dangerous buildings populated by fiends and outlaws. In addition, she herself is up to much the same kind of misadventure. This whole trip, in fact, is part of a tortuous, inventive route to increase her personal gain. Her very personal gain.

She raps on the ceiling.

"Here will do," she calls, over the hissing of the pistons. The wheels grind to a halt against the cobbles. She's on the corner of Trongate, could almost be visiting a hat shop, looking for a suitable frippery to wear to her next afternoon garden party—if she weren't dressed in rather unusually somber clothing and if she were not draped with a dark, voluminous cloak of thick velvet.

"Tenner," said the driver, turning to spit into the gutter.

"That's outrageous," she said.

"My usual rate for such a precious cargo. Sir Catter wouldn't like to think his daughter were bein' carried round by some fly-by-night villain, now would he? 'Specially in these parts of town. A woman needs lookin' after round here, don't she?"

He leered at her with a mouth full of broken teeth.

Violet passed him the note, her fingertips feeling greasy although she didn't touch his grubby mittens.

Once the cab had spluttered along the street and was lost among the afternoon traffic, Violet slid down the alley between the baker's and the music hall. The smell of hot bread made her mouth water, as it always did. Or perhaps it was anticipation of another sort.

The door was heavy, but Violet had learned the trick. With one sharp kick of her leather boot, it sprang in the hinges and gave enough that she could tug it open. She lifted the cape to cover her face. The smells down here were of the night soil variety—thick enough to make you retch.

The lift was a fearsome cage—rusted so thick that it appeared made out of dried mud. Flakes of old paint came away on her glove when she closed the doors behind her. She swallowed her fear. Four floors, she said to herself, pulling the lever to raise the lift upward. The higher she rose, the more lightheaded she felt. Her palms were damp, and she rubbed them against the soft fur of the cape.

He knew she was coming. Of course he knew. Would he be waiting for her? Automatically, she reached to her face and buried her hand in the wild black frizz of her hair. She drew her shoulders back and watched the floors roll slowly past outside the crisscross lift bars. Something clicked as she rose higher: A cog complaining of the strain. Cables stretched to their breaking point.

Violet closed her eyes.

The lift drew to a halt. She got out and arranged her skirts before ringing the bell.

"Hello," he said, pulling open the studio door.

"You were expecting me."

"Of course." He stood watching her. His—she didn't know exactly what to call it—his machine hand, the prosthesis, gripped the door frame.

"It is cold out here, sir."

"Come in, come in." At once, he flung open the door and turned to the dim chaos of his studio. Violet followed with as much dignity as she could muster, even though her knees felt horribly like they were not connected to the rest of her. As if she were cobbled together, like Gustav, a broken person who'd been remade and was now something other than entirely human.

"Care for a drink?" he threw the question over his shoulder.

"Yes." She needed something sharp.

Gustav lived like a wild animal. His workshop was also his home. Violet had been shocked, on her first visit, to see a heap of blankets and animal skins tumbled in a corner, disheveled and obviously recently slept in. Women like her were not raised to visit the sleeping quarters of males. The sight of Gustav's bedsheets was enough to make her cheeks burn. But Gustav laughed when she blushed, and now, after two subsequent trips out here to Hell's western outpost, she had taught herself to ignore the depraved manner in which the man chose to live.

"I've made some modifications," Gustav said as he reappeared and handed her a shot glass. "I think you'll be pleased."

"I know what I want."

"And you are all the more admirable for it." Gustav said. He raised his glass to her. When he threw back his drink, Violet's treacherous gaze hooked onto his throat, the jut of his Adam's apple. Her eyes slid inexorably down, toward the second, more shadowy jut, the slight protuberance at his crotch. It wasn't the first time she'd been secretly fascinated by the workings of a man's body. Only Gustav's seemed, somehow, so much more... vivid than those of other men.

"Unusual," Gustav said. Violet's eyes jerked up to meet his. She swallowed, and tasted the fumes of whatever potcheen he'd just served her.

"What is?" she asked.

"A woman who has the gall to demand what she wants. But then, you are born to a family that is used to doing whatever it pleases."

"I'd be grateful if you would not mention my family," Violet said. "While I'm here, I'm your employer, not anybody's daughter. Is that clear?"

Gustav stared at her.

"You've been amply rewarded for your compliance," Violet continued. "It would be wise not to forget that."

"And it would be wise of you to learn not to try to buy someone's loyalty," Gustav said, his voice low.

"I beg your pardon?" Violet clutched her glass. Somehow, it was empty. Her mouth was burning dry.

Gustav didn't answer. Instead, he set his glass down with a click and moved toward the bench in the center of his studio. The table was strewn with detritus, piled high with spanners and cutters and hammers and glass tubes, all discarded over scribbled plans and intricate drawings. Gustav abandoned projects when his attention was drawn to something else, the newest, ever more exciting inventions that his brilliant, daring mind came up with. Here and there among the rubble, there were tiny marvels. Violet noticed a clockwork bird, its feathers minutely engraved and its one wing perfectly constructed. She knew without asking that it was a working model; that it would fly if it were ever finished.

Because Gustav was a genius. It was how she'd heard of him, all those stories the servants retold in backrooms when they thought none of the gentry were listening. The outraged claims of her married lady friends, the hotly whispered secrets. What she'd overheard. How he'd fought as a young man, in the Clockwork Revolution, and nearly been killed. And how he'd rebuilt himself. A firebrand beholden to no one, living on the edge of society, building his awful toys for the idle rich.

"I think you'll find it still fulfills your demands," Gustav said. His voice was flat now, like any servant's. His face turned away, Gustav pulled the tarpaulin from the lurking shape in the center of the room.

The chair was a beautiful piece of craftsmanship. Anyone would be taken with the skill of the carving, the finely wrought detail on the headrest, the way the wooden spindles virtually melted into the metal. The seams were invisible. It looked almost as though it were something alive. Violet's mouth watered as she ran her eyes over the curves of it. In particular, she lingered on the special additions, the hidden components that made the "fainting chair" such a very special piece of art.

"Rather wonderful, isn't it?" Gustav said. His hand stroked the undulating backrest, as if it were the shoulder of a friend. "I've grown quite attached." With this, he held out his hand— not the flesh and blood hand, but the other one, his wire and steel simulacrum.

Violet hesitated for a fraction of a second. Long enough for a shadow to pass over his eyes.

"It won't hurt you, you know," he said, voice full of spite. "I do control it."

He reached for her hand and took it, his grip surprisingly warm, as though the metal fingertips had a pulse, and the smooth battered leather of the palm were still living skin. Still, Violet flinched.

"I'm sorry," she said, shrinking back.

"You? Sorry?" Gustav raised an eyebrow. "A Catter, apologizing to a miscreant and a rebel?"

"Don't," she said, tugging at her hand. But his grip was firm. Of course it was. It wasn't entirely human. He probably couldn't read her signals, Violet thought, trying to stop herself from panicking. Couldn't feel her try to shake him loose. There was no feeling in his arm, after all—

"Oh, come now," Gustav said, almost whispering. He smiled at her. "We have to try out your machine, after all."

"No!"

"No? It was a very expensive commission, my lady. Surely you wish to satisfy yourself that it works?"

"I trust you," she said, hopelessly. His hand held her wrist casually, belying the strength of his hold on her.

"Do you?" he said. "Do you really?"

Their eyes met. His were a deep, dangerous brown, like metal that had rusted, been tempered by time and experience. Violet was no weak, simpering girl. But she wasn't used to meeting people as forthright as Gustav. The men in her circle were powerful, buoyed up by riches and inherited empires. They put on a good show of force and bravado.

Gustav was different. He had virtually nothing, yet he carried himself with the ease of a prince. With his rough, ragged shirt-sleeves and his wild, shoulder-length hair he managed to wear the look of a man beautiful enough not to need polished boots and well-cut clothes. It was the way he moved, Violet supposed. The way he held himself. The way he...touched her.

She was silent as he pulled her toward the center of the room.

"You want me to sit?" she asked, obedience coming far more naturally than usual.

It was, in fact, a fainting couch, he'd told her. Not for sitting in. She would lie prone over it. Facedown. The thought did indeed make her feel faint.

"First things first."

His voice was as low and quiet as an idling engine. "Remove your clothes, please."

Violet felt the blood drain from her face.

"How dare you."

Gustav merely inclined his head. "Violet." It was the first time he'd used her name. "Remember the measurements I asked for?"

Though she thought it impossible, she blushed harder. Her face must be as beetroot red as a scolded child's. She gave a hard nod. How could she forget? Sharing her intimate details with a stranger—it had been the most intrusive and excruciatingly embarrassing conversation. Well, almost. Asking for the machine itself should surely have been her worst nightmare. That first visit, that exhilarating leap into the unknown. She had felt herself on the edge of life, that day, ready to scream or swallow the muzzle of a gasgun. Desperate enough to do something insanely reckless. *You're hysterical,* she'd told herself, and then she'd gone out to find a steamcab.

She had found herself in Gustav's infernal den, and she had met the man with a bravado and daring to match his own. "For my health," she'd said, almost smirking. "As my dear friend Amelia was advised by her own physician."

Of course, she wasn't married. But meeting Gustav, she was certain that this detail would not bother him. Not with a purse full of coins and not with a customer as formidable as the daughter of Lord Catter himself. She'd almost felt dizzy, as she stood in front of Gustav's laughing, bold brown gaze. For once, the idea struck her that she might use her power for her own satisfaction, rather than let it use her.

At the same time, she had felt herself so overtaken by rising sensation that she had barely trusted herself to stay upright. As though her body might swoon with the rushing tides of pulse and breath, as though she might lose control at any moment.

The feeling had returned.

"Measure twice. Cut once," he said. "I cannot check the fit through thirty layers of lace."

"This is necessary?" she said.

"It is, if you wish your commission well made," Gustav said reasonably. "And I did warn you this would be an intimate process."

"Your threats have not been forgotten!"

"I merely reminded you of the need for discretion. A project like this is not without risks, as you know. Sensitive information must be kept under wraps, for protection."

"Whose protection? I think you care not for my honor, sir! If my father knew what you were doing…"

"He'd disown you," Gustav said mildly, refilling his glass and taking a leisurely swallow. "You'd be cut off with nothing. Milady."

Violet trembled. But it was rage, not fear, that spurred her onward.

"You would not emerge unscathed," she said. "Remember that."

"No. But I think of the two of us, you have more to lose." He came close, then, and the smell of whisky on his breath swept over her. "Far more at stake than your inhibitions, don't you think?"

"You're enjoying this," she said, reaching for the button at her throat. "You want to see me broken."

"Not broken," he said. "Merely—undone."

She shrugged.

"I am not afraid of your scorn," she said.

Then there was no sound, only the muffled pop of her buttons and the swish of silk as she pulled her bodice apart. She would not let him see her cowed.

"I have defied men greater than you, sir."

"Yes. But I bet you never let them see your underwear," he said, idly, walking round his machine as if he'd lost interest in Violet's striptease already.

She barked a laugh at him.

"Don't fret, madam." He eyed her gravely. "Remember, I am doing this for your pleasure."

"Pleasure. You make it sound like a mere whim."

"Were not for the whims of the rich, I'd be a pauper."

"It's more than idle fancy!"

"How so?"

"I am not married, sir."

"I had noticed," Gustav said.

"Unmarried ladies are not greatly popular, you know. Even if they have chosen to be so. If I wish to live alone, I must—Oh, what would you understand about it? Having your whole life mapped out already. Having to fight for every scrap of independence."

"Perhaps more than you think."

Gustav was bent over the machine, adjusting a strap. Violet looked at his false fingers, noticed how delicate they were, how skilled the movements. As she watched, a calm came over her, like a draft of cold air after a thunderstorm. She dropped her arms. Her heart fluttered in her breast, like a bird trying to escape a calico cage. Violet removed her dress in silence, only the rustle of fabric disturbing the air in the studio. Outside, there were shouts in the street and the whistle of steamships passing, floating into the Upperspace where they would circle above the smog and bustle of the city.

"Good," Gustav said lightly. "Now, here." He touched her arm more gently than she'd thought he could, with his warm, flesh and blood hand, and motioned for her to lie, facedown. With as much grace as she could muster, Violet kneeled on the padded leather and slid down until her body was nestled against the curves of the chair.

"Part your legs, this way," Gustav murmured, touching her calves very gently. He circled her, making small adjustments to her position, checking that she could reach the levers and handles. Lying prone, with her cheek against the cushion, Violet noticed a curious sensation. Despite her agitation, the chair invited her body to unwind. It supported her, like the body of a lover, she imagined—it was firm, generous, enveloping. Rising to meet her between her legs, with dips and hollows at her breasts, chin and knees, it molded to her shape perfectly.

The leather warmed and softened under her, and she felt herself melt into the chair—had she ever felt this cared for, this mellow? A fleeting word tickled the back of her thoughts. Was this how it felt, she wondered, to be loved?

"Ridiculous," she murmured.

"Beg your pardon?"

"It fits," she replied, "very well."

"Of course," Gustav said. "But we need to test the working of it. Here, let me."

Violet bit her lip. Gustav's hand had fallen on her thigh. He dragged her legs apart, not roughly, but as though she were a doll to be posed and adjusted according to his whim.

"Ready?"

Violet murmured her assent. Gustav bent down low so that his mouth tickled her ear.

"Don't struggle, now. This will be easier if you hold yourself still."

He took her left hand and led it to the polished wooden handle.

"Just very easy, now, pull this back."

Violet did as she was told. Underneath her, cogs ground against each other. A pulley creaked. There was a loud sigh, as steam escaped, and an insistent hum as the power ran from the central steampillar and entered the machine. And she felt pressure rise against her pubis, the chair extend and curl upward, as though a large, stiff tongue were pushing against her, digging between her legs. The chair shook and hummed, as though the tongue were singing to her, a song so unbelievably warm and expansive it terrified her.

She pressed her mouth tightly closed.

"Good. A little more," Gustav said, his voice tight. She felt his hand burrow into her drawers, and let out a gasp.

"Shh," he said, laying his other, mechanical hand on the small of her back. "I'm just checking."

It was enough, she thought, to be lying half undressed in the crepuscular, squalid studio. Enough that she had shared her most shameful and abominable desires with him and found herself trapped in a cage of her own making. That he would now lay his hands on her—

"Stop," she said, suddenly. With no little difficulty, she pulled herself upright. Her bodice was awry and her clothes crumpled. Yet her defilement had not made her a mewling wreck, at least.

A hot coal burned in her breast. This feeling was familiar. Violet was angry.

"Sir," she said. "This has gone far enough. I cannot tolerate you mocking me any longer."

Gustav stood, his face a mask.

"I do not mock," he said.

"I came here," Violet said, standing and pulling at her clothes, trying vainly to cover herself though everything seemed to be slipping. "I came here because I needed something from you."

"And I have made it," Gustav said. "Haven't I fulfilled the brief?"

Violet looked down at the chair, which was still buzzing, gently. Its curves suddenly seemed treacherous, its embrace just another cage that sought to trap her.

"You don't understand," she said. "How could I have thought you ever would?"

To her fury, tears rose up to accompany the words, spilling generously from her eyes. She turned her head away.

Gustav sighed.

"I believed I was providing you with a machine to service your needs, my lady."

"No. More than that." Violet fixed her eyes on the closed doors of the furnace, behind which burned the engines that kept the buildings running.

She had never fully understood the exact workings of the city, the giant burning columns that provided the power harnessed from the steam, the railways that crisscrossed the streets, carrying coal and wood, the curious and complicated machinery that converted that power into useful apparatus— she knew only that when she needed something, it appeared.

Her every wish, dream or fancy, instantly fulfilled—just so

long as it was approved by her mother, father, the gentlemen of the court, and the unwritten and unbendable rules of etiquette that governed her everyday life and it seemed, by some unarguable and inexplicable logic, kept the world running smoothly.

"I needed something to sate my wants," she said, her voice flat and dim. "A machine that would assuage my frustrations—"

She bit her lip. "The inner life of a lady, sir, is not as peaceful as you may imagine."

Gustav laughed.

"I do believe you're admitting it at last."

"Sir?"

He stood and approached, scratching his stubble with his machine-hand. Violet had an inkling that he knew it frightened her. She suspected he enjoyed the shiver that she could not quite suppress.

"That underneath all that fine lace, you have what everyone else has."

Violet narrowed her eyes.

"Could you stop yourself from being coarse for once? Do you even have it in you?"

"I'm not talking about your body's natural appetites." Gustav nodded at her. "That's your own imagining, my lady."

"I'm talking about…" he laid a hand on her chest, where the shelf of her bosom rose and fell faster than it ought to, "…your heart."

His hand was warm. He kept it there. Nestled in the valley of her breasts, she was surprised to find it comforting, rather than threatening. She looked up at him. For once, there was no rusty fire in his eyes, only a deep and quiet warmth.

"I do not need to love," she said.

"Or to be loved? Forgive me, but I do not believe you."

She pulled away, but he tugged her back, replaced his hand.

"It beats," he said, softly. "I can feel it."

"Yes, it beats. Whether I wish it or not."

Violet raised her chin.

"When I lie abed, alone in the darkness, I am at last able to let go of the damned smile I must wear day in and day out, the cursed, cultivated, ladylike mouth that I paint on in the morning and loathe from the moment I wake until the hour I retire. I jam my hand between my legs. I stroke myself. I induce such paroxysms that I could scream."

Gustav did not let his eyes drop.

"And yet it is not enough," he said. "Is it?"

Violet stepped forward. She kissed him hard. Hard enough that his stubble scraped her cheek. At first, her tongue darted into his mouth as fast as a flickering flame. Then, as they sank against each other and his warmth flowed into her body, she let it meander a little, over his lips, to taste the salt there, the fire of the whisky.

He broke away, breathing hard.

"My lady," he said, "Violet."

"Quiet," she said. "I am not paying you to talk."

"I trust you are not paying me to make love to you, either."

Violet held his face in her hands.

"I have spent my life paying people to do what I wish. I have never wanted for anything. Why should I stop now?"

"Because what you want can't be bought."

They stood with their faces inches apart, so that their hot breaths met and swirled together. Violet felt again the grip of his metal hand and this time she wanted him with a violence that almost overwhelmed her.

"What do you want?" she whispered. "What is your price?"

"Everything," he said. "Everything you own."

She searched his eyes.

"You think I'll give up all that, to soothe the lust in my heart?"

"Not lust. The one thing you are really afraid to admit."

"Which is?"

"Love," he said, simply. "To live here, with me. As a free woman."

Violet laughed. "It seems a veritable bargain."

Gustav didn't laugh back. Instead, he held onto her with his machine hand and started, with the other, to loosen her corset. The lacing pulled from the eyes with a little ripping sound.

"Give up your life," he said, "and you will win me."

"My flat?"

"Abandon it." He tugged at the laces around her waist. As they came free, she exhaled noisily.

"Thirty servants. A steamtrap and driver."

"Set them free."

He pulled the shell of her corset away in two halves, as though he were removing the shell from some sea creature. Underneath, her bare skin was marked with lines where her underclothes had bitten into her skin.

"A place at court. Invitations to the very best parties."

Gustav raised an eyebrow. He took hold of her petticoat and ripped it apart, tearing it from her waist to her knees. Violet shrugged, and stepped out of the ruined skirt. She laughed as though she had breathed in for the very first time.

"The proceeds of my trust?"

Gustav paused. "How much?"

"More than I need."

He nodded; traced a line from her chin, down her collarbone, to the gentle curve of her breast, where he circled, as if entranced. Her eyes dropped to the twitching fingers of his metal hand.

"How did you lose it?" she asked.

"I was impatient," he said, lifting his wooden-tipped fingers, as if to surrender. "I wanted to master the world. Be the greatest inventor that ever lived. And I refused to listen to anybody."

"Sounds familiar."

She took the hand and examined it. He held it still, not flexing the spring-loaded joints, not curling the delicate, beaten-tin fingers.

"I built it myself," he said.

"That must have been difficult."

"Yes. But now it works. It is part of me," he said at last. Violet looked up at him, then bent to kiss the worn leather of the machine palm. She drew the hand down, to her drawers, and placed it between her legs, pressing against it through the slit in the cotton.

"It works?" she said.

Gustav nodded. He pulled her toward him, crushing the awkward metal of his hybrid hand between them, making her moan.

"Like any man, my body is weak," he said. "Only I have been blessed with a hand of my own devising." He interspersed each sentence with caresses, raining kisses down on her bare neck and shoulders like molten lava. "With it, I can create miracles."

The blunt tips of his fingers pressed and pushed at her, the polished wood hard, but curiously supple too, so that it felt he was making love to her with a wondrous mix of urgency and tenderness, the sensation circling, rising and dipping to some intricate pattern of his own creation. Violet felt a scream build in her belly, low and urgent, as though her voice were not her own.

With his other hand, Gustav had freed his cock from his trousers and pushed her against the couch, lifting her buttocks so they perched on the curve of the headrest.

His first thrust was almost desperate, rushing her hard and deep so that she cried out involuntarily. At the sound, he lunged again, and bit down hard on his lip.

"Forgive me," he started to say.

"Never," she replied, and pulled him to her. This was what she had been seeking, she realized, as he sank into her, meeting the rock of her hips with the jut of his own. This unbearable proximity, this suffocating closeness; to be filled with him, to swallow him up: this was the prison she would never wish to leave.

He ground against her, and his mechanical fingers drummed a fantastic tattoo around her sex, thrumming there on the most sensitive part, the little screw that held it all together, as she thought of it.

They beat against each other as if locked in a struggle, both reaching, clutching hold, writhing as if climbing the ladder of each other's body. She felt herself rise and grow furiously dizzy, calling out to him as she did so, slamming against him as if she could join their flesh by violence.

As the sensations grew ever more urgent, she dug her fingernails into the flesh of his back. He moaned and bit down on her neck. That moment, she wanted to be marked by him, wanted them to both be changed, irrevocably changed. As she milked his cock and wrung a climax out of his heated, struggling body, his mechanical hand worked at her and she felt herself tumble, a wound-up machine gone wild, spun out of control, overtaken by the exquisite and miraculous machinery of the body itself, fueled by blood and spit and desire, attracted irresistibly to this man by some inexplicable force, both damned and redeemed by this fabulous creation, this wonderful cage, this beautiful trap that she found herself, for once, glad to be contained in.

Their ecstasy split the moment in two, and they collapsed

onto the couch, knocking levers and bruising themselves on protruding parts. Violet lay across her incredible machine, overtaken by waves of laughter as Gustav rose and disentangled himself, reached for the bottle and returned to lie with her in glorious, foolish disarray.

"May we live long and never leave each other," he said, his dark eyes locked on hers as he took a swig from the open bottle.

"And cherish our freedom," she said, taking the bottle from him. "Us penniless outlaws." She spilled whisky and he leaned forward to lick it from her arm, sending a fresh wave of laughter rippling through her.

"May we make our own miracles," she said.

"And recognize them when we find them," he said, bending to kiss the whisky from her lips.

RESCUE MY HEART

Anya Richards

The corridor connecting my private lift to the pleasure balloon *Ecstatica* sways, and Ruiz de Cortez places his hand on mine as though to stop me stumbling. The motion is so familiar no assistance is necessary but I don't pull away. Indifference will mask that; for me, the contact of skin on skin is both pleasure and pain. The landward breeze blowing across the harbor and through the louvered walls ruffles my skirts and hair but does nothing to cool my fevered skin.

Glancing sideways at him, I note the changes time has wrought. When he first entered my parlor the familiar stride and proud carriage made my heart stumble. He looks the same now, albeit more prosperous. His flight jacket gleams with gold buckles, and not many can afford supple roebuck breeches or patterned long boots. However, this close, I see additional lines fanning out from the corner of his eye and bracketing his hawkish nose. At his temple a swath of silver threads through the straight, midnight locks, which are secured at his nape with an emerald-green ribbon.

The captain has aged but, God help me, in ways that make him even more beautiful.

And he has come to finally collect on a promise I now wish I had cut out my tongue rather than make. But how could I know, ten years ago, he would ask of me something that would destroy what was left of my heart?

"I cannot ensure I will be able to achieve what you want," I warn, as we enter the airship proper. "Hardwick may not let her go, nor even allow me to take her from the room. Be that the case, there is nothing I can do."

"Better to purchase her outright than steal her," he replies, slanting me an unfathomable look. "But if you can do neither, I'll be content with the effort."

Had he approached me even three months before there would have been ample opportunity for him to whisk Angelique van Groot away from my city. But then it would have been me, Beatrix Morgan, rather than Griffen Hardwick blocking his way.

That knowledge and this man, both redolent of unfulfilled dreams, make me inexpressibly sad.

Pausing out of earshot of the guards, I give Ruiz my hardest stare, and one last chance to change his mind. "Are you sure this is what you want? After this my debt to you is paid."

Is it love? I want to ask, but the words stick in my throat.

The familiar sparkle is missing from his light brown eyes, and I never before saw him so grim. "Yes, your grace. If I had been there to help her bail her brother out of jail, she wouldn't have fallen into Hardwick's hands."

I turn away, unsure of my ability to completely mask my ragged emotions. "So be it."

The guard opens the door and we step into what will no doubt become my greatest nightmare.

People are scattered around the closed and stuffy room, indulging in myriad sexual acts—some in pairs, others in groups—many employing the mechanical devices still rare in the rest of the colonies. Here in Port Royal, the wickedest city in Christendom, nothing is forbidden and the automated fuckers, suckers, attachments and personal pleasure enhancers are a common sight.

"Her Grace, the Duchess of Palisadoes, and Captain Ruiz de Cortez," intones the major domo, and almost everyone stands, except those immobilized on the larger machines, and one woman who has been caught at the moment of climax. As we walk across the room toward our host I am saluted on all sides by erect cocks and nipples and accompanied by the high-pitched cries of the writhing spender.

Hardwick cannot stand, paralyzed as he is, unable to move anything but one hand and his oversized, balding head. A skull with flesh, sunken eyes and a bony nose, he is the stuff of nightmares and, watching our approach, a small smile tips the purple-hued gash that is his mouth. His lap is lightly covered by a cloth, leaving the rest of the emaciated, vaguely gray form bare. Beneath his feet, as a footstool, Angelique dares not lift her head to acknowledge us, deference to her owner trumping all protocol. Hardwick dips his head toward me, the degree of incline calculated to be within reason and yet still slightly insulting.

"Well met, your grace. Good of you to finally accept one of my invitations." With a flicker of a glance, he acknowledges my companion, "Captain."

The rasping voice sets my teeth on edge. He would, of course, recognize Ruiz's name, for everyone knows the story of how he found and took me to England to claim my inheritance. Many hate him for it, either for his luck or for instigating the turning over of one of the world's greatest fortunes to a woman, worse yet a mulatto.

I return Hardwick's meaningless smile with one of my own. "My friend has not been in Jamaica for upward of five years, and I would have him enjoy himself...in whichever way *he* chooses."

Hardwick's eyes narrow, but it is the tightening of Ruiz's arm beneath my hand that makes me realize my mistake. Insulting Hardwick means nothing to me. He, and others like him, will always resent my place in the world. Slavery may have been abolished, made pointless by the advances in mechanization, but it still lingers, insidious and unmistakable. My rise to wealth and power has left a bitter taste in many mouths. It is my duty to turn that bitterness to bile at every turn.

No, it is allowing Ruiz to know I have tracked his movements that is my greater error in judgment.

"Well," Hardwick replies, his gaze moving around the room and then lingering on Angelique's crouched form before returning to my face, "I hope you both will feel free to indulge with us tonight, Duchess. After all, it is only with your kind auspices this party can occur."

With a lift of my eyebrows, I too glance around the room. The participants are still standing, awaiting the signal to recommence their orgy. They all stare, no doubt wondering at my attendance, for although I own the entire floating city I never mingle with those who come to indulge their peccadilloes.

I shrug, and allow Ruiz to lead me toward a chaise lounge. "Parties like this would occur whether Port Royal existed or not," I reply, sitting and fanning out the silk of my skirts, knowing the white velvet upholstery is a perfect foil for my red dress and chocolate skin. "In fact I wonder at your making the journey here, rather than entertaining at home."

Another dig, and Ruiz, in the midst of sitting beside me, sends me a sideways look. Hardwick's mother, a woman of impeccable and unassailable rectitude, would have a conniption should he hold such a gathering in London.

"Ah, but where else can I find such convivial company and delightful weather?"

And where else could he try, in every way he can, to seek my weaknesses and hopefully a way to blunt my power?

If not for my ingrained suspicion, he would have already succeeded. Believing Angelique my friend, I harbored hope she would be the companion and lover I so yearned for. On learning she was his slave and spy I thought my heart shattered. Now, seated beside the only man I ever loved, in the company of the woman I still hunger for, I know I have but sipped at the cup of pain.

As though reading my thoughts Hardwick gestures and, as the entertainers return to their activities, one of his lackeys lifts his feet from Angelique's back. She does not move, but remains on elbows and knees, legs drawn up beneath her, face tilted down, hidden by a swath of golden hair. Although still keeping my gaze on Hardwick, from the corner of my eye I glimpse the pale, enticing skin, the beautiful curves of arse and planes of back. I refuse to look more closely.

"Please, feel free to participate in any way you desire." Hardwick's eyes glitter, fever bright.

It is tempting to walk around, if just to escape the proximity of these three people. Ruiz has settled close enough that his heat and scent enfold me, reminding me although I had thought him part of my past I now must admit he has never been far from my thoughts. I am fighting desire and hurt, for I had dreamed when he came to collect on my debt what he wanted would be *me*, not a lover lost to Hardwick's machinations.

Pain stabs at my chest, forms a cold ball in my belly. I won't survive the night if I cannot master these emotions. Locking them away takes all my will.

"Ruiz expressed an interest in attending," I send Hardwick another meaningless smile, "for he heard no one surrounds himself with more beautiful women than you."

The caw of a crow, his laugh is harsh and disturbing. "And surely you concurred?"

"Of course," I force amusement into my voice, holding his yellow-tinged gaze with ease of long practice in the art of dissembling, "'Tis a well-known fact."

"I am glad you think so. Come, Angelique, sit up. Interesting as I am sure the view of your arse is, I would display you in a better light."

Like an automaton she rises, shuffling on her knees to face him, the ruby-clad collar around her neck flashing like wet blood. On direction she spreads his legs and turns to sit, the back of her head against his thigh, her gleaming hair a waterfall over his sickly flesh. I should not look, but having never seen her naked, I do, allowing myself to follow the contours of throat and peach-tipped breasts, slim torso and flaring hips. Downy hair shades the juncture of her thighs and I long for her to open, reveal her sweet cunt, so I can carry the memory forever.

I look to her eyes, longing for the remembered softness of her gaze, the hint of laughter and lust, even though I know it to have been a lie. She is expressionless, and the breath sticks in my throat—the heat of the enclosed room and stench of sex suddenly overwhelming.

The urge to run makes me turn away, pretend interest in the antics of two women sharing a floor fucker of immense length and girth. They are laughing, one trying to mount the phallus while it is already switched on, while the other holds her friend's labia open, trying to align her properly with the up-thrusting cock. They are probably slaves but I envy their freedom and familiarity, affection and unselfconscious touching.

When last have I enjoyed another's body, freely given, with no thought of what gains could be had from lying with me?

With shrieks of laughter the women achieve penetration, the one on top bouncing about for a few moments before settling deeper onto the juddering phallus, taking half its length. It stretches her almost comically and laughter wells within, until I see her obvious delight. When her friend presses an open-mouthed kiss to the wet flesh between her thighs, making her moan with pleasure, heat floods my belly and, for a moment, I allow myself to dream...

Ruiz stirs beside me, and I glance over to see him also watching the women, a distinct bulge forming at the front of his breeches. Like me, is he imagining us fucking, me on top, with Angelique's tongue dancing from my clitoris to his sac, back and forth, until the combined power of our coming together and her caresses drive us both to dizzying completion?

He turns, and although he is impassive I read concentrated desire in his hooded eyes. The heat shimmering beneath my skin travels inward, shudders through my veins and drips, like the finest wax, down into my cunt. Should any other man stir these feelings in me, I would take him to my quarters and fuck him until he begged for mercy, secure in my ability to walk away thereafter. But Ruiz would be the one to leave, and I don't know if I could bear it.

Yet there is something in his eyes that will not release me—a promise or a dare—and he shifts almost imperceptibly closer. My hands almost itch with the need to touch and I clasp them together on my lap so as not to give in. Hardwick's voice murmurs but, still captured by Ruiz's darkening gaze, slowly giving in to my heightening desire, I ignore it.

"Your grace, master suggests I offer myself to you and Captain de Cortez for your pleasure."

Angelique's whispered words are a dash of iced water, and I look down to where she kneels before me, head bowed.

"Do anything you like, your grace, barring penetration." Hardwick is goading me, and rage rises with each of his words. "That privilege is mine alone."

Without thought I reach out and lift her chin. Emotionless and quiescent, her face reveals nothing, but in her cerulean eyes is a shimmer that can only be tears and, as I watch, her lips quiver in an ephemeral cry of pain before firming once more.

Often, in the lonely stretches of night, I wondered if her slavery was of necessity or choice. Did she thrive on his twisted possession, devoted to a man whose cock cannot rise without mechanical assistance and whose altered flesh is, by design, horrific?

Perhaps it is a falsehood to believe I have found the answer, but now I know what I must do, and the decision leaves me relieved and resolved.

"Perhaps I shall indulge, just a little," I say, and my fingers drift down toward Angelique's breast. It is a delicate game I play, and it must be timed to perfection. "She is a delicious morsel, although..." I slant a brief glance at Ruiz. "...I had my heart set on rather more substantial delights tonight."

Fixated on watching my fingers slip down to her collarbone and rise again, Hardwick hesitates, licks his lips and, in the silence left by his lack of response rises a sudden cacophony of moans and sighs, as if the entire room climaxes at once. A flush stains his sallow cheeks and his hand twitches convulsively.

"No need to deny one pleasure for another, your grace." The rasping voice quivers with excitement. "Here you can safely indulge both."

Agonizing laughter wells in my chest and is suppressed. If only he knew how much I wished I could. But even with the possibility laid out before me I will not chance the exposition of yearning such an encounter would create.

Cupping Angelique's breast, feeling her nipple tighten against my hand, I turn to Ruiz. In his eyes lie too many questions and I avoid them by twining my other arm around his neck, urging him closer, letting my lips soften in mute invitation. There is a moment of resistance, and then he surges forward.

The first commanding touch of his lips, his almost feral growl, causes desire to become a molten army marauding through my blood, twisting in my belly, flooding my cunt. Accepting the hard thrust of his tongue, the soft yielding of Angelique's flesh beneath my hand, I am slave and master, seducer and seduced and, with this dichotomy, complete.

Ruiz deepens the kiss, thrusting his tongue between my lips, demanding my response. I freely, joyously give it as Angelique moves closer, parting my legs so as to nestle between them. Only the silk of my gown separates our bodies, and I feel the brush of her fingers on my calf just as Ruiz slips his hand into my bodice.

I am lost, as though broken from the tether of my life and floating away—a casualty of a hurricane-force wind. Not even the now-vague memory of Hardwick's presence can lessen my pleasure at being surrounded by the touch and scent of the two people I love best. Lust is the physical manifestation, the only one I dare express, but my heart sings to have received this one chance to experience their attentions.

Forcing myself to break away is the hardest action I have ever taken, but if I do not I will forget all in their arms, and my plan will go awry.

Pulling back, I look across at Hardwick. His gloating, lascivious stare causes a chill to trickle down my spine.

"Indulge me, Hardwick. Let me see the mighty cock I have heard so much about."

Ruiz stiffens and a shiver cascades through Angelique as at Hardwick's barked command the cloth is whisked away. Only years of training stop me from recoiling from the sight of the monstrous appendage lying between his stringy thighs.

Red and lived, flaccid it is at least a foot in length, bulging with implanted rings and studded with knobs, some with sharp, squared-off edges. With a movement of his hand a pump springs to life, and the phallus begins to rise, not stopping until it stands, like a hideous caricature of all that is depraved, a full fifteen inches into the air.

Angelique presses closer, the frantic beat of her heart a match for my own.

"*Madre de Dios,*" Ruiz murmurs, horror deepening his usually almost imperceptible accent, and I tighten my fingers on his nape in warning.

"Magnificent," I breathe, hoping Hardwick doesn't notice the underlying revulsion, or the motion of my hand on Angelique's breast. "Let me see it in use." Looking down at Angelique, I order her to him with a gesture of my head. "Go."

"*Geliefde...*"

I do not understand the word, but the plea in Angelique's whisper, in her eyes, is almost my undoing. There is no way to reassure her. All I can do is briefly squeeze the tender flesh still nestled in my fingers and gesture once more. "Go, now."

Ruiz moves, whether to stop her or to pull away from me, I cannot tell. I hold him still and although the pain in Angelique's eyes slices through me, I nudge her urgently with my knee. Finally, just as I am close to losing my composure, she turns and crawls to Hardwick.

From all accounts, there is a ritual Hardwick employs with

each sexual encounter. He feels no sensation below his neck and now depends on degradation and pain to find his twisted form of satisfaction.

Belly writhing in agony, I watch Angelique straddle his lap and reach between them to grasp the dreadful appendage, her fingers unable to meet around its girth. Even from this distance I see her trembling. She offers him her right breast and my heart lurches.

"No," Hardwick says, turning his head, voice thick with lust, "The other one. The one she touched..."

With seeming reluctance Angelique angles her left breast to his mouth. The purplish tongue darts out, circling her nipple before he fixes his teeth on the tip and closes his lips around it.

Angelique cries out, and again Ruiz makes as though to rise.

"Wait," I murmur, "wait."

Angelique lowers herself toward his cock. Still retaining the grip on her nipple, Hardwick pulls, painfully stretching her breast in a bestial tug-of-war. My entire body stiffens in anguished suspense as the tip of the phallus settles between her thighs.

Hardwick gasps, releasing Angelique, as the poison I put on her nipple takes effect. Eyes widening until it appears they will pop from their sockets, his neck arches impossibly back. Foam bubbles to his lips and, with a cry of alarm, Angelique scrambles backward, losing her balance and falling before Ruiz can catch her. Attendants rush forward, screams break out around the room. I swiftly rise and shout for the guards stationed outside the door.

No one stops us when we leave, although Ruiz carries Angelique's still form in his arms. I pause only to remove the collar from her neck and throw it to the floor. Once outside I lift my skirts and run, Ruiz beside me, racing death back to my apartments.

The skin around Angelique's lips is blue, her breathing so shallow fear clamps around my chest. I force the antidote into her mouth, rub her throat until she swallows, Ruiz crouched beside us the entire time. After giving orders to and dismissing my staff, we wait, unable to leave her side until her color normalizes and she takes a full, deep breath. Without conscious thought I reach for Ruiz's hand, and the heat of his strong fingers steadies me.

Her eyelids flutter and Angelique begins to shiver.

"Bring her through to the bedroom." Is that my voice, so tremulous and faint? "A warm bath will help."

Ruiz carries her and lowers her into the tub, uncaring of the soaking he receives. The tenderness on his face as he strokes her cheek is almost my undoing, but I force back the tears and sponge water over her shoulders, trying to avoid looking at the bruises forming on her poor, battered breast.

Finally her eyes open, the confused, unsure gaze tracking from his face to mine.

"*Geliefde,*" she whispers. "What...?"

"I'm sorry," I can hardly get the words out past the choking relief, "I hoped it wouldn't affect you, but could think of no other way."

"Way...?"

"Poison," Ruiz murmurs. "Although how she managed it, I don't know."

I show them my ring, the secret compartment beneath the seal and residue of powder inside. "I hoped it wouldn't enter your body through the skin, but couldn't be sure, so I only put it on one nipple." The memory of her offering Hardwick the other breast flickers through my mind, and I falter, unable to continue.

"And Hardwick?"

"Dead," satisfaction is patent in Ruiz's voice.

"You're free," I add, although a band tightens with sickening force across my chest.

Angelique closes her eyes for a moment and when they reopen they're shimmering.

"Free? To do whatever I desire?"

She looks back and forth between us and both Ruiz and I smile, nodding. Reaching out to us, she uses our hands to rise and gathers us against her warm, wet body.

"Then take me from here to the bed over there, *geliefde*," she says in a voice that fairly rings with joy, "And prove this to me."

Over her head I meet Ruiz's gaze, see in it something that makes my heart leap and the familiar heat uncoil deep inside. And as though in the throes of my most dearly held dream, I hear myself say, "Yes."

Urgency, near desperation grips me, as though in disbelief of reality. Part of me wants to go slowly, savor the sensations, the contrasts between Angelique's softness, Ruiz's strength, but I'm afraid something will interrupt, come between us.

So I won't let them linger over the removal of our clothing, and I frantically touch his muscular chest, her tender belly. And I cannot stop kissing them, one then the other, taking Angelique's lips with open-mouthed fervor, ceding to Ruiz's masterful demands.

An inferno builds inside me, banking higher with each thrust of tongue against tongue, each glorious, aching caress, but one moment blurs into the next until I am blindly rushing toward a goal I long for, and dread.

It is Ruiz who stops me, holding my arms down on the bed above my head, one immovable thigh trapping my writhing form.

"Shh," he croons, "*amada,* there is time."

"No," I cry, bucking against restraint, "No, quickly, before—"

I cannot articulate my fear but he seems to understand, bending to kiss me once more, resisting my frenzy, gentling me with the slow, tender sweep of his tongue. Fury abates and then, only then, do I truly feel. *Everything.*

The heat of his body on one side, Angelique's on the other, the smoothness of his lips and her hands, the crisp hair of his chest and press of her nipples, the hardness of his erection on my hip. The scent of our bodies mingles with the arousal tingeing the air, and above the thudding of my heart I hear the harsh rush of excited breathing.

He lifts his head, stroking my breast, teasing the already tight nipple, and the sensation of that calloused digit echoes through my veins.

"Yes, *geliefde.*" Angelique's lips find my ear, softly tracing the inner curl, and I arch at those simple, irresistible pleasures.

Freeing my wrists, Ruiz kisses the side of my mouth and then down along my neck to my breast. Angelique follows on the opposite side, and I tangle my fingers in their hair, holding them to me. The hot slide of tongues, the nip of teeth, the long, firm draw of mouths are amplified over and over, until I shudder with each gasping breath, already nearing climax.

Fingers pull my thighs wider apart, travel up, caressing the trembling flesh until finally slipping between the lips of my cunt. I cannot curtail my cry of bliss, the way my hips lift to greet the penetration, the swirling on my clitoris. Just those touches take me to overwhelming, devastating release. Something cracks inside—in the darkness where loneliness lives—liberating me, giving me strength and courage and hope.

Now we flow together, finding each pleasure point on each other's bodies, tasting and discovering in all the ways that lovers can. There is nowhere I am not caressed, nowhere I dare not stroke or lick, and the only rush is that of desire finding its natural culmination, over and over again.

Curled around his body, I explore the texture of Ruiz's cock with my tongue, the heft of his sac with my hand, glorying in his deep, agonized sounds of passion, and in the knowledge they are made against Angelique's cunt. Then he and I share those wet, blushing folds, making her cry out with the lashing of our tongues, the double incursion of our fingers.

I hunger for them, feast on them and am feasted on in return. Lying between Angelique's legs, sharing kiss after kiss, Ruiz buried deep within me from behind, I once more feel the inescapable twist of desire. Each powerful thrust of his hips drives his cock into me with devastating pleasure, propelling me, in turn, against Angelique's clitoris. Reaching back, I grab his buttocks with one hand, the other braced on the headboard, holding us all in place. Angelique begins to spend, arching into me, and the beauty of her moment of bliss inspires my own, which in turn carries Ruiz to completion.

He slumps, holding his weight above us on shaking arms. I am surrounded by them, whole in a way I never was before, and I don't realize I'm crying until they untangle us and begin to kiss the tears from my cheeks.

"Ah, Bea, please, *amada,*" Ruiz sounds broken, as though my tears bring him pain even greater than my own. "Don't cry."

I am Beatrix Morgan I remind myself, the Duchess of Palisadoes, scion of the great Henry, whose daring and vision created his own private country, and whose son had the courage, after the earthquake of 1692, to take his wicked city skyward. I do not snivel and weep like a baby. Gathering the threads of composure, I look from one to the other of my loves.

"I don't want you to leave," is all I can manage before covering my face with my hands, and weeping inconsolably.

"Leave?" Angelique sounds both frightened and outraged. "Why would we leave?"

"I don't know," Ruiz pulls me closer, as though to emphasize his words. "I have no wish to go."

"What did you tell her, Ruiz, to make her rescue me?"

For a moment the only sound in the room is my sniveling.

"Once she said she would grant me any favor, so I asked her to," his voice is hushed. "I wasn't sure the truth would suffice."

I push him away so hard he almost falls off the bed and I sit up to glare at him.

"What truth, de Cortez?"

Angelique's hand on my shoulder soothes some of my ire, but I cannot relent until I know all.

"He has always loved you, *geliefde,* pined for you all these years. He didn't think you would want him, not with all you now have." Angelique's voice is soft, but it cracks like a whip against my heart. Ruiz's face tightens, and he looks away. "I think," she continues slowly, "he came not only because he cares for me, but because he knew we love each other too."

"You knew how I felt about Angelique," I accuse him, unable to prevent my voice from trembling, "and said nothing?"

"Just as you knew exactly how long it had been since I last came to Jamaica," he snaps back. "Do you think you are the only one with spies, or who keeps an eye on those they love?"

All I can do is stare at him in disbelief, my mind whirling with possibilities and doubts.

"Will you stay?" I finally ask, looking at them both. For that is the most important question of all.

They smile, as though the answer should be apparent.

"If you wish it, your grace," Ruiz replies, somehow able to make a courtly bow while both seated and naked.

"Well," I reply slowly, feeling joy bubble upward like champagne, making me light-headed, "my grandfather kept a harem. I only want you two. Besides, who would dare complain? There has to be some advantage to being head of a sovereign state. But," I hold up my hand as they both move toward me, "only on the condition you tell me what *geliefde* and *amada* mean." I shrug, "My education didn't stretch to languages."

"Beloved," they both say together, and I repeat it as a promise when I sink into their arms.

"Beloved..."

ABOUT THE
AUTHORS

VIDA BAILEY is an aspiring writer who holds those who parent, hold down their day job and still manage to publish stories in infinite awe. She has published stories in Alison Tyler's *Hurts So Good* and Sommer Marsden's *Dirtyville* anthologies. You can find her at heatsuffused.blogspot.com.

MARY BORSELLINO writes short erotica, pop culture analysis and punk young adult novels. She desperately hopes that somebody someday writes a steampunk pastiche of Oscar Wilde's *Dorian Gray*. Her website is maryborsellino.com.

A 2009 RITA finalist, **MELJEAN BROOK** is the *New York Times* bestselling author of the Guardians paranormal romance series and the Iron Seas steampunk romance series. *The Iron Duke* is her seventh full-length novel. Meljean holds a bachelor's degree in English literature from Portland State University. She lives in Oregon with her husband and daughter.

ELIZABETH COLDWELL lives and writes in London. Her stories have appeared in numerous anthologies from Cleis Press, Total-E-Bound, Black Lace and Ravenous Romance among others. She can be found at elizabethcoldwell.wordpress.com.

Multi-published author **CHRISTINE D'ABO** loves exploring the darker side of romance and passion. She enjoys taking her characters on fantastical journeys that change their hearts and expand their minds. Christine is published with Ellora's Cave, Samhain Publishing, Cleis Press, Carina Press and Berkley Heat. Please visit her at christinedabo.com.

On her own and with coauthors, **ANDREA DALE** (cyvarwydd. com) has sold two novels to Virgin Books UK and approximately one hundred stories to Harlequin Spice, Avon Red and Cleis Press, among others. Her steampunk pornographer persona is named Penny Dreadful.

SYLVIA DAY is author of more than a dozen novels, written across multiple sub-genres. A wife and mother of two, she is a former Russian linguist for the U.S. Army Military Intelligence. She lives in San Diego, California with her family. Visit with her at sylviaday.com.

SACCHI GREEN writes in western Massachusetts. Her stories have appeared in a hip-high stack of publications with inspirational covers, and she's also edited seven volumes of erotica, most recently *Girl Crazy*, *Lesbian Cowboys*, *Lesbian Lust* and *Lesbian Cops* from Cleis Press.

NIKKI MAGENNIS is a Scottish author and artist who has written erotica and erotic romance for Virgin Black Lace, Harlequin Spice and Cleis Press, among others. Find out more at nikkimagennnis.blogspot.com.

ANNA MEADOWS is a part-time executive assistant, part-time lesbian housewife. Her work appears in *Best Lesbian Romance 2010*, *Best Lesbian Romance 2011*, *Red Velvet and Absinthe*, *Girls Who Bite*, and on the Lambda Literary website.

After living a checkered past, and despite an avowed disinterest in domesticity, multi-published author **ANYA RICHARDS** settled in Ontario, Canada, with husband, kids and two cats. To find out more about her writing, drop by Anya's website at anyarichards.com.

LISABET SARAI has published six erotic novels, three short-story collections and dozens of individual tales. She also edits the single-author charity series "Coming Together Presents" and reviews erotica for Erotica Readers and Writers Association and Erotica Revealed. Visit Lisabet online at Lisabet's Fantasy Factory (lisabetsarai.com).

CHARLOTTE STEIN has published many stories in various anthologies, including *Fairy Tale Lust*. She also has novellas out with Ellora's Cave, Total-E-Bound and Xcite, and you can contact her here: themightycharlottestein.blogspot.com.

LYNN TOWNSEND is a displaced Yankee, mother, writer and dreamer.

SASKIA WALKER (saskiawalker.co.uk) is a British author

ABOUT
THE EDITOR

Described by *The Romance Reader* as "a budding force to be reckoned with," **KRISTINA WRIGHT** (kristinawright.com) is an author, editor and college instructor. She has edited the Cleis Press anthologies *Fairy Tale Lust: Erotic Fantasies for Women* and *Dream Lover: Paranormal Tales of Erotic Romance* and her forthcoming anthologies include *Best Erotic Romance 2012* and *Lustfully Ever After: Fairy Tale Erotic Romance*. Her first anthology, *Fairy Tale Lust: Erotic Fantasies for Women* was a Featured Alternate of the Doubleday Book Club. Kristina's erotica and erotic romance fiction has appeared in over eighty print anthologies. She received the Golden Heart Award for Romantic Suspense from Romance Writers of America for her first novel *Dangerous Curves*, which was published by Silhouette Intimate Moments. Her articles, interviews and book reviews have appeared in numerous publications, both in print and online. She is a member of Romance Writers of America as well as the special interest chapters Passionate Ink and Fantasy, Futuristic and Paranormal. She is a book reviewer for the Erotica Readers and Writers Association, the book club moderator for *SexIs Magazine's* Naked Reader Book Club and blogs weekly at Oh Get a Grip! (ohgetagrip.blogspot.com). She holds degrees in English and humanities and has taught English Composition and World Mythology at the community college level. Originally from South Florida, Kristina has lived up and down the East Coast with her husband, Jay, a Lieutenant Commander in the Navy. They currently live in Virginia with their two young sons.

TO OUR READERS:

For more than thirty years Cleis Press has been among the vanguard, publishing books that reflect our mission to help create a world in which we are all free to live our authentic lives.

Whether you've been a loyal Cleis Press reader or are just now discovering our list, we thank you for supporting our press.

Your purchase of this book helps us thrive.

Visit us at www.cleispress.com.

More from Kristina Wright

Best Erotic Romance
Edited by Kristina Wright

This year's collection is the debut of a new series!
"Kristina is a phenomenal writer...she has the enviable
ability to tell a story and simultaneously excite her
readers." —Erotica Readers and Writers Association
ISBN 978-1-57344-751-5 $14.95

Steamlust
Steampunk Erotic Romance
Edited by Kristina Wright

"Turn the page with me and step into the new worlds...where airships rule the skies,
where romance and intellect are valued over money and social status, where lovers boldly discover each other's bodies, minds and hearts." —from the foreword by
Meljean Brook
ISBN 978-1-57344-721-8 $14.95

Dream Lover
Paranormal Tales of Erotic Romance
Edited by Kristina Wright

Supernaturally sensual and captivating, the stories in *Dream Lover* will fill you with
a craving that defies the rules of life, death and gravity. "...A choice of paranormal
seduction for every reader. All are original and entertaining." —*Romantic Times*
ISBN 978-1-57344-655-6 $14.95

Fairy Tale Lust
Erotic Fantasies for Women
Edited by Kristina Wright

Award-winning novelist and erotica writer Kristina Wright goes over the river and
through the woods to find the sexiest fairy tales ever written. "Deliciously sexy action to make your heart beat faster." —Angela Knight, the *New York Times* bestselling
author of *Guardian*
ISBN 978-1-57344-397-5 $14.95

Ordering is easy! Call us toll free or fax us to place your MC/VISA order.
You can also mail the order form below with payment to:
Cleis Press, 2246 Sixth St., Berkeley, CA 94710.

ORDER FORM

QTY	TITLE	PRICE
———	————————————————————————	———
———	————————————————————————	———
———	————————————————————————	———
———	————————————————————————	———
———	————————————————————————	———
———	————————————————————————	———
———	————————————————————————	———
———	————————————————————————	———

SUBTOTAL ———————

SHIPPING ———————

SALES TAX ———————

TOTAL ———————

Add $3.95 postage/handling for the first book ordered and $1.00 for each additional book. Outside North America, please contact us for shipping rates. California residents add 8.75% sales tax. Payment in U.S. dollars only.

* Free book of equal or lesser value. Shipping and applicable sales tax extra.

Cleis Press • Phone: (800) 780-2279 • Fax: (510) 845-8001
orders@cleispress.com • www.cleispress.com
You'll find more great books on our website

Follow us on Twitter @cleispress • Friend/fan us on Facebook